# Interview with Love

## Reviews for Lisa Y. Watson's first novel

*Watch Your Back*

"This novel is in no way predictable, which makes it an easy and intriguing page turner. The main characters have so much passion between them that both the loving and hostile words that drip from the pages will be felt by the reader. This story will stick in the mind of the reader."
—**B. Nakia Garner,** *RT BOOK* **Review Magazine, 4 Stars**

"Lisa Watson draws a fabulous tightrope of betrayal, scintillating romance, and suspense in her debut novel!"
—**L.A. Banks,** *New York Times* **and** *USA Today*, **Vampire Huntress Series**

"Bitter secrets, dark betrayals and ready-to-explode desire.
    Finding a thief has never been so dangerous or so hot!
    The plot will keep you guessing until dawn.
    Lisa Watson is a writer you don't want to miss!"
—**Christina Skye,** *New York Times* **best-selling author of the CODE NAME series.**

# Interview with Love

# Interview with Love

## Lisa Y. Watson

**www.urbanbooks.net**

Urban Books, LLC
78 East Industry Court
Deer Park, NY 11729

ISBN 13: 978-1-60162-700-1
ISBN 10: 1-60162-700-9

First Mass Market Paperback Printing December 2014
First Trade Paperback Printing December 2010
Printed in the United States of America

10 9 8 7 6 5 4 3 2 1

Distributed by Kensington Publishing Corp.
Submit Wholesale Orders to:
Kensington Publishing Corp.
C/O Penguin Group (USA) Inc.
Attention: Order Processing
405 Murray Hill Parkway
East Rutherford, NJ 07073-2316
Phone: 1-800-526-0275
Fax: 1-800-227-9604

"*Watch Your Back* will have you reading it all in one sitting. A good first release for Lisa Y. Watson."
**—Dianthia R. Lemons,** *Romance In Color* **Magazine, 4 Stars**

"Newcomer Lisa Watson has delivered a very intriguing read. The writing is succinct and the dialogue is brisk and real. I love the interactions between Devon and Jayde. I would highly recommend this book."
**—M. Glover, 5 Stars**

"This author is a gifted and talented writer. From the moment you open the book and start reading you are hooked and will not be able to put the book down. Her writing style is easy to follow and allows you to get into the characters like you are part of the story. The playful banter and passion between the main characters Devon and Jayde is wonderful and funny. Chapter after chapter this book is fantastic. There are twists and turns and it keeps you guessing and gasping."
**—Lori Mosel, 5 Stars**

# DEDICATION

*Interview with Love* is dedicated to my mother, Harriette Y. Dodson. Your "Last Button on Gabriel's Shirt" loves you very, very much.

And to all the family and friends that are always watching MY back. I thank you!

# ACKNOWLEDGMENTS

God truly moves in an infinite amount of ways. He's graced me with a gift that allows me to touch so many people. Also, my Dad, George A. Dodson, Jr., and all the other angels in my outfield. I appreciate the help!

Eric, Brandon, and Alyssa. Thanks for letting me rotate the wife, mommy and writer hat as needed! I love you guys!

Carl Weber, Natalie Weber, Brenda Owen, and my Urban family. Heartfelt thanks for giving me the opportunity to tell my stories.

My crazy, undying thanks to my cousins, Dr. Patricia D. Raspberry of Black Raspberry Consumer Insights, and Angela Raspberry, Executive Creative Director at Black Raspberry Consumer Insights, and Associate Creative Director at Doner Advertising. Your expertise gave Vaughn and Sienna depth and soul. I appreciate every call, text, e-mail, and rap session. This book would not have been written without you both! Much love from your Cuz!

# Acknowledgments

The Critique Boutique: C. Adele Dodson, Tina Ezell-Hull, Pat Simmons, and Steffi Wheeler. Your opinions, suggestions, and encouragement were greatly appreciated and very instrumental in getting *Interview with Love* off the ground and out the door! I love you guys!

Thanks to everyone at *RT BOOK* Reviews Magazine. You all do amazing work!

Nicole Ferweda—You are astounding and forever in my corner. I just wanted you to know I appreciate your being there.

To my Steele fiction authors and readers—You guys are awesome! That's for graciously allowing me to defer my stories while I got this one done!

The Inner Circle: I would not be who I am today without the love and support from each and every one of you. My cup runneth over!

To each and every person who has ever read anything I've written. You all keep me going. You keep me motivated and constantly striving to improve who I am, and what I write! Thank you all for the e-mails, blog posts, tweets, texts, and visits while I'm at bookstores waiting for someone to buy my books! LOL!

To the Berry Sisters: Alyce and Robin. Thanks for bringing me into the fold, my tall, gorgeous sisters! You are two of the most talented women I'll ever know!

# Chapter One

## Business as Usual

He was the kind of man that couldn't help but pique a woman's interest; unless she was a nun. He was above average height, his skin like a flawless piece of chocolate. Sienna Lambert, Ph.D, hadn't missed the looks he had given her over the last two hours. Picking up the usual signs, she had done her best to shut him down. She was completely professional in her interactions with him and the rest of the focus group participants. Yet here he was—in all his not-so-covert masculine glory.

"Miss Lambert?"

It hadn't been ten minutes since the session had ended and he was back. Sienna lowered the notes she was perusing and looked up. "Yes, Terrance? Did you have any additional comments you'd like to share?"

He flashed a wide grin, "Not exactly. I thought we might be able to chat for a minute. You know, without all the other folks hanging around."

Yes, she did know. *Not again!*

Sienna stood up tucking her folder securely under her arm. She adjusted her glasses. "Sure. What's on your mind?"

"I just figured . . . um, are you local?"

She posted a very polite smile on her face. "No, I'm not. I'm just here for another few days to wrap up."

"Man, that's too bad." He twisted his mouth into a brilliant smile.

*Isn't it, though?* She thought.

"I was just going to ask you if you'd like to accompany me to dinner. I don't normally do this, but I don't care for eating alone." His tone dropped. "It's surprising how often I end up doing just that. I can't imagine it holds much interest for a woman as lovely as you."

Sienna cast a glance back to the one-way mirror that separated the screening room from the respondents. It was amazing how often she got propositioned in front of her clients. It was equally interesting how the men forgot that they were not alone and there were people watching— and listening.

"I'm sorry Terrance, but I'm going to have to decline. I have quite a bit of work to do before tomorrow's session and—"

"Well, if you don't have time," he interrupted. "Maybe a quick drink, or . . . whatever."

Suddenly, Sienna's BlackBerry vibrated in her suit pocket. She reached in and retrieved her telephone. "I'm sorry, I have to take this." She apologized turning away. She hit a button on her phone and read the newly arrived text message. *Looked like you needed rescuing.*

Sienna's right thumb tapped out a quick reply. *Owe you!!* She turned back toward the eagerly waiting man. "I'm sorry, but I'm going to have to leave. It's been a pleasure meeting you."

His eyes skimmed over her before he replied, "Believe me, it was all mine."

After she collected the rest of her belongings, Sienna gave him a final smile. With purposeful strides she walked to the exit at the back of the room where her client was waiting—and watching.

Once the door closed securely behind her, Sienna sagged against the barrier while taking a deep breath. Absentmindedly, she smoothed her hair into its already secured bun.

"Amazing, wasn't he?"

Sienna looked up to see Sherry Bradshaw standing nearby. A quick glance around confirmed that the other executives observing the session were already gone.

"I haven't seen his equal in quite some time." Sienna confessed.

"He'd make a woman dizzy just looking at him." The woman sighed, loudly. She patted her heart over her navy blue suit jacket. "It's not too late to change your mind you know, he's still standing there."

"What?" Surprised, Sienna pushed away from the door and leaned to the left. Her head was inches from the glass as she peered back into the focus group room. Sherry followed suit. She lifted her riotous red hair away from her face to stare through the window. Sure enough the man was still standing there confidently. His gaze traveled lazily over the mirrored boundary. Twice, he almost made eye contact with her. She reared back as if he could actually see her. "He's persistent, I'll give him that."

"Maybe he's waiting for you to come to your senses," Sherry chuckled, moving back away from the glass. "Are you sure you wanted to turn him down?"

"Flat," Sienna said, with firm conviction. She held her index finger in front of her. "Rule number one: Never date the respondents."

"I don't think dating is what he had in mind."

"Rule number two: Don't trip the light fantastic with your test subjects."

"Don't what? I've never heard of that one."

"My definition is a bit different from the original meaning. Mine means don't sleep with them."

"Oh. What's number three?"

"A bad idea never, ever, looks better after a few drinks."

The woman's eyes widened considerably. "Dr. Lambert, are you serious with all these rules?"

Before turning her attention back to her client, Sienna watched the living Adonis she'd just turned down shrug his shoulders and saunter out of the room. His move clearly signaled that he thought it was *her* loss. She felt not one twinge of regret. "Absolutely."

"I can't argue with logic like that," Sherry mused before changing the subject. "I want you to know that we truly appreciate your flying here to conduct the focus groups. Our collective schedules this week would've made travel kind of hectic for us, especially Mr. Dexter. You coming to the corporate office made it much more convenient for him."

Sienna hadn't thought twice about flying there to accommodate the chief executive officer, Antonio Dexter. The president and CEO of Dexter Clothiers, Antonio, was an older gentleman with an olive complexion and a bright smile. He was very personable and instantly put those around him at ease.

He had dark hair and light-brown eyes that hinted at both intelligence and good humor. Sienna was amazed at how tall and athletic he was. She'd heard he was in his late fifties, and she noted upon meeting him that he wore it well. She hadn't been able to meet his brother Eduardo, the chief operating officer of the company because he was out of the country on business.

"It was no problem." Sienna spoke up realizing she hadn't answered yet. "The facility here is working out wonderfully. Besides, I'm always thrilled to visit New England. It's beautiful here."

"I love New Hampshire, too. Then again, North Carolina is beautiful as well. I'm sure you must miss it."

"It is and I do."

"Actually, the younger Mr. Dexter has property in North Carolina. I've been there on a few occasions. He spends a great deal of time there when he's not traveling."

"It's beautiful country. I never tire of looking at it."

"I wouldn't doubt it. So do you have an idea when you'll be finished with your report?"

Sienna scanned her portfolio. "Since the last group is tomorrow afternoon, I should have it to you on Tuesday. Will that be okay?"

"That will work just fine. I've got three ad agencies pitching for the Best Kept Secrets campaign. We should have our selection made by the end of next week. I'd like to go over your findings before then. I've got to tell you, I'm very excited about this product."

"It's worth being excited. Men's undergarments more comfortable the longer they're worn? They sound truly state-of-the-art."

"They are. You should see the team that created them. Some of them look like they've never seen the light of day."

They both laughed. "Well, it's an exhilarating proposition to men everywhere and from all walks of life."

"Don't we know it," Sherry replied, "but not just men, Dr. Lambert, women the world over will be reaping the benefits, too."

Later that evening, Sienna sat cross-legged on the bed in her hotel room. After a long, very hot shower she put on her comfy cotton pajamas. Her hair was swept up into a loose pile on top of her head, a style she rarely wore in public. Papers and a plate holding a half-eaten turkey club sandwich arched out in front of her. Glancing over at the nightstand clock, Sienna stifled a yawn. It was well after midnight. Though her next group wouldn't start until six o'clock tomorrow evening, she still wanted to give herself plenty of time to prepare her questions and go over any last-minute details.

When she caught herself nodding several times, Sienna knew it was time to call it a night. She eased her glasses off and placed them in their case on the nightstand, then leaned back against the plush hotel pillows to stretch languidly.

Rubbing the sore muscles at the nape of her neck, she laughed aloud as she recalled her respondent's pick up lines. He was supremely confident that she would eventually change her mind and go out with him.

"It'll take much more than a hot physique and a smile to get me to break one of my rules," she quipped, rolling off the bed. Sienna gathered the papers and slid them back into her laptop bag. The next stop was the table where she deposited the plate of food. Lowering the metal lid back over the plate, Sienna padded to the bathroom to brush her teeth. She retrieved a small hour-glass from her toiletries bag, flipped it over on the sink and commenced her two-minute brushing regime.

As she rotated the motorized toothbrush around in her mouth, her mind wandered. The living Adonis that tried to pick her up earlier popped into her mind. Sienna didn't doubt for a second that he had recovered himself and was bestowing his charms on the next lady-in-waiting. It wasn't hard for her to imagine him wearing a new pair of Best Kept Secrets, or that they would fit like a second skin. Sienna almost felt sorry for the unsuspecting ladies. She had no doubt seeing his handsome physique parade around in new underwear would be the equivalent of a superhero sporting a shiny new red cape.

Sienna adored her job. She was irrevocably in love with being a consumer psychologist. She poured over the soft data gathered to give her clients insight into consumers' thoughts. Their patterns, motivations, and the emotional connections all tied in when they considered their purchases. The products people used, the food they ate, the cars they drove, and the clothes they wore were all conscious choices influenced by the way companies marketed their lines. It was fascinating to her.

When Sienna had started Lambert Insights, Inc., it was the most rewarding thing she'd ever done. It was also the most terrifying. To start with nothing and build her dream from the bare bones to the living, thriving company it had become, made her want to weep with humility.

Edgy, Sienna paced around the hotel room. The excitement coursed through her veins with each turn on the patterned carpet. Anticipation revved her up the way a well-loaded coffee with an espresso shot did. This was it. Out of every aspect of her job this was the part she loved the most. When the hostess escorted a new group in on Sienna's cue, the smile she wore was always genuine. The well-screened participants were eager, excited and ready to have someone listen to what they had to say. They were thrilled that someone had asked for their opinions about a topic they could relate to. It was a cohesive group bouncing responses off each other that gave them a common patch of ground.

On occasion, there would be a respondent that didn't want to engage in meaningful, communicative dialogue. Sienna would never let their clipped, monotone responses dampen her spirits or deter her from doing her job. Those moments were infrequent and when they occurred she would simply tune the facility coordinator in to the issue. The respondent was removed from the room in a swift manner before he or she affected the collective group.

It was the unpredictable occurrences that made the long hours, the endless airports, and take-out food bearable. The bloodshot eyes she received from pouring over handwritten notes and audio data from the sessions was worth it. The decent and sometimes indecent proposals she received from men were trivial compared to what she'd feel tomorrow at the final moment she put all her experience to the test. *The interview.*

Sienna closed her eyes and harnessed the energy required to keep a group of strangers entertained, connected, and responsive to her over the next two hours. It was like going into battle each time she welcomed her next group. It was a wonderful, fantastic, creative battle that caused her stomach to knot and her heart to beat with excitement. *Showtime.*

A quick knock and then the door opened. In walked a woman smiling at Sienna with six men in tow. "Good afternoon everyone," she said, cheerfully. "Welcome. Feel free to take any seat and then we'll get started." She waited until every man was seated comfortably and her hostess had left before lowering herself into her chair.

"My name is Sienna Lambert, and I'd like to take a few minutes to go over what we'll be discussing for the next two hours." She turned slightly in her chair. "Behind me you'll see a mirrored wall. This is a one-way mirror and behind it are my clients. This evening they'll be watching us and taking notes on our conversation and your responses to my questions. They are just as interested in what you have to say as I am, however in the interest of keeping the energy flowing freely and our conversations relaxed, their group will stay behind the scenes. Now if you'd like you can all turn around and wave at the mirror and say hello to break the ice."

There were chuckles throughout the group. A few turned around and waved at the wall.

"Great. Another thing I'd like to mention is that there is a microphone and video camera recording what we're saying. Most of this is to ensure that I can focus my attention on you all and leave the heavy note taking to them." Sienna joked.

"This is an open dialogue, okay? There are no right or wrong answers. We are here to hear what you have to say and to get your honest opinions on men's undergarments. I know it's after five and that most of you may be coming from work and have had a long day. Trust me, we appreciate your willingness to be here and to participate in this study. I think it would be great if we could go around the table and get each of you to introduce yourselves. Please start by telling us your name, if you live alone, with a spouse and or kids, a partner or friend, when was the last time you purchased underwear and who you were with when you bought them. Oh, and tell me if they were boxers or briefs. We'll start on my left."

After the group introduced themselves, she continued. "Now I'd like you to name all of the factors you consider when shopping for underwear. We don't need to go in order, but just make sure you speak up and talk one at a time. That will make the audio more clear when I'm listening to the playback of our session later. It will help me remember who said what, okay?"

"For me, the most important factors are price, comfort, style, and color," Barry noted.

"Me too," Daniel agreed. "When I'm in court I'm sitting, standing, and approaching the bench. I don't have time to worry about trying to—you know—adjust."

Sienna made a few notes. "I can see how that would be inconvenient."

"I look at the track record of the brand name. Once I find a brand I like, I stick with it," someone chimed in.

"Since I drive a bus, I'm sitting all day," Justin added. "I have to be comfortable. Color's irrelevant, unless you're French or something."

"Well I'm not French," Dr. Sutton said, looking around. "But color is a factor when I'm choosing new underwear. My top three would be comfort, color, and then style."

"Now, tell me what makes a great pair of underwear for you all?" she asked.

"It doesn't bind or cling," Barry spoke up quickly.

There was a collective head nod around the room.

Two hours had passed and Sienna glanced at her watch. She stood and walked to the front of the room. "Last question guys and we're done." She positioned an easel at the head of the table. "As you can see, we have a large pad of paper with two stick figures. My two stick buddies here are each wearing a suit. Our man on the left is wearing a perfect pair of very comfortable underwear. Imagine how this guy feels."

"He's feeling great," one man called out.

"He's pressed, starched, and he's feeling like he's the man," another added.

"So what I'm hearing is how he's feeling about himself is directly tied in to how well his clothes fit?"

"Absolutely," Frank commented. "He's happy."

"He's got the look and the confidence to do whatever," Michael responded.

Sienna pointed to the pad. "Now, let's look at his buddy over here on the right. He's also wearing a suit, but he has a pair of ill-fitting underwear on. How do you think he feels?"

"He's thinking, 'How the heck can I adjust without being obvious,'" Justin said loudly.

"Definitely cranky," Dr. Sutton replied. "That pair of underwear is going to be detrimental to his day."

"Nothing worse than underwear that don't fit right," Daniel added. "Personally, I think it's a perfectly acceptable form of torture."

Frank shifted uncomfortably in his seat. "I bet I know what he's thinking. Stick man's thinking as soon as I get home these freaking things are going in the trash and I'm hitting the shower!"


Sienna was typing notes onto her laptop when the flight attendant announced that everyone should stow all electronic devices. Her fingers flew over the keyboard to get her current thought on the page before she shut down her computer. *Done!* Sienna smiled triumphantly, while she hit the icon to save her work. Once she powered down, she snapped it closed and then slid the lightweight machine into its bag. Gently, Sienna maneuvered it under the seat. She eyed the obtrusive seat of the passenger in front of her. It was practically resting in her lap. With a small sense of satisfaction, Sienna shoved the tray in its upright position with a bit more force than necessary.

The captain's voice resounded overhead. He briefed the passengers on the weather and what time they would land at Raleigh–Durham International Airport. Sienna scanned the sky outside her window. The pink and blue tinged clouds floated lazily over the horizon as the sun set on another day. *Another long, incredibly-productive-kick-butt-and-take-names kind of day.* There was no way she could contain the grin that slid across her face. Though she remained humble, Sienna couldn't help but feel satisfaction in the work that she'd done. Her final focus group for Dexter was complete and the men were a riot.

Her face turned red just remembering the session. The discussion was almost finished when one of the respondents wanted to discuss a subject that had not been covered. He thought it important to mention that there were plenty of men that enjoyed wearing women's underwear, and not just for sexual reasons, but because they were comfortable, held more of a variety then men's underwear, and were available in a lot more colors, textures and styles. He was quick to point out that it may not be the best choice if one were ever in an accident, but that they were comfortable nonetheless. That proverbial bucket of worms had started a discussion that became so animated Sienna had to all but physically steer the group back to the topic at hand.

Later, going over her notes and the tapes had been incredibly insightful. The creative energy bouncing off the six respondents was almost tangible. Their beneficial feedback prompted Sienna to wonder if Dexter Clothiers should consider adding a Best Kept Secrets line for women.

At that moment the plane touched the runway with several quick bumps. The sound of the plane reversing engines resonated loudly throughout the cabin. As their speed slowed so did Sienna's breathing. Calm seeped into her. Lambert Insights' report was in the hands of Sherry Bradshaw and the other execs at Dexter Clothiers, and she was back in North Carolina safe and sound. Only now would she allow herself to bask in the knowledge that business was stable and doing well. The company was finally in the black and making strong headway in the profits department. It was time for some serious celebrating.

Sienna maneuvered her way out of baggage claim twenty minutes later, to the nearby shuttle for satellite parking. She swung her bags on the raised platform inside the bus and sat in a seat across from it. Her thoughts drifted to the official wrap up of her biggest client. Oh yeah, she was definitely hauling Vivian out for a night on the town to celebrate.

While the bus ambled monotonously down the road, Sienna retrieved her Date Minder from her purse. She scanned through the pages until she got to that day. Scribbled half-way down the page was the exact location of her car. Three trips ago, she'd spent thirty minutes in the pouring rain trying to find it. From then on she'd written it down.

Once her bags were stowed in the trunk, Sienna touched her door handle. Her car beeped and the door on her Hybrid Toyota Camry unlocked. She slid behind the wheel and placed her purse on the passenger seat. She pressed the button to start the car while retrieving her navigation unit from the glove box. "Hi, Lola," she said, affectionately to her GPS.

With a firm press she clicked the unit onto her windshield before turning it on. Tapping the *Go Home* button, she waited while the system calculated her route. As she pulled out of her space,

Sienna pressed a button on her steering wheel and spoke loudly. "Dad, at home."

"Dialing," a female voice replied.

A few rings later, a male voice answered. "Hey, honey."

"Hello, Colonel," Sienna said, cheerfully.

"There's my little girl," Retired Army Colonel, Gordon Lambert replied, with a warm voice. "How was your trip?"

"Better than I anticipated. We did it, Dad. We knocked this one out of the park."

"Fantastic, sweetheart! "Now, where are we going to celebrate? Sushi? Indian?"

"I don't know. I'm still reveling in my good fortune."

"Good fortune had nothing to do with it. It was good old fashion hard work, kiddo."

"Thanks for the vote of confidence. I'll ponder where we're going for dinner and get back to you." Sienna maneuvered onto the on-ramp for I-540E. "How's Mom?"

"She's doing fine. Told me to tell you she has three more recruits signing up."

A visual of her father marching her step-mother, Cassandra's pre-teen class around her dance studio made Sienna giggle. "Dad, I don't think a group of ballerinas march."

"Well, plies then. Anyway, what are you up to tomorrow?

"I'm going to spend tomorrow doing absolutely nothing."

"Much needed I'm sure. Where are you now?"

"On I-540, about to take the Leesville Road exit."

"Oh, you're almost home. Ring us once when you get in so we'll know you made it in safely."

"Yes, sir," Sienna said in a stern, serious voice.

"At ease," he laughed before hanging up.

It wasn't long before her car turned into her townhome community. She pressed a button overhead and her garage door eased open. She waited until it was safely closed behind her before she exited the car. Sienna removed her luggage from the trunk, wheeled it into the entryway, and then walked to the keypad to disarm the alarm. After flipping the lights on, she went in search of the cordless phone.

"Great," she muttered after realizing it wasn't left on the charger. Sienna retrieved her cell phone out of her pocket and dialed her father. As instructed, she let the phone ring once, and then hung up.

Her gaze traveled toward the kitchen, but she ignored the temptation to snack. Instead, she set her alarm in Stay mode and hefted her bag up the stairs.

Twenty minutes later, her nighttime regimen was done. Easing under the bed covers, Sienna retrieved the cordless phone on her nightstand to check voicemail for messages. A few calls were telemarketers attempting to sell her time shares or magazine subscriptions she didn't need. Without listening more than a few seconds, she pressed the number three on the keypad to delete their messages. The next call was from a friend reminding her when the next Zumba class was. She continued listening.

There was a message from Sherry Bradshaw's admin assistant. She wanted to remind her that they needed her RSVP for the company outing by Thursday.

"What outing?" Saving the message, she got out of bed and padded downstairs. Flipping her dining room light on, she glimpsed a stack of mail on her table courtesy of her best friend and business partner, Vivian Adair. Taking a seat in a nearby chair, Sienna flipped through the mail. She spotted a few pieces from her office. Setting the personal letters aside, Sienna focused on the office correspondence. She discovered an invitation addressed to her in bold print.

After ripping the envelope open, she eased the invitation out. She read it twice. A smile plastered itself across her face. *I've been invited to a Best Kept Secrets Launch Party at Eduardo Dexter's summer estate.* Her eyes dropped lower on the thick card stock to read the details. Normally she didn't co-mingle with the client unless it was business, but the outing could prove to be great PR for the company and she was looking forward to meeting the younger Dexter. Decision made, Sienna doused the light and ran back upstairs. Excitedly, she picked up her phone and resumed checking messages. This time when a woman's voice resounded in her ear, her breath caught in her throat.

"Hey, it's Sasha. I tried to call you a few days ago, but you didn't bother calling me back—an oversight no doubt. Call me when you get in."

Sienna immediately hit the delete key. Angrily, she tossed her glasses on the table. "Hell will freeze over first," she said, aloud.

# Chapter Two

## Foul Ball

Three days later, Sienna pulled into a large circular driveway in front of what could only be described as a mini-castle. The estate was on the main channel of Lake Norman in Catawba, North Carolina. The drive from her house had taken just under three hours. She stopped the car and slid the gear into park. With quick strides, an attendant intercepted her. He held the car door with one hand and assisted her from the car with his other.

"Good afternoon, ma'am. May I have your name, please?"

"Sienna Lambert."

The young man repeated her name into a headset. "Hello, Ms. Lambert. You can follow the pathway around to the rear of the house. Someone will be there to assist you."

"Uh, okay." Sienna retrieved her bag from the back seat. She strolled along the cobblestone driveway toward the extensive lawn. She couldn't resist gazing up at the multi-leveled roof lines. She tried to repress the urge to gawk, but it was difficult especially when she spotted several turrets.

"Wow," she said, aloud while walking around the side toward the back of the home.

The stone, brick, and hardishake home had massive windows on three sides. She could imagine the panoramic views of the lake and the several nearby islands. When Sienna reached the back, there was a woman standing at a small lectern greeting guests. *This is too much.*

"Good afternoon, Ms. Lambert," the woman smiled warmly, and then handed Sienna a name tag and a packet. "Have a wonderful time."

"Thank you," Sienna replied, continuing on.

The extensive back yard looked like a miniature theme park. There were various stations with different attractions. She opened the packet in her hand and saw a detailed list and map of where to find each activity. Volleyball, croquet, baseball, and water polo were available, as well as huge water slides, paddle boats, and jet skis.

Sienna hadn't known what to expect so she'd chosen a sleeveless summer dress with sandals.

Always prepared, she'd also packed a small duffle bag with a swimsuit, shorts, a T-shirt, athletic shoes, bug repellant, and sunscreen.

"Sienna." A voice called from her left.

Turning, she glimpsed Sherry and other members of her team advancing.

"How are you, Ms. Bradshaw?"

"Sherry," the woman corrected. "I'm fine, and thrilled you could make it."

"Thanks for inviting me. From what I've seen so far," Sienna said, falling into step next to her, "our host has gone all out."

"Isn't it a blast? You haven't had a chance to meet Eduardo, but you will. He is just as amiable as his brother Antonio."

"I can't wait to meet him." Sienna glanced around. "Honestly, I don't know where to start first."

"No rush. Want something to drink? Wine? Margarita?"

"Iced tea or lemonade would be just fine."

"Rule number three: Never drink at parties held by clients?"

Sienna laughed. "Only co-mingle with the clients if it's business."

"I think you're going to have to make an exception to that rule," Sherry informed her. "I'll introduce you to the Best Kept Secrets models. We've got men in all shapes and sizes. They're sure to appeal to every woman's eye. The press is here, too. They'll be doing a photo shoot after Antonio gives the welcome speech officially kicking off the new line." She practically dragged Sienna along. "Later, I'll introduce you to the executive and creative directors from the ad agency we're going with, Chase & Burroughs."

"Sounds great." She was about to ask a question but Sherry held up her hand. "Uh-uh. No more shop talk," she whispered, conspiratorially. "Right now we're going to run down a waiter and get you a drink, and then I'm going to introduce you to our very capable, very gorgeous cover models. I'll bet there's someone here that will rival your admirer from the focus group."

"Now that," she said, in a hushed voice, "would be a tall order."

After listening while the brothers introduced their new line, Sienna found a great spot on the patio to drink her lemonade and people watch. Some of the models were gathered around the pool for an interview. *There are definitely some beautiful people here,* she mused. Flipping open her cell phone, Sienna dialed Vivian.

"You should've come with me," she said, without preamble.

"Darn, I knew it! Hunks galore? Unlimited adult beverages and all the food I could've eaten?"

"Yes, yes, and yes."

"Shoot!" Vivian grumbled. "House?"

"Massive."

"Landscape?"

Sienna looked around. "A photographer's dream."

"You see? I told you family obligations are highly overrated."

"Viv, your sister was having a baby and you were the coach," Sienna reminded her.

"It's not like it was her first," Vivian groused before laughing at her own joke.

"You are too funny. By the way, did she have a boy or girl?"

"Boy."

"That's fantastic. Tell her I said congratulations. She's got to be thrilled to have a boy after three girls."

"Trust me my brother-in-law is beside himself with joy. He'll still be outnumbered, but at least there'll be another man in the house to get yelled at for leaving the seat up."

Sienna could believe it. "When does his plane land?"

"In another four hours. My sister has decreed that it's the last business trip he's going on so close to her due date."

Sienna visibly shuddered. "She's seriously thinking about another one? Four isn't enough?"

"Who knows. Take a picture from your phone for me."

"I'll try. I may not be able to zoom out that far. I'll probably have to paddle a boat over to the nearest island to take one."

"An island? Oh, I'm so jealous," Vivian lamented. "Have fun and I'll send you a photo of the little man later."

"Deal," Sienna promised before hanging up.

"Finally." Sherry loomed over her. "We need another body in the outfield. Come on, you've been drafted."

She dropped her phone in her bag and stood up. "I, uh . . . I'm not that good at sports."

"You'll do fine. The balls never get that far, anyway," Sherry informed her. Looping her arm through Sienna's, she dragged her along. She eyed the bag slung over Sienna's shoulder. "My instincts tell me there are extra clothes in there, so let's go get you changed."

When they were done, Sienna walked out of the lower level French doors. After her wardrobe change, she'd re-checked her bun to ensure no errant hair had escaped. She'd swapped her eyeglasses for prescription sunglasses. Gingerly, Sienna lowered a baseball cap into place.

"Okay, you're up." One of Sherry's assistants came up to greet her. "I'll keep your bag for you."

"Thanks," Sienna replied holding her stomach. She took several deep breaths to quell the queasy feeling. "I hope I do okay. Sports aren't exactly my forte."

When she looked up she was alone. Sherry's assistant was already gone. "Great. I'm standing here talking to myself. How lame is that?"

Moments later, Sienna sidled up to a crowd of people by the canopied seating that passed as the dugout. "Fantastic, you're here. Come on, we're getting creamed out there. We have to pow-wow," a man standing next to Sherry said.

He glanced toward Sienna. "You any good?"

"Um, not really. The last time I played any-thing ending in b-a-l-l was in high school."

"Okay, you'll be playing outfield."

After a few more deliberations the small team dispersed.

Another teammate handed Sienna a glove. "Break a leg."

"Thanks?" She forced herself to smile despite the sweat forming at the nape of her neck. *I can do this. No big deal.*

Sienna did well in the outfield. She only had to go after one ball. She'd surprised herself when she ran for it, grabbed it and lobbed it toward third base. She'd jumped for joy when the man running to third base at break-neck speed was pronounced out. With more confidence than when she'd started, Sienna swaggered toward home plate as the opposing team headed toward the open field.

"You're doing great, Sienna," Sherry proclaimed.

Her teammates readily agreed.

Sienna's face lit up. "Thanks. I'm feeling pretty good. This is a lot of fun."

She cheered her team on and clapped at each point they gained. When they struck out she'd clap anyway to encourage the next player to the mound. She was still clapping when someone called out that she was up.

"It's . . . my turn? So soon?"

"Yep. Batter up, Lambert."

"Just take a deep breath and swing," someone called after her.

"Don't choke," another person yelled out.

*Rule number four: Always impress the clients and potential clients by appearing outgoing and fun.* With that mantra ringing in her ears, Sienna headed for the plate.

\*\*\*

Later that afternoon on the makeshift baseball diamond, Sienna discovered two things about herself: The first was that she could enjoy a spur of the moment activity as much as a well-planned one. The second, that she wasn't as adverse to sports as she had imagined. Each time her bat connected with the baseball it sent a surge of adrenaline through her, especially when she actually hit the thing.

"Head's up, Lambert."

Swinging, she hit the ball with a loud crack. Dropping the bat, she took off toward first base. As she ran past each base, Sienna could hear the cheers of encouragement from the crowd. *I can definitely get used to this*, she mused.

When it was her team's turn to hit the outfield, Sienna was stopped short by the self-appointed captain of their team. "Lambert, you take third base."

"Okay." Nervously, she headed toward it. This would be her first foray covering a base.

Before she knew it, her team was down by four runs. Her mouth was dry and her feet ached, but she wasn't about to give up. She'd bonded over the last hour with the people on her team and there was no way they weren't going to win this thing.

Another player stepped up to home plate with bat in hand. The heat outside combined with her anxiety caused her to sweat. Sienna was wiping her perspiration soaked shirt against her eyes when she heard the loud thwack. The batter threw his bat to the ground and jetted toward first base.

"Look lively," her teammate yelled from second base. "It's coming your way."

Tilting her head up, Sienna tried to keep her eye on the ball. The sun was making the job difficult. Blinking rapidly, she moved back and forth across the grass in an effort to catch the ball. *There it is,* she said to herself. She raised her glove and calculated when the ball would drop into it. Peripherally, she could see a man bearing down on her position, his team cheering him on. Excitement made her heady. There was no way he would make it to third base before she caught the ball. He'd be out. She would make sure of it. Her face was scrunched in concentration. *Get the ball, get the ball.*

Voices were shouting at her to get the man out. "I got it," she cried out. Several seconds later, the ball plopped heavily into Sienna's glove. Two seconds after that her world went pitch black.

# Chapter Three

## The Wrong Idea

"Sienna? Sienna, can you hear me? You've got to wake up," Sherry said, worriedly.

"We found smelling salts. Let's try these," another person replied.

Vaughn Deveraux quirked an eyebrow. "Smelling salts? They still make those?" He held out his hand. "Okay, let's give it a shot."

Sherry was crouched right next to him. "You think those will work?"

"We're going to find out."

Vaughn waved the bottle under Sienna's nose with slow, deliberate movements. Her body jerked sharply. Her head turned side to side before she sputtered and her eyes popped open.

Vaughn watched her blink a few times. He was sure she was trying to focus.

She turned her head toward him. He smiled reassuringly into her confused face before he leaned down and whispered into her ear, "Welcome back." He watched as various emotions crossed her face. She glanced around. Eventually, her gaze traveled back to him.

"Who are you? Why am I on the ground?"

"I'm the guy that just barreled into you while sliding into third base." Vaughn was concerned about her, but he was a tad bit annoyed that she had blocked his running line.

"Oh," came her whispered reply.

"Let's help you up."

"Do you think we should move her?" Sherry glanced at Sienna. "Maybe we should call an ambulance."

"I'm fine, see?" she stood up to prove the point. Immediately Vaughn noticed the color in her face drain away. When she swayed, he moved his arms to grasp her shoulders. "Steady, I got you." He looked down at her. "I think we should get you looked at."

"No need," Sienna spoke up quickly. "I just got the wind knocked out of me that's all. I'm perfectly fine."

Vaughn's gazed flickered over her body. Her shorts had grass stains in various places, there was a cut on her right knee and her once neat bun was hanging haphazardly down the nape of her neck. Now that she was upright, he noticed she was almost eye level with him. With a teasing grin, he winked at her. "That you are."

"Is everything okay here?" someone called from a distance. Every head turned to see the Dexter brothers approaching with an entourage of people in tow.

The throng of onlookers parted immediately to let them through.

"Sienna's had a bit of a tumble," Sherry assured everyone. "She'll be fine, though we should probably let her rest a bit."

A photographer started snapping pictures. A reporter came to the forefront.

"Sienna? I didn't get your last name."

Instinctively, Sienna turned her head toward Vaughn's chest. *Uh-uh,* she said to herself. There was no way she was going on record looking like a bleeding, bedraggled mess.

Without being asked to Vaughn eased her closer to his side and away from the curious journalist.

"Sherry, you can take her inside to get freshened up," Eduardo replied ushering them toward the house.

*It figures,* Sienna groaned to herself. *The first time I meet Eduardo Dexter face-to-face and I look like a science experiment.* "Thank you, Mr. Dexter," Sienna replied, sheepishly.

The older man folded her arm through his and took off toward the house. "Nonsense, young lady it was truly my pleasure. Sienna noted during his speech earlier that he was as charming and good looking as his brother. Up close and personal, his appeal drew you in like a well-placed magnet.

"Now if you need anything Dr. Lambert, you just alert my staff and they'll take care of you. If they don't, you come get me."

"I'm sure I'll be just fine Mr. Dexter."

"Mr. Dexter's my older brother," Eduardo teased. "I think we'll save all that formality for him."

Out of the corner of her eye, Sienna noticed the reporter scribbling furiously on his note pad. She put some effort into the daggers she glared at him, but considering her appearance she didn't doubt the intimidation she was going for fell way short of the mark.


Sienna checked herself in the mirror one final time. It had taken forty minutes to shower and repair the damage to her hair, but she felt better.

Placing her grimy clothes back into her duffle bag, Sienna straightened up the bathroom. The housekeeper had told her where to find the laundry chute to drop her towels. *A laundry chute?* Sienna had to laugh. She had never used one before and took great delight in lowering the used towels into the small compartment and seeing them slide out of view. "Now that's cool."

She returned to the bedroom she had used and gave it a once over to make sure she hadn't left anything out of place. Confident that everything was tidy, she returned to the lower level family room.

She wasn't surprised to see Sherry sitting there waiting. The shock came in seeing the man she'd collided with seated next to her.

"There you are," Sherry stood and walked over to Sienna. "You look none the worse for wear and tear."

"Isn't it amazing what a shower can do?" she joked.

"We're having a water slide race in a few minutes. I'm going to be one of the referees. I just wanted to be sure you were doing okay. Catch up to you later?"

"Sure. Thanks for everything."

After Sherry left, Vaughn's gaze returned to Sienna.

"She's right. You don't look like you've been through anything more traumatic than a paddle boat ride."

She laughed. "Looks can be deceiving," she extended her right hand. "I'm Sienna Lambert. Thank you for helping me, Mr.—?"

He grasped her hand in his. "Deveraux. Vaughn Deveraux."

"It's a pleasure to meet you, Mr. Deveraux."

"Call me Vaughn. The feeling is mutual though I'm sure you'd have preferred it be under less strenuous circumstances."

"Actually, I found out for the first time today that I don't mind baseball."

He released her hand. "That's good to hear, but make sure you watch your back. As you can see it can get physical sometimes."

"True. I forgot to ask, did I get you out?"

"Uh—"

Something about his expression tipped her off. She eyed him with amusement. "Yes," she almost yelled. She winced at the instant throbbing in her head. "I knew it!" she said, lowering her voice. "I got you out. You can't even deny it with a straight face."

Vaughn laughed in a rich baritone voice that boomed in the quiet room. He ushered them outside into the sunlight. His hand automatically drifted to the small of her back. Snagging an iced tea off a nearby table, Vaughn handed it to Sienna before getting himself one. He found that the urge to tease her was not something he could resist. "I hate to tell you this, and after you worked so hard, but it was a foul, Sienna. You didn't get me out."

"What?" she said loudly and then cringed at the pain it caused her. "You mean to tell me I was knocked unconscious, I nearly suffered a concussion and you were safe?" Exasperation tinged her voice. "I can't believe it."

Vaughn eyed her apologetically. "Afraid so. The umpire awarded me the base."

She looked confused.

"The foul is called an obstruction," he explained. "A fielder can't block the base from the runner."

"I guess they forgot to tell me that rule," she said, dryly."

"Don't feel bad, you did great," he winked. "It's hard to get me out. It's not something that happens that often."

"Oh please," she retorted as she lowered herself gingerly into a nearby chaise lounge.

"Would you hold this for a second?" he asked handing her his glass. Vaughn walked over to a nearby seating area to grab a vacant lounger. He sidled it up right next to Sienna sitting sideways on his so that he faced her. "So, what do you do when you're not taking one for the team?"

She chuckled at his joke. "I'm a consumer psychologist. Dexter Clothiers is a client of mine."

"Really?" he perked up. "Mine, too."

"Oh, I thought you were one of the cover models."

Surprise registered across his face. "Me? No, I leave the modeling in the very capable hands of my younger brother, Pierce. He's a retired football player. I'm the creative director at Chase & Burroughs. You know it's too bad we're on the campaign. Pierce would've made a perfect addition to the line. He has a great deal of experience with women asking questions about his briefs," he chuckled.

Sienna shook her head with amusement.

"Actually, we just found out we got the new line."

"Congratulations. I conducted a few focus groups for it."

Vaughn leaned closer to her. "I know. We read your reports. You got some great feedback that will be very useful for a few ideas we have, and the groups sounded very interesting."

"That is an understatement." Recalling the interviews Sienna couldn't help but laugh.

They chatted genially for quite some time. Each completely engrossed in their conversation. Both discovered they had much in common. In the midst of their banter Vaughn handed Sienna a piece of strawberry cheesecake from a nearby waiter. "I can't believe we both live in Raleigh and we've never met."

She didn't respond until after she'd reverently placed a piece of the chilled dessert in her mouth. She moaned aloud. "That was sinful."

Vaughn's fork clattered loudly on his plate. He cleared his throat.

Sienna didn't seem to notice his discomfiture. "I can believe we've never met. I work a lot. Most of my time is spent growing my business. If I have any free time I'm usually spending it with family."

"Same here," he said absentmindedly, as his eyes followed the progression of her dessert laden fork to her mouth and back.

Sienna looked up. Her gaze locked with Vaughn's. She was the first to look away. "So how's your campaign for Dexter going?"

He sat back slightly. "They seemed really impressed with what we pitched to them last week. A few of our teams are still in the late-night-concepting phase on some additional ads, but I'm confident my team will hit a home run when we're done.

She rolled her eyes at the pun. He winked.

Vaughn continued talking about his company's progress. Sienna's expression was still attentive so he continued. "We've got an idea for one commercial where this guy is wearing Best Kept Secrets. He's trying all sorts of things with them on. He's jogging, skiing, dancing, and a few other activities. Then he sits down on this chair and after a few seconds a wide grin slowly comes across his face. Then a caption pops up on the screen. "Best Kept Secrets. You gotta SEAT to believe it."

While he was talking, a look briefly crossed Sienna's face. He went silent.

"What?"

Sienna shook her head. "Nothing."

Vaughn eyed her perceptively. "You don't like it?"

"Uh . . . it's not that I don't like it—per se."

He gave her his undivided attention. "Then what was it exactly that caused that look of disapproval to flitter across your face?"

She remained silent.

"Oh come on, don't chicken out. If there's something wrong with my team's idea just tell me."

Sienna looked at him as if trying to gauge what his reaction would be.

"Just tell me."

"Okay. I think the last concept you had about the focus being on a seat that the guy is sitting on—well—it's kinda hokey."

"Hokey?"

"I'm just saying, it isn't as strong as some of your other ideas."

Vaughn's jaw flexed. Her tone grated on his nerves, reminding him immediately of an argument he'd had with his executive creative director just days before. This time when he spoke he couldn't help the annoyance that caused him to reply, "Hokey. Gee, is that a technical term, Dr. Lambert?"

Sienna bristled. "No, it isn't. I merely—"

"Said it was too rudimentary."

"I said it wasn't as good as your other ideas," she clarified. "The simplicity of it had nothing to do with it. It was the concept that was lacking."

Whatever interest he'd had for Sienna fizzled faster than the air let out of a balloon. He wasn't used to the women he was trying to impress ripping into him about anything, and never, ever, about his work. This was something that simply never happened. Vaughn was definitely out of his element.

Sienna read his expression and keyed in on his body language. She looked incredulous.

"Why are you upset? You can't expect every idea you have to hit the bull's eye dead center."

Vaughn sat back on his lounge chair. The air between them crackled with tension. He cleared his throat. His eyes raked over her. "So, purchased many pairs of men's underwear, have we?"

"Excuse me?"

"I'm curious how often *you* purchase men's underwear."

"As a rule—number five to be exact; I never discuss personal business with clients."

"I'm not a client," Vaughn pointed out. "My client is a client. Just answer the question. When's the last time you and men's underwear were up close and personal?"

"What does that have to do with anything?"

"Well, you don't like the concept about the seat, which by the way a guy would totally get. So it must be because you don't wear them—or buy them."

"For your information I've purchased plenty of men's underwear before."

Vaughn snorted. "Birthday, Father's Day, and Christmas gifts for your dad don't count."

Sienna's eyes narrowed. "You have no idea who I purchase anything for, and for your information I don't have to *wear* men's underwear to know what I like—or what's a crappy idea."

Vaughn threw his hands up. "Oh, so we've gone past hokey and are now in crappy territory."

Sienna couldn't believe the crazy turn their conversation had taken. She stood up and grabbed her bag. When she spoke this time her voice was edged with censure. "I'm astonished, Mr. Deveraux, that what started out as an amiable conversation between us somehow took a sharp turn for the worse. You are supposedly a professional, yet you seem incapable of listening to constructive criticism without insulting the person giving you their opinion—fascinating," Sienna replied smoothly.

Stiffly Vaughn stood up. Her last comment really got under his skin. "I'm glad to see you're feeling well enough to turn the psychoanalyzing sign back on. It's been a pleasure meeting you, Dr. Lambert," there was an edge to his voice when he said Doctor. "Hopefully, if we ever cross paths again, you'll know to step out of the way before you get run over." he began to walk away.

"Who knows Mr. Deveraux; maybe next time you'll be the one that gets knocked on your—seat." She replied in a voice so sweet a dentist would have gotten a cavity.

# Chapter Four

## Undercover

Vaughn felt like a total idiot. As he maneuvered his car onto the interstate to head home, he thought again about his behavior towards Sienna Lambert. He winced as he replayed their conversations—all of them—over in his mind. Granted, their first meeting had started with him knocking her out, but from the moment she regained consciousness, they had hit it off. Vaughn couldn't explain why her criticism of his team's idea for the line had irritated him enough to go for her jugular, but it did. This wasn't his first day on the job. He had been in advertising for ten years and was used to having his ideas challenged all the time. Considering what he had to deal with at work on occasion Sienna's comments had been tame.

*So why the all out battle with her?* His reaction didn't make any sense. He'd been trying to impress her. Even when she'd been battered and bruised Vaughn had felt that first spark of interest, after he got over her blocking his play, of course. Being a sports junkie made him appreciate her physical side that much more. Though he really couldn't understand what the severe hairdo was about, there was no way it detracted from her facial features. She didn't appear to have an ounce of make-up on and she still looked incredible. Overhearing the occasional conversation between women in his office clued him in that a woman looking as beautiful as Sienna Lambert did, sans make-up, was a bonus. She was tall, well-proportioned and he was glad to see nowhere near being skin-and-bones. That sickly look most women coveted made him cringe. She was shapely. Her already bronzed skin was enriched by the summer sun. She was breathtaking.

While they were talking, he'd tried hard not to appear to be staring. He'd turned his gaze to the lake and then various points around the back yard. A minute later he couldn't help looking over at her with that smile he reserved for women he was trying to impress.

"So much for that," he said, sarcastically. Despite his best intentions things had gotten pretty ugly toward the end. Agitation made him fidgety.

Vaughn hit a button on his navigation screen and dialed his best friend, Carlton Petersen. When his buddy answered he spoke. "Got a problem."

"Hang on. Let me schedule my client's next appointment. Be right back."

Vaughn listened impatiently to music in his ear as he waited for Carlton to return.

"Sorry, buddy. You've got my undivided attention. That being said, you've got twenty minutes before my next client comes so make it good."

"Since when is giving someone a massage more important than a problem of mine?" Vaughn groused.

"Since she's paying me—and you're not."

"Point taken," Vaughn recounted the story for his friend in fluid efficiency leaving nothing out. "So there you have it. Stupid, huh?"

Carlton was silent for a few moments before he burst out laughing. Vaughn bristled. He squeezed the steering wheel until his knuckles came into view. "That isn't what I had in mind."

When Carlton spoke, his voice was laced with mirth. His Trinidadian accent was hard to miss. "Are you serious?"

"I wouldn't have mentioned it if I weren't serious," he snapped.

"So you're waiting for me to confirm you made a jackass out of yourself in front of this lady?"

"I already know that, Carl. What I was hoping to get was some insight on why. It makes no sense."

"You make no sense. This is the craziest thing you've done since the time you—"

"Will you focus?" Vaughn said, with impatience. "How do I fix this?"

"Apologize to the woman for your reprehensible manners. How can she not forgive you? It's not that often we admit to that, you know."

"I'm glad to see you're having a ball at my expense."

"Of course, it's what I'm here for."

Silence ensued. Finally, Carlton broke the sound barrier. "Angella's been asking about you. She wants to know when you're taking your best girl out."

Hearing mention of his nine year-old goddaughter made him calm down a bit. He loved being around her. The moment he'd held her little body in his big arms and she didn't cry, he was hooked. The fact that she was as big a sports junkie as he was only made it more fun.

"The next two weeks are bad for me. I'll be swamped at work all this week, and the following week I'm on travel. I'll have to make it two weeks from now."

"That's fine, man. She knows your job gets hectic sometimes."

"Still, I hate to put her off. Tell my Angel she and I will hang out when I get back. We'll play a round of golf and grab dinner."

"She'll love that," Carlton replied. "Now about this mystery girl—"

"Sienna. Her name is Sienna Lambert. She's amazing, Carl. She has a great sense of humor, she's intelligent, personable, her smile is contagious, and her body is on point. I'm positive there's nothing artificial on her—anywhere."

"Fascinating. My advice is quit worrying about it. Just call her up, apologize and then ask her out—sexy body and all."

"After the train wreck of our first meeting, the last thing she would see me as is dating potential. Besides, it's easier said than done," Vaughn sighed. "I don't have her number."

"You mean you aggravated the woman past the point of no return *before* you got a number?"

More chuckling ensued. Vaughn gritted his teeth.

"You're resourceful, buddy. I'm sure you can find a way to contact her. Sorry, but I have to run. My next client is here. Keep me posted."

"Don't I always?" Vaughn countered before hanging up.

Vaughn's mood hadn't improved by the time he got home. He was looking forward to a hot shower, crashing on his couch and getting caught up on some of his recorded shows. When he pulled into his driveway, he groaned aloud. A shiny red Audi R8 was parked sideways. Vaughn stifled the groan that hung on the edge of his lips. *Pierce.*

Of all the days to get an impromptu visit from his younger brother, this day was the absolute worst.

Vaughn gave the sports car a wide berth and pulled into one of the vacant stalls of his garage. Entering the house, he passed through several rooms with no sign of his brother. He headed downstairs to the basement and straight into the "Man Cave." His brother was playing pool and listening to music. When Pierce looked up, he flashed his brother a grin. "Hey, dude. What's up?"

"Too much," Vaughn groused going straight to the mini kitchen. Vaughn pulled a beer out of the refrigerator, and then retrieved a bottle opener from a drawer. He flicked the top off and pitched it into the trashcan.

"Really?" Pierce leaned over the table and sank a ball into a corner pocket. "Care to elaborate?"

Vaughn retrieved his favorite pool stick from a mounted rack. "Not yet." Ignoring his brother's game, he started racking up balls. Pierce followed suit. Once they were lined up Vaughn sent the cue ball hurtling down the table. The balls scattered with the force of the collision. They had played two games before Pierce broke the sound barrier.

"Okay Vaughn, you've had time to stew, and I've allowed you to beat me for some time now. I think you need to tell me what's going on."

"Allowed me to beat you?" Vaughn snorted.

"Don't act like you're a better pool player than me, big brother. I take your shirt every game we play. Chase does too, and considering how often he gets back home, I'd say that was pretty pathetic."

Vaughn thought about their middle brother, Chase. He was in the Army stationed in Germany. He rolled his eyes. "Not every game."

"Quit deferring. What's the matter with you?"

"I had a crappy day. No more, no less."

"This is hardly what I would call the norm, bro. Even with the headaches you bring home from work. You've never been this—edgy before," Pierce took his shot. "If I had to bet my money I'd say it was a certain psychologist that's got you all worked up?"

Vaughn's ball missed the pocket by a large margin. Annoyance flashed in his eyes. "Carlton's got a big mouth."

Quit complaining. He merely called to warn me that you'd be in a piss poor mood. Besides, this way you don't have to repeat how you tanked with the ladies."

"It wasn't ladies," he clarified. "It was just the one and there's nothing happening between us."

"Because you blew it," Pierce countered.

"If you have nothing to input other than sarcasm, you know the way out."

"Stop getting so riled up. I agree with Carl on this one. Just flash your pearly whites and combine it with an apology— she'll be all yours."

"It's not like that. She isn't one of the superficial women you're used to dating, Pierce. Sienna has more character, and a higher IQ."

"Don't knock what you haven't tried," Pierce quipped. My ladies are into a good time. I go all out to make sure they get it, too. No harm, no foul."

Vaughn gave up on the pool game. He grabbed his drink and stalked over to the couch. After he flopped down heavily, he put his feet up on the nearby ottoman. "Spare me the details, Pierce."

"I'm just saying—"

Vaughn looked up. "I wasn't kidding."

"Suit yourself," Pierce retrieved his duffle bag off a nearby table and headed toward the entertainment system. He grabbed the remote for the projection screen and flicked it on. "I brought over a DVD of me commentating on Sports Time last week. You can tell me how you like my new suit."

"Pierce, I love you. You're my brother and all, but I'm not about to comment on how good you look in a suit."

"Don't hate the player," Pierce laughed plopping down next to him. "This segment has the new sports drink I'm endorsing. Cha-ching," he pretended to press the spin button on a slot machine.

Pierce talked throughout the entire one hour segment. Considering how many times he backed up or pressed pause on the DVD player, it was an hour and a half of non-stop chatter.

He truly had to laugh at Pierce's enthusiasm for his subject matter—himself.

Eventually, his mood couldn't help but improve. There were times when despite himself Vaughn had to laugh at his brother's antics—both live and on DVD.

In the middle of Pierce mimicking one of the football coaches on the screen, Vaughn elbowed him. "Thanks, man."

Pierce shrugged it off with a laugh. "That's what I'm here for. You do realize that it's a Saturday night and I'm here with you. There will be hearts breaking all over Raleigh tonight."

"I know," Vaughn replied playing with the bottle in his hand. "I know."


Sienna was in her office a week later proofreading a memo when Vivian came in.

"The mail just arrived, she said, cheerfully. "The invoices have been completed and are ready to go out."

"Thanks."

Vivian set the letters and a small FedEx package on Sienna's desk and walked out.

It was almost fifteen minutes before Sienna pulled her gaze away from the stack of papers in front of her. Bypassing the letters, she grasped the padded envelope. Seeing the return address she flipped the package over. She tugged at the flap to open it.

"What is this stuff made out of, *Crazy Glue*?" she replied, yanking forcefully on the seam.

Finally, she was successful. She eased the contents out of the package and onto her desk.

Her smile was almost blinding as she held up the garments in front of her. "I owe you big time, Sherry."

She placed the items back in the envelope. The papers she was working on were neatly stacked and put in her laptop bag. It took a few moments, but eventually her desk was back in some semblance of order. Sienna retrieved her purse out of a lower drawer. Balancing all her items, she walked to the door, flipped her light off and headed down the hall.

"I'm leaving, Viv. I'll be working from home for the rest of the evening, so call me or e-mail if you need anything."

"It's Friday night," Vivian bellowed from down the hall. "Girl, get a life," she shouted.

"I've got one—and you're sitting in it," Sienna yelled back.

She hurried out of her office on N. Boylan Avenue and around to the side parking lot to retrieve her car. Once she'd deposited her things on the opposite seat, Sienna slid in, secured her seatbelt, and started the car. She plotted her course on her GPS, *Lola*, and then turned on the satellite radio. CNN piped through the cabin speakers. She listened to the day's headline news as she drove out of the parking lot and headed home.

The first thing she did when she got there was change out of her work clothes into something comfortable. After standing in front of the refrigerator so long its door alarm went off, Sienna retrieved a yellow, orange, and red pepper out of the crisper, a few green onions, and some asparagus. Next were shrimp from the freezer, olive oil, and seasonings from the cabinet. While listening to *Watercolors*, a smooth jazz station on satellite radio, she made quick work of fixing dinner. She retrieved her favorite pasta dish and a wine glass from the cabinet. The weather was perfect for dining al fresco so she fixed her plate, poured a glass of wine, and then headed to her deck. Sienna kept the door open so that she could hear the music.

Taking the first bite of food, Sienna's eyes drifted closed. "Perfect," she smiled. Unable to help it, Sienna's thoughts strayed to her encounter with Vaughn Deveraux. He'd literally swept her off her feet in the beginning, but it had gone all pear-shaped in the end. She still wasn't clear why her disapproval had provoked such a vehement response from him.

His inference that she didn't understand the concept because she couldn't identify with the product was asinine. This was what she did for a living. She darn well knew what she was talking about. She grabbed her dishes and went back inside. Fresh irritation sparked anew just recalling their disagreement. Sienna cleaned up the kitchen. The white FedEx package sitting on the counter caught her eye. She stalked over to the counter to retrieve it. "I don't understand men's underwear, huh, Mr. Deveraux?"

Sienna pulled a pair of Best Kept Secrets briefs out of the envelope and walked into her living room. Vaughn's words and his condescending tone had sparked her competitive side. "It's game time Mr. Know-It-All," she said aloud. Sienna slid her lounging pants down her legs and stepped out of them when they hit the floor. Next item to be discarded was her panties. She had to laugh at the picture she would paint if anyone happened to be peeking through her window. Slowly, Sienna eased the underwear up her thighs and over her hips. Once they were in place she stood there motionless. "Hmm," she turned around several times. She walked into her foyer and stopped in front of the large mirror. "Well, aside from the opening in the crotch they look good. Now let's try moving in them."

Sienna turned up the radio and danced around to some "old school" tunes. She felt a bit silly when she broke into the Running Man. "So far, so good. Let's see how you handle exercise." Sienna turned and took off up the steps. She took them as fast as she could. Her breath came rapidly out of her mouth as she climbed the stairs and then ran down them.

Sienna ran up and down the steps several times. She was on the way down when the phone rang.

"Hello?" she said, a little breathless.

"Do I even want to know what you're doing?"

"Hey, Vivi. I'm conducting an experiment."

"With whom?" she snickered.

"Not whom, what. Men's underwear."

"I told you you've been working too hard."

"Would you be serious? Sherry gave me samples of the Best Kept Secrets line. I have to tell you Viv, the underwear is amazing. I've been doing everything in them and I can't even tell I have them on, aside from the air occasionally sneaking thru the manly opening."

"Uh-huh. So, why are you doing this again?"

"To prove a point. He thinks I don't know what I'm talking about just because I have never worn men's underwear. Well now I have, and his pitch is still corny."

"Who?"

"Vaughn Deveraux."

"He's the creative director at Chase & Burroughs, right?"

"Yes, he's the CD all right. Not so sure about the creative part though. More like Certified D—"

"Sienna!"

"I was going to say dufus."

"Wasn't he the one you hit it off with at the party?"

"It was just a friendly conversation, but yes, until he acted like a complete jerk."

Vivian laughed. "So what are you going to do now?"

"I'm going to finish my experiment and give Mr. Deveraux a report of my findings. You know, these things are so comfortable it's no surprise that a woman would want to wear them," Sienna paused for a moment. "Vivian, that's it."

"What's it? You've lost me again, Sienna. I can only follow you around so many bends," she said with exasperation.

"Never mind, I'll tell you later."

"Oh no, you don't. You can't leave me hanging like this. Tell me what you're up to and I mean right now," Vivian threatened.

"Can't. I have to hurry if I'm going to go through with this. I have to see Mr. Creative Director to give him a piece of my mind, and something tells me, I know just where to find him."

# Chapter Five

## The Pitch

"Finally," Vaughn grumbled, eyeing his co-worker. "We were about to send up a flare signal."

"Sorry, I had to go back for the wasabi," he retorted unloading the heavy bags on the table. "Good thing I checked before I'd driven all the way here."

"We are eternally grateful." Vaughn helped unpack the brown bags of plastic containers. His team swarmed around the conference room table, opening, closing and passing the food around. "Hey, who got Dragon rolls?"

"Me," a woman replied, stepping around the table to intercept him.

"You're parting with at least one," he informed her.

After a few minutes of chaos, everyone was seated at the table eating their sushi. Sitting at the head of the table, Vaughn dipped his spicy tuna roll in a mixture of wasabi and soy sauce. He popped it into his mouth and chewed a few seconds before speaking. "So, we're ditching the *Seat it to believe it* print and TV ads in favor of the one with multiple guys going throughout their day wearing Best Kept Secrets." Vaughn stood and pointed to the story boards in order.

"The guy with the big imagination seated at his desk all day, the one washing windows fifty feet in the air, the race car driver, the Alaskan fisherman, the EMT guy in the ambulance working to save someone's life, the missionary in the Costa Rican rainforest. The common theme between them is their need to be comfortable. They have to be prepared for anything. They don't have time to worry about whether or not their underwear are riding up into their—"

"Excuse me, Mr. Deveraux, there is someone here to see you," a woman called from the conference room door.

Vaughn glanced at the clock hanging on a nearby wall. It was after eight. "Okay," he said, lowering the last picture. "Guys, keep working on the copy, I'll be back."

He followed his associate into the reception area. When he saw who it was, he stopped short. "You're almost the last person I expected to see."

Sienna had stood up when she saw him enter the reception area. "Sorry to bother you when you're working," she said, stiffly. "But I need to speak with you. It's rather important."

Vaughn walked up to her. "Sure, follow me," he said, guiding her down the hall. "How did you even know where my office was, or that I was still here?"

"I Googled," she informed him. "When someone picked up, I asked if you were still here. She told me you were in a meeting so I figured I'd take a chance." As she walked silently beside him, Sienna couldn't help but ask, "So, who's the last person you expected to see?"

"My sixth grade teacher, Mrs. Whittier."

Her gaze turned to his profile. "Why?"

"Well, considering she died over twenty years ago, she'd be the absolute last person I'd expect to see."

Sienna didn't laugh at the joke.

He opened the door to his office, flipped the light on, and then stood aside to allow her to enter. Vaughn noted her serious expression and her body language. A twinge of guilt gripped him. He cleared his throat. "You said it was important. I'm all ears, Doc."

She frowned. "Why do you call me that?"

"Less formal than, Dr. Lambert."

"You could just call me, Sienna."

"I could," Vaughn agreed, "but after our last meeting I figured all possibility of a friendship between us was out the window."

"That wasn't my fault."

He nodded. "You're right, it was mine."

When he didn't continue, they lapsed into silence.

"I can't believe how comfortable they are," she exclaimed suddenly. "And they stay in place no matter what you're doing. Trust me, I've tried lots of things to test them out and they haven't budged."

Vaughn was baffled. "What?"

"Best Kept Secrets. They're incredible. It's amazing; I couldn't find one thing wrong with them. Consumers are going to love these things. If all goes well with the men's line, I think Dexter Clothiers should seriously consider developing a women's line. Granted, your pitch is still off, but—"

He held up his hands. "Wait a minute. You came to my office at almost eight thirty at night, pulled me out of a meeting with my team to tell me you tried on men's underwear?"

"Not just tried them—loved them," she clarified. "I'm serious."

"I don't doubt it," he countered.

"I even came up with a pitch for them. Wanna hear it?"

Vaughn leaned against his desk. He still looked incredulous. "By all means, Doc. Enchant me."

"Okay." Sienna paced a few feet from his desk. She held up her hands in excitement. "Best Kept Secrets: So seductively comfortable, even a woman would wear them!"

Vaughn opened his mouth to speak but she cut him off. "Well, that's all I came to tell you. I wore them, I liked them and I think by your standard that makes me qualified to give my opinion now. And my opinion is that you create ads that consumers will be able to connect and identify with. We've really got an amazing product here, Mr. Deveraux. Granted, the line can speak for itself, but I don't think it should have to."

Before he could comment, she'd walked out. He was still leaning against his desk feeling like he'd just witnessed a tornado blow through his office, ebbing as quickly as it arrived.

Annoyance crept into him, but it wasn't directed at her. He'd missed the opportunity to apologize for his behavior when they'd first met. Not that she'd given him much time to utter a syllable much less a full-blown sentiment. That being said, he was impressed.

"You, Sienna Lambert, are unusual." Vaughn shook his head in awe. Walking around his desk, he sat in his chair and put his feet up. Retrieving his cell phone from his back pocket, he held down the second button on his phone activating the speed dial. When Carlton picked up the phone, Vaughn quickly replied, "How can I *not* like her? She's completely unpredictable and looks better in men's underwear than I do."

There were a few seconds of silence before his buddy spoke. "Whoa, how'd you get her out of hers and into yours? I didn't even think you two were talking. When did you and the psychologist—"

"Not my underwear, Carl, the client's underwear."

"So she and Dexter are—"

Vaughn let out an exasperated sigh which in all honesty he wasn't sure was directed at his best friend, or himself. "Sienna tried them on to shut me up. She even came up with a tag line for the ad to boot," he couldn't keep the admiration out of his voice. "And she was right—it is better than mine."

"So what now, buddy? Chalk it up to lesson learned and move on?"

"You know better than that. Dr. Lambert and I were starting to become friends before I messed it up. We're going to finish what we started."

***

Sienna slammed her car door and then winced at the harsh sound. Her breathing came out in rapid shudders. *The jerk!* She felt supreme satisfaction when she had sailed passed him with his mouth practically hanging open. "Serves him right," she said, into the silence before starting her car.

As she pulled out of the parking space behind Vaughn's building, Sienna couldn't help but wonder at her bravado. Was it all just to prove him wrong, or was it because she wanted to see him again? "Probably both," she admitted aloud. She'd been good and mad when she went to his office determined to give him a piece of her mind. That anger fizzled a bit when he walked into the reception area. *All six-feet-whatever of him.*

Truthfully, Sienna had been hard pressed to stay mad when she glimpsed a smile tugging at his lips at seeing her. Then she recalled how their wonderful day at the picnic had been shot to smithereens because of him. That gave her the push she needed to say her peace and leave.

*The jerk!* She repeated in her head. She was too geared up to feel sleepy. She wasn't far from her parents' house in Wakefield Pines so she dropped in.

When Sienna pulled into their driveway, she spotted her father's silhouette in the mirrored door. By the time she'd cut the engine and got out, he was on the porch waiting for her.

"Hi, Dad," she greeted as she walked up the stairs.

"How's my beauty queen?"

She shook her head at the reference. She disliked being reminded of a time in her life she preferred to forget. "Just fine. Is Mom awake?"

Gordon kissed his daughter and then followed her into the house. "Of course. She just got finished doing some class on FitTV. She's in the exercise room."

"Don't you guys sleep?" Sienna asked heading toward the basement stairs.

"This coming from someone that knocked on our door at nine thirty?" her father chuckled.

"How'd you know I was out here?"

He winked. "Father's intuition."

"Good to know," she laughed heading for the basement stairs.

"Oh, by the way. Have you spoken to Sasha lately?"

Sienna didn't bother to mask the sarcasm. "Why, should I have?"

"Sienna."

"Spare me the soldierly lecture, Dad."

"I wasn't going to lecture you, sweetheart. I just want you two to get along better, that's all."

"Duly noted. Now, can we drop the subject?"

Sadness etched her father's features. He nodded. "Consider it dropped."


Once in the basement, Sienna followed the hallway toward the exercise room. She poked her head in the door. Her stepmother was on an exercise mat on the floor. "Hey, Mom."

"Hi honey," Cassandra Lambert smiled cheerfully. If she was surprised to see her stepdaughter at such a late hour, she refrained from comment. "What brings you by?"

Sienna sat down on the recumbent bike and fingered the handlebar. "Actually, I was in the neighborhood and figured I'd stop in."

"Really?" Cassandra stood up and walked over to a nearby shelf to grab a towel. As she wiped her face, neck, and shoulders she scrutinized her stepdaughter. "Well, that's lucky for your father and me." Kneeling, she retrieved her mat from the floor. She rolled it up and walked over to lean it against the wall in the corner of the room. "Are you hungry?"

"Mom, it's almost ten."

"What difference does that make? How about some dessert? We've got your favorite—rainbow sherbert."

"No thanks, I'm fine," Sienna replied flicking the pedal on the stationary bike.

"Darling, is everything okay? You seem like something is on your mind."

"Just a long day that's all. There's not much to tell."

"That's not what my gut tells me," Gordon replied from the doorway.

"Daddy," Sienna admonished. "You shouldn't be eavesdropping."

"I was doing nothing of the sort. I knew the moment you walked onto the porch something was wrong. My instincts are never wrong."

"Yes, dad we know. You have the most accurate instincts known to man."

"Don't laugh, young lady. They served me well during my military career."

Sienna walked over and hugged her father. "I thank God for it, too."

"We both do," Cassandra chimed in.

"Okay, now that we've had our family moment, what's got you so out of sorts, kiddo?"

Sienna looked at her watch. "Dad, it's kind of late and I've got to get going."

"I hope you aren't planning to drive back home at this hour," Cassandra cautioned.

She burst out laughing. "I live ten minutes away."

"Giselle came a few days ago so clean sheets are already on your bed."

Sienna hadn't realized how tired she was until she contemplated having to drive home—all ten minutes of it. She almost yawned aloud. She turned to Cassandra. "Thanks, Mom. I think I'll take you up on your offer to stay over."

Cassandra hugged her. "Sweety, you never need an invitation to stay here. It's your home, too. Now, let's go find that sherbert."

Gordon perked up. "Sounds good to me," he replied heading down the hallway. "While we're at it, Sienna can fill us in on what she's trying not to fill us in on."

"It's not that serious," Sienna grumbled.

"You let us be the judge of that, darling," Cassandra replied.

# Chapter Six

## A Clean Slate

Sienna took her glasses off and rubbed her eyes. She'd had a presentation across town that morning, two conference calls, and it wasn't even lunchtime yet. She hadn't slept well when she'd spent the night at her parent's house. The bed was comfortable enough, but the twenty questions over rainbow sherbert had been a bit much. She told her parents about her run-in with Vaughn at the party and their unusual conversation afterwards. Oddly enough, neither one tried to tell her what to do, and both had been supportive—until she mentioned the underwear experiment. That tidbit of information elicited her father's signature raised eyebrow. It was reminiscent of Vaughn's expression when she'd told him about her experiment.

*Vaughn.* There had been no contact with him since she went to his office. She didn't think she'd hear from him, but part of her had hoped she would. *What did you expect? You read him the riot act, told him his work was sub-standard, and didn't let him get a word in edgewise.* Sienna fingered the tight knot at the back of her neck. *Still, it would've been great if they could have become friends*, she scolded herself. *Rule number six: Never waste time wondering "what if?"*

"I wasn't going to anyway."

"Do you always talk to yourself?"

Sienna gasped and sprang to her feet. The chair she was sitting in snapped back against the wall.

"Sorry, did I startle you?"

She glanced across the room to see Vaughn lounging against the door jam. She ignored the happiness at seeing him that shot through her. "No problem." She stared at him. "What are you doing here?"

"When last we met, you didn't let me get a word in edgewise, so I thought I'd stop by *your* office so that I could get a chance to finish my sentence."

"Oh." Sienna's cheeks reddened. "Come in."

"Thanks," Vaughn replied, closing the door behind him. He sauntered toward her.

"Um, how did you find my office?"

Vaughn sat in the chair across from her desk. "I Googled," he grinned.

Sienna lowered herself back into her seat. "Resourceful aren't you?"

"When I need to be."

"Hey, Sienna would you—"

Vivian stopped midsentence when she noticed Sienna wasn't alone. "Oh, sorry, I didn't know you had a meeting," she apologized.

Sienna stood up. "I don't—I mean I didn't—until now."

Vivian walked toward the desk. She glanced between Sienna and the man now standing, too. He extended his hand. "Good afternoon, I'm Vaughn Deveraux."

"Yes. Yes, you are," Vivian remarked, with a wide smile. "It's a pleasure to meet you, Mr. Deveraux, I'm Vivian Adair. I'm the office manager, webmaster, and photographer extraordinaire."

"You wear a lot of hats," Vaughn noted.

"Don't I know it," Vivian agreed. She glanced pointedly at Sienna.

Sienna ignored her friend's not-so-subtle stare. "What's up, Vivian?"

"I've got the new website layout you wanted to see. I can come back later if now isn't a good time?"

"No, it's fine. I'll take it." Sienna walked around her desk. "Thanks. I'll look it over and get back to you later."

"You're welcome." Her friend grinned. "Pleasure to meet you, Mr. Deveraux."

"Please, call me Vaughn. It was great to meet you as well, Ms. Adair."

"Vivian," she corrected.

Sienna walked with her to her door. "Girl, you're all kinds of crazy," Vivian said, softly as they walked.

"I'll find you shortly," Sienna whispered closing the door behind her friend.

"Sorry about that," she replied, turning toward her desk.

She was brought up short by Vaughn standing right behind her.

"No big deal."

Sienna backed up as much as she could, considering that the door was right behind her. "So, what brings you by my office and in the middle of the day no less?"

"Underwear. What else?"

"Excuse me?"

He flashed a wide grin. "I can't believe you wore men's underwear just to prove me wrong."

"What other reason is there?" Sienna countered.

Though he tried to contain it, amusement rumbled deep inside him. It was just too strong a feeling to suppress. Eventually, the laughter bubbled over. Vaughn shook so hard with mirth his eyes started watering. He tried to stop, but failed miserably. After a few moments, he looked up expecting to find Sienna seething with anger or indignation. Instead, she too was laughing uncontrollably.

"Rule number seven." Sienna wiped the tears from her eyes. "Always keep them guessing."

"As to which direction you're going to pull the rug out from under them?"

"Not exactly."

"Yes, exactly."

They shared a smile, but after a moment Vaughn turned thoughtful. He took a deep breath. "Sienna, I owe you an apology. The other day—I was way out of line. I still haven't figured out what prompted me to act so reprehensibly. He ran a hand over his jaw. A day earlier, Linda Wilkins, my executive CD, chewed me out about another campaign we were working on. I don't know. Maybe something about your critique reminded me of her. Not that I'm trying to make excuses." He looked at her. "There are none."

"It's okay," Sienna replied trying to lighten the mood.

Vaughn moved closer. "No, it's not okay. I ruined what was turning out to be a day—full of surprises."

Sienna nervously smoothed her hair back into her already flawless bun. "I have to admit, I haven't had one to equal it since I sat on a mound of fire ants one year at a family picnic."

"You don't seem to have very good luck at outdoor functions," he teased.

"Tell me about it."

"Have dinner with me."

Sienna's head popped up so fast she gave herself whiplash. She grimaced at the tingling pain that shot up the side of her neck. It was her turn to look baffled. "What?"

"I'd like to take you out to dinner. It would help considerably if you'd say yes."

"Look, if this is about the horrific way you behaved—"

"Partially," he interrupted. "Mostly it's because I'd like to continue talking to you, but I have to get back to work."

"Are you serious?"

"I do have a meeting this afternoon and—"

"Not about work," Sienna said, impatiently.

"About dinner? Quite." He bent down until he was eye level with her. "Is that a yes?"

An image of her and Vaughn at an intimate table for two with candles, wine, and music popped into her head. He looked hot and was leaning in for a—.

"Sienna?"

"Hmm?" she said, blinking.

"What do you say?"

"I don't know, Vaughn." Sienna frowned pushing the daydream aside. "We haven't exactly had the best track record."

"Which admittedly has been my fault. I'd like to have the opportunity to fix that."

"Can I think about it and let you know?"

"Sure." Reluctantly, he retrieved his business card and wrote his home number on the back. "If you call me tonight you'll have to try my cell. I probably won't be home till late."

"You really put in some long hours."

"Yes I do, but not tonight. I'm taking my Angel out for a night on the town."

Sienna blinked. The smile on his face was captivating. She couldn't keep the edge out of her voice. "If you have a date with such a paragon, I wonder why you're asking me out."

Vaughn tried not to smile. "That 'paragon' is nine years-old, and my goddaughter, Angella Petersen. Her father, Carlton, is my best friend. Her mother died of ovarian cancer when she was a baby. I help out as much as I can."

Sienna's cheeks reddened. She bit her lower lip and looked away. "I'm sorry I said that. Embarrassed party of one? Your table's ready."

Vaughn put his hand on her shoulder. "Hey, no worries, I'll talk to you later?"

Sienna nodded.

Vaughn gave her a final smile before heading to the door. He paused before he went out and turned around. "Thanks for coming to tell me about your experiment. I'm sure I'll have detailed questions about it later." He winked.

"I would be surprised if you didn't," Sienna joked.

"Have a good day, Doc."

"You too, Vaughn."

The moment he left Sienna bolted to the door. Slowly, she opened it and peeked down the corridor. She watched him until he disappeared from view. She counted out a full minute before she cautiously left her office. Sienna speed-walked in the opposite direction and went directly into Vivian's office.

"Took you long enough," her friend replied, eyeing a proof sheet.

"He just left. Vivi, he asked me out."

"Tell me you said yes," Vivian said, warily.

"I said—I'd think about it."

That got Vivian's attention. She raised her head and slid her glasses up over the braids in her hair. "Have you lost your mind?"

"Maybe," Sienna said, defensively. "Anyway, it's not a date-date. He said he wants to take me out to apologize for being rude. We haven't exactly gotten off to the best start, you know. Besides, we're not even friends."

"I could see the sparks bouncing off the walls the second I walked in. I'm not blind. I can tell you like him."

"So," Sienna countered.

"So, he likes you, too."

Flopping down on Vivian's arm chair, Sienna leaned back to stare at the ceiling. Her stomach was still doing tumbles. "You think so?"

"Is this you fishing for compliments, or are you completely oblivious to the man staring the clothes off you with his eyes?"

"Both, I guess. You see?" Sienna lamented. "This is why I don't go out on dates. It's too much stress."

"I got an idea that could help that. You could always interview him. That should make you feel better," Vivian teased.

When Sienna didn't immediately respond, Vivian look up with an appalled expression on her face.

"I'm kidding," Sienna replied. "I'm not going to interview him. Besides, there's nothing between us."

"Whose fault is that?"

"Technically? I'd say both of ours."

"All the more reason to remedy the situation, and what better way to do that than over a good meal and a glass of wine, or beer, or—"

Sienna sighed, loudly. "Will you be serious?"

"You thought I wasn't? Call that fine man back right now and accept his dinner invitation."

"No way. I just put my foot in my mouth and trust me I've got to let some time go by before I talk to him after that embarrassing moment. Rule number eight: After intense embarrassment, twenty-four hours must elapse before seeing the person again."

"Do you make this stuff up on the fly?"

"Maybe," Sienna hedged.

"Sienna," Vivian said, patiently. "You do realize that half the chaos in your life you bring on yourself? Seriously, stop analyzing it to death and go execute."

"Fine," Sienna said, with mock annoyance. She got up and walked back to her office. She shut the door and went to her desk to sit down. Reaching into her pocket, Sienna retrieved his business card. She stared at it. "No, I can't call now. He just left. It would look funny if I call so soon," she rationalized aloud. Sienna put the card back and took a deep breath. *I'll call him later.*

The day got away from her. Sienna was non-stop busy until she left at seven o'clock that evening. Dinner was a carry-out Kosmic Karma pizza from Mellow Mushroom. As Sienna drove down Glenwood Avenue, her thoughts turned to her social life. Aside from work, she didn't really have much of a life outside of the office. Most of her time over the last few years had been spent growing her business. Its success had been her number one priority. Now Lambert Insights was doing well and business was steadily growing. Maybe it was time to live a little.

Later that night Sienna, in her pajamas, paced across her bedroom floor. She popped another frozen Crème Puff into her mouth. "Now is a perfect time to call, right?" she said, between bites. She glanced at the clock. It was quarter to nine. The card he'd given her was on the nightstand near the phone. "He said he would be taking out his goddaughter, Angella. He'd still be out. Wouldn't he? Perfect!" She decided to call his house and leave a message so that she wouldn't have to actually speak to him.

Decision made, Sienna crossed the room and sat on the edge of her bed. She sat the plastic container on her nightstand, ate another puff for good measure, and then picked up her cordless phone. She dialed Vaughn's home number. She hung up before the first ring.

"What if he answers? What then?" Sienna pondered.

Vivian's voice sounded in her head. *Then you talk to him. Now stop debating it and just do it.* "Okay, okay," Sienna said, aloud. She tried again. Her foot tapped against the carpeted floor anxiously. Her dessert laden stomach churned loudly. After the fourth ring, his answering machine picked up. Sienna heard his voice in her ear followed by a beep.

"Hi Vaughn, this is Sienna. I, uh, wanted to let you know that I decided to accept your dinner invitation. Give me a call to let me know what day and time is convenient for you." She left her home and cell phone numbers before hanging up the phone. Sienna fell back against the bed. Her heart fluttered against her chest. "I said yes." She took a deep breath. There was no going back now. She'd left a message, one that he would be checking before the night ended.

"*Nothing major, just a casual dinner date between two people trying to get to know each other better.*" Images of her last daydream drifted into her thoughts. He looked incredible in a dark suit. She had on a dress that complimented her in all the right places. In this vision, her hair was down and curled softly to frame her face. He was gazing at her like she was featured on the menu. A live jazz trio played a soulful melody nearby. Suddenly, Vaughn grabbed her hand and pulled her up from the table. He twirled her around once and guided her to the dance floor.

"Stop it," she said, snapping herself out of her own fantasy. Her hand snaked out to grab the dessert off her table. She felt so warm the frozen treat would probably melt on contact. "I'm a psychologist," she reasoned. "No need to freak out. Emotions, I can handle. Besides, I've interviewed hundreds of people before. This is just one man, right?" Sienna thought back to the man that hit on her in New Hampshire. The one she'd dubbed the living Adonis. "I have nothing to worry about—we're just friends. Besides, Vaughn doesn't even have a shiny red cape." *Yeah,* her conscience replied. *But something tells us he doesn't need one.*

# Chapter Seven

## Angel

"It's my turn," Angella Petersen whispered in Vaughn's ear.

He passed her the popcorn. "I knew I should've gotten you your own tub," he teased. "You said you only wanted a little."

"What are you talking about, Uncle Vaughn? I've only had a few handful."

"Uh-huh. If that's the case, why is it almost empty?" he queried.

His goddaughter squinted her eyes in the limited light and peered into the darkened popcorn container. "Because you've got bigger hands than I do?"

Vaughn chuckled and poked her. "Good try, Miss Petersen, but I'm not buying it."

Angella poked him back. "Shh. The movie's starting."

"Brat," he whispered.

Two and a half hours later, they made their way out of the IMAX Theatre at Marbles Kids Museum. "Thanks for the movie, Uncle Vaughn. I loved it," Angella said, hugging him.

"It was awesome, wasn't it?"

"Dad's going to freak when I tell him what a good time he missed." Angella followed Vaughn out the door. She wrapped her arm around his as they walked back to the parking lot behind the building.

"He knows anytime we go out, he ends up missing out on all the fun. Serves him right," Vaughn joked. Opening her car door, he got her settled into her seat before he closed the door. By the time Vaughn slid into the driver's seat Angella had secured her seat belt.

"Where to now?" she inquired.

"Now, I drive you home, Angel."

She glanced over at Vaughn. "It's still early," she complained.

"Little girl, it's eleven o'clock. That could hardly be considered early."

"Sure it can."

"Not for a nine year-old," Vaughn clarified.

"Well, are you taking me to soccer practice? You promised you would this time."

"I remember. I will be at your door bright and early."

She settled back into the leather seat and watched the lights zoom by. When he got on I-540 going west she turned toward him. "Uncle Vaughn, can we stop by the airport to see the planes land?"

"Not a chance. Besides, Observation Park is probably closed by now. How about tomorrow?"

"Won't you have a date or something?"

Vaughn's head snapped up. "Excuse me?"

"Well, it is the weekend. You should get out. Maybe you could call your new friend?"

Vaughn was going to have a nice talk with Carlton when he dropped Angella home.

"Someone's been eavesdropping."

"Uncle Vaughn, you know how loud Daddy talks. I can't help it if I happen to overhear stuff. The walls aren't concrete, you know."

"Uh-huh. We're not exactly friends, yet. Munchkin. I've only seen her a few times."

"But you'd like to be," Angella pressed.

"Sure, Sienna is a wonderful lady. She's smart, has an unusual sense of humor, and she's flat out beautiful."

"Does she have a sister?"

Vaughn laughed. "I don't know. Like I said, we haven't exactly had a chance to converse much."

He nudged her. "Playing matchmaker for your dad again?"

"Somebody needs to. All he does is work."

"He wants to make sure you are well provided for, Angel."

Angella turned her face toward the window. "Because Mom's gone," she said, flatly.

Vaughn felt that familiar tug in his chest whenever Carlton's wife was mentioned. She'd died when Angella was only three. Vaughn took his godfather duties very seriously and had immediately stepped in to help his best friend cope with losing his wife and raising a toddler. He took her hand in his. "Sweety, are you okay?"

"I just want Daddy to be happy." she sniffed.

"Angel, he is. Each day he gets to wake up to your smiling face makes him happy."

She turned toward him. "How do you know?"

"Because he told me. That was a direct quote from him, kiddo."

That made her smile. That one gesture made Vaughn's heart lighter. He took the off-ramp onto Route 55 heading toward Apex. "Wanna stop at McDonald's and get a McFlurry?"

"Dad would kill me if I had something sweet this close to bedtime," Angella replied automatically.

Vaughn noticed that she didn't say no. He grinned. "Oreo or M&M's?"

Angella's eyes twinkled mischievously. "Oreo. Definitely Oreo."

An hour later, Vaughn was sitting on the patio with Carlton having a beer. He took a swig, and then sat the bottle down on the glass table. "You have some explaining to do."

Carlton's eyebrow rose. "Really? About what?"

"Let's start with why my goddaughter is inquiring about a possible date for me with Sienna Lambert."

His friend had the temerity to chuckle. "I suppose she may have overheard us on the phone."

Vaughn rolled his eyes. "Ya think?"

"What's the big deal? I think you ought to consider asking the woman out."

"I did, remember? She turned me down. I was hoping to get to know her better, but it doesn't look like it's going to work out."

This time it was Carlton's turn to roll his eyes. "You're in advertising, Vaughn. Since when don't you have another pitch on hand?"

Vaughn was thoughtful for a moment. He glanced over at his friend. "There's more. Angel thinks it's high time you got out there as well. You know, look for something serious."

Carlton sat his beer down. "She said that?"

"Yep. She wants you to be happy. She asked me if Sienna has a sister."

"Does she?"

"You two are definitely related," Vaughn said, dryly. "I'll tell you like I told your offspring. How do I know? Sienna and I haven't talked long enough to cover any personal details, so back to you."

Vaughn couldn't see his buddy's face, but the timbre in his voice when he spoke was tortured. "I can't."

Silence permeated the night. Eventually, Vaughn spoke. "Carl, I am absolutely the last person that would ever try to diminish your grief, but it's been six years. You don't think you're ready to go past casual dates?"

Carlton looked over at his friend. Sadness etched his features. "I can't," he repeated.

"Why?"

"I love her too damn much."

Vaughn lowered his head. "I'm sorry, man. I didn't mean to push."

"You weren't. I know it's what Angella wants—more than anything, but I just can't extend myself that far. Not yet, at any rate."

\*\*\*

By the time Vaughn arrived home it was almost two in the morning. He had taken the roundabout way to get back to his house to have some time to think. His best friend was still mourning the death of his wife. Vaughn knew he'd loved her, but to still be that devastated six years later gave him insight into the depth of Carlton's love and commitment.

Once he parked his car in the garage, he entered the house through the connecting door. He walked through the mudroom into the kitchen not bothering to cut on any lights. Vaughn dropped his keys and wallet in a dish sitting on one of the granite countertops. Mentally and physically tired, he made his way through the dark house and up the wide staircase to the second floor. When he entered his room, he flipped the switch on the wall. Bright light flooded the massive room.

Vaughn slid the dimmer switch down until the glow was muted. He walked into his walk-in dressing room. He stripped his jeans, socks, and silk shirt off and threw them in the hamper in the corner. Padding into the bathroom, he went straight for the shower to turn on the water.

When the temperature was almost scalding, he stripped his briefs off and slid under the streams of water pouring out of the rain shower head. After he'd showered and brushed his teeth, Vaughn doused the light and headed into his bedroom. With a towel still wrapped around his middle, he sat at the top of the bed. He glanced over at the telephone on his nightstand and noticed that the voicemail indicator was lit. He dialed his access number and waited.

A look of surprise crossed his face at hearing Sienna's voice.

"Hi Vaughn, this is Sienna. I uh, wanted to let you know that I decided to accept your dinner invitation. Give me a call to let me know what day and time is convenient for you."

Vaughn skipped the message back a few seconds to write down her phone numbers.

He saved the message before hanging up and then leaned back against the pillows. "Huh," he said, aloud. Unable to contain the wide grin plastered across his face, he glanced over at the notepad on his table. He was sorry he'd missed her call, but looked forward to speaking with her in the morning. He would phone her while he was at Angella's soccer game. The next question in his mind was where to take her on their date. Vaughn doused the light, flung the towel toward the general vicinity of his closet and got under the covers.

Lying on his back, he folded his arms behind his head and stared into the darkness. "Nothing ordinary or stuffy for you, Doc," he said. "We need to get you out of your comfort zone." An idea popped into his head causing him to laugh into the silence. "That'll work." Vaughn couldn't wait to see how she handled his idea. He knew it was mischievous of him, but he couldn't help it. She'd set him on his ear by wearing men's underwear just to get under his skin. Vaughn figured it was high time he returned the favor. Her figure materialized in his mind's eye. He could see the shocked look on her face at his choice. "Sweet dreams, Sienna," Vaughn murmured. "I'll most definitely see you tomorrow."

# Chapter Eight

## The Build Up

Being awakened from a deep sleep, and an even better dream, by the shrill ring of a telephone wasn't exactly the way Sienna envisioned starting her day. Turning over, her hand immediately reached for her cordless phone. She jammed the talk button. "Hello?" she said, groggily, her head face down in the pillow.

"You're still asleep?"

"Viv?" Sienna yawned. "Why are you calling me so early?"

"Early? It's eight thirty, Sienna. Since when do you sleep so late?"

"Since I didn't get to bed until two in the morning." She rolled over onto her back and then flicked her hair out of her face. "What."

"Did he call?"

"You woke me up to ask if Vaughn called?"

"Of course, I'm calling to see if Vaughn called. You can't be surprised."

"No, I haven't spoken to him, yet. Now, if you'll excuse me I'm going back to bed."

"Why? You're up now. You might as well—"

"Goodbye, Vivian," Sienna replied before her thumb connected with the off button.

Thirty minutes later, the phone rang again. Annoyance set in. This time when she answered the phone her voice was curt. "Can't you let me sleep in peace?"

"I suppose I could, but then I wouldn't get to hear your sexy morning voice."

Cold water doused over her head couldn't have woken Sienna up any faster. "Vaughn," she replied, instantly awake.

"Good morning, Doc. I'd ask you how you are," he chuckled, "but apparently someone already beat me to it."

"Vivian called a while ago," she confessed sitting up in bed. "Normally I'm up by now, but I didn't get to sleep until after two this morning."

"Me either. If I'd have known you were up, I would've called," he taunted.

Loud shouting and clapping rang in Sienna's ear. A puzzled look crossed her face. "Are you at a football game or something?"

"Close. I'm at Angella's soccer match. The visiting team just scored a goal."

Sienna booed into the phone causing Vaughn to laugh. "That's what I wanted to do, but that wouldn't be politically correct of me. Plus, I didn't want to cause a riot. Parents take the game way more seriously than the kids."

"I'll bet."

"So, I got your message."

She liked the way his voice took on a playful tone. "Were you surprised?"

"Pleasantly. Are you available tonight?"

*Rule number nine: Never, ever appear too eager.* "I'm not too sure. I'll need to check my schedule."

"Okay, in that case if you want to call me later . . ."

*Rule number ten: If a president has been elected since your last date, ignore rule number nine.* Sienna laughed. "I'm kidding. What time?"

"How about I pick you up around five thirty?"

"That would be great," She gave him her address. "So, what's the dress code?"

"Casual is fine."

"Where are we going?"

"Now that, Dr. Lambert, is confidential. You'll just have to wait and see."

Intrigued, Sienna's mind sifted through the possibility of. dinner, candles, and soft music. She could picture him just inches across from her, leaning in so they could. . . ."

"Sienna?"

There was no response.

"Doc?" Vaughn said, a little louder.

"Hmm? Oh, sorry," Though he couldn't see it she blushed at being caught daydreaming. "What did you say?"

"I said that I'd see you later on, and for you to have a great day."

"Thanks. You do the same," Sienna told him, before hanging up.

She fell back against the pillows. The smile that was plastered across her face rivaled the sun streaming into her bedroom window. After she'd replayed their conversation in her head—twice— she called her best friend. As soon as Vivian picked up the phone Sienna filled her in happily.

"Saints preserve us," Vivian said, loudly into her ear. "So what time and what'cha wearing?"


After the game, Carlton drove Angella home, so Vaughn phoned his younger brother to invite him to lunch. Surprisingly, he answered his home phone and was available.

"I have to admit I'm kind of shocked," Vaughn confessed.

"Consider it your lucky day. Meet me at 510 in thirty minutes."

"You're on. Where are we eating?"

"*Hi5*, of course."

Vaughn wasn't surprised. *Hi5* was a sports bar and restaurant located within the trendy building known as 510 Glenwood Avenue. Condos were on the top floor, restaurants and other shops on the street level. A constant on his brother's short list was someplace to eat, drink and watch sports. Absolute must-haves for a retired football player, and having his favorite things under the same roof was an added bonus.

"I'll meet you there, but I'm not staying all day, Pierce. I mean it."

"What's so dire, Vaughn? You went out yesterday with Angella, so what's the rush? It's not like you have a hot date or anything."

When Vaughn remained silent Pierce whistled into the phone. "You have a hot date?" Pierce said, incredulous.

"It's a date," Vaughn confirmed. "We just met so I wouldn't qualify it as hot."

"The psych major accepted your apology?"

"That she did."

"Finally, some of my charm is rubbing off on you. Mom would be proud. Remind me to tell Chase the next time I call him."

"Clock's ticking, little brother. See you in twenty."

\*\*\*

True to his word, Vaughn left in plenty of time to drive home, shower, get re-dressed and then relax until it was time to leave. Sienna told him she lived in the Wakefield Pines community which was only about fifteen minutes from his house. Once he was on the main road, he called her. "I just wanted you to know I should be there in about fifteen minutes. Is that okay?"

"Oh sure," Sienna replied. "I'll see you shortly."

After she'd hung up, she glanced frantically at her friend. "I've got less than fifteen minutes," her voice was panic stricken. "Will this work or not?"

Vivian was lounging in the love seat in Sienna's bedroom. "Girl, as I told you an hour ago, you will look great in whatever you choose to wear. The operative word here being *choose*."

"Viv, you aren't funny," Sienna said, sarcastically. She threw the discarded dress on her bed before dashing back into her closet.

The wooden hangers were being scraped loudly across the metal pole. Drawers opened and shut repeatedly and over the loud commotion Sienna talked to herself.

"I'm hearing some very unladylike language from in there," Vivian remarked about her friend's grousing. "Hey, I thought you two were just friends? Do you take this much time to get dressed when you go out with all your 'just friends' or is Vaughn special?"

"This isn't funny," Sienna retorted, in a muffled voice. She hobbled out of her closet with a mound of clothing in her arms.

Vivian watched her friend shuffling across the room with a pair of pants around her ankles. "You do know you're over analyzing again, don't you? Sienna, just pick something. You'll look beautiful no matter what you're wearing."

"He said casual," Sienna gasped as she kicked the jeans off, and then went face down into her mattress. Slowly climbing up over the mound of clothes, she powersurfed through her outfits. "Does that mean dressy casual, sort of casual, or all the way casual? There are too many variables here."

A piece of dark clothing went sailing past her friend's head. "Sienna, I just looked at the clock."

"So?"

"So crazy person, you're out of time. Either you pick something and get dressed, or I will dress you myself."

"Okay," Sienna snapped. "I can do this. Give me twenty seconds."

"Fine." Vivian eyed her watch. "Go."

Motionless, Sienna's eyes scanned quickly over the extensive clothing. She flicked a few things out of her way before she settled on a choice. "Done."

"Good. Go," Vivian said, pointing toward the doorway.

Sienna dropped the robe she'd been wearing and put on khaki Capri pants and a raspberry colored short-sleeve tee-shirt. White canvas shoes with white ankle socks finished out the ensemble. Vivian tossed her the matching zip-down jacket, and then followed her into the bathroom. When Sienna began twisting her hair into a bun Vivian frowned. "Why in the world are you wearing your hair like that? It's a date, not a symposium."

"I'm comfortable with it like this."

"Precisely my point. Throw caution to the wind and wear it down. You have lovely hair, girl. Why hide it in that ridiculous style? Rule number . . . what number are you on?"

Sienna was thoughtful. "Eleven, why?"

"Rule number eleven," Vivian said, loudly. "Stop wearing outdated hairdos even your grandmother wouldn't wear—and she's dead."

Sienna observed her reflection in the mirror. Her dark, wavy hair lay against her shoulders.

She contemplated following Vivian's advice. When the doorbell rang, she quickly brushed it back into a ponytail and secured it with a scrunchy before donning her glasses.

Her best friend sighed. "You look like someone's mother's school teacher."

"Do not," she quipped before running out of the room toward the stairs.

Sienna reached the bottom of the stairs and forced herself to walk slowly across the foyer to the front door. She slid her tongue over her teeth and blew into her hands. Satisfied that she wasn't offensive she opened the door.

"Hi." Vaughn smiled at her.

"Hi yourself." She grinned. "Come in."

She stepped aside to allow Vaughn to enter her home. When he moved further into the room she closed the door. "Welcome to Lambert Landing,"

Vaughn's gaze roamed the room. He was amazed at how bright it was. Hardwood floors and neutral paint made it welcoming.

"Would you like a tour of the first floor?"

"Sure."

Sienna took him through each room. He noted that the ceilings had to be ten feet tall with crown moulding throughout. White columns flanked the entryway from the living room to the dining room. The decorating was done in warm tones. A white love seat and two dark brown chairs were arranged with the fireplace as the focal point.

When she got to a room off to itself with glass doors, he stopped her.

"You play the piano?"

"Yes. My mother insisted. She was a piano teacher."

He turned to face her. "Are you any good?"

With a devilish grin Sienna walked over to the piano. Leaning over the keys, she played a few bars from Scott Joplin's, The Entertainer. When she stopped Vaughn clapped.

"I'd say that was a resounding yes."

She ushered him back into the main living space. Vaughn perused the pieces of African art, sculptures, and scenic desert pictures around the rooms. "Wow, this is a beautiful home, Sienna. This is some serious space for a townhouse."

"I know. The minute I saw it I knew there would be no more hours spent looking at houses and driving around. I was home."

"It suits you." Vaughn's gaze traveled over her. "You look beautiful, too."

His compliment made her smile. "Maybe the house is rubbing off on me."

They stared at each other for several seconds until the sound of footsteps coming down the stairs drew their attention.

"Don't mind me, I'm just leaving."

"Hi, Vivian, great to see you again."

"Likewise, Vaughn." Vivian squeezed Sienna's arm on the way out. "Have fun," She mouthed.

The solitary sound of the door being shut reiterated that they were alone and still standing in the middle of the foyer. Neither had moved and they were still facing each other. After a few moments, Vaughn cleared his throat.

"Are you ready?"

"Sure. Just give me a sec." Sienna went to retrieve her purse. "So, where are we going?" she inquired when she returned.

"I'm not telling. It's still a surprise." He opened the door to let her out.

Sienna walked onto the brick landing. Vaughn followed her closing the front door behind him. She leaned in to lock it. They walked a few feet down the brick walkway to the driveway in front of her garage. Her cool air-conditioned skin warmed rapidly in the summer heat. Vaughn opened the car door to his silver Audi convertible.

"Thank you." She eased in and fastened her seatbelt.

"My pleasure," Vaughn replied, on the way around the car.

He slid into the driver's seat. After he started the car, he turned to her. Would you like me to put the top up?"

"Oh no, you don't have to. I'm fine. I love convertibles. I used to have one when I was much younger."

"I had my dad's old sedan until I graduated from college. After I'd been at my real job for a year, I treated myself to an upgrade."

She laughed. "Do tell. What did you upgrade to?"

"I got a Toyota Camry."

Her eyes widened. "That's the car I drive now. I have the Hybrid."

During the drive they chatted about their likes, dislikes, and philosophies on life. There were a few points they differed on, but not much. Vaughn was filling her in on his worst client when Sienna glanced around. "We're on Briar Creek Parkway. Come on, you can tell me now where we're headed can't you?"

"You haven't guessed by now?"

"No," she confessed. She thought about the upscale restaurants in the area.

Vaughn couldn't contain his mirth. "I definitely would've thought you'd figure it out by now." He turned right and drove up an incline. Sienna was perplexed. "We're getting your car washed before dinner?"

The laughter echoed throughout the car. When he drove further up the driveway Sienna took in the massive yellow, red, and blue structure. She turned to him. "Frankie's?"

"Yep."

Vaughn found someone coming out up front. He turned his signal on and waited for them to back out. He took the time to study Sienna to see if she was mad about his choice. She merely looked curious. *That has to be a good sign.* He told himself. A few moments later, he eased into their space. He got out of the car and walked around to open her door. He held his hand out. Sienna placed her palm in his. He closed his hand with hers still inside it. "Come on, Doc," he laughed, pulling her behind him. "Let's go have some fun."

# Chapter Nine

## Expect the Unexpected

The large double doors opened with a swoosh. Cooled air wafted around her. When they stepped inside, Sienna took a second to assess the situation. Orderly chaos was the first thing that came to mind. The Laser Tag studio and a restaurant were to the right, to the left, more games than Sienna had ever seen outside a theme park.

"Come this way." Vaughn guided her toward the cashier. He purchased fun cards for both of them. When he was finished, he eased her over to the side out of the line. "So, what would you like to try first?"

Her eyes widened. "I don't have a clue."

Vaughn grinned. "How good are you at the old school games?"

The first thing they tried in the Arcade was Ms. Pacman. Sienna beat him soundly and was thrilled. Next, they played a shooting game. They went on a virtual hunting expedition to shoot Elk. Vaughn won by a landslide.

"Oh my gosh, they have Skee Ball," Sienna enthused. "I haven't played that since high school." This time she dragged Vaughn behind her.

Kids with their parents in tow weaved in and out of their path. It didn't bother Sienna in the slightest. A game that looked like Wheel of Fortune caught her eye. "Hey, let's go Bass fishing," she joked sliding her money card in the card reader. She grabbed the large lever and pulled down as hard as she could. The dial spun furiously before it landed on 450 tickets. "I won," she shouted, excitedly. The dispenser doled out her tickets in rapid succession. She turned to him. "You have to try this thing."

"Okay." Vaughn slid his card and pulled the lever. It went around several times and stopped on 85 tickets. He laughed as Sienna scooped them up and added them to her mound of tickets.

They walked by another game. This one had a giant metal claw. Sienna saw the huge stuffed animals and stopped in her tracks.

About six-dollars later, Vaughn handed Sienna a huge stuffed animal. "For you."

Sienna hugged it to her possessively. "Thank you, Vaughn. She beamed up at him. So what's next?" she scanned the crowd.

"How about we get dinner and then we'll check out the outside?"

Sienna grinned. "There's an outside?"

They waited inside the restaurant to be seated. After a few minutes they were shown to a booth. Sienna slid in with her prized possession. Vaughn followed. The waitress handed them both menus. They both ordered Iced Tea. While they were waiting they scanned the menus.

"Do you know what you want to eat?"

Sienna shook her head. "It always takes me forever to order. You?"

"I think I'm going with the ribeye and shrimp."

Her gaze traveled distractedly over the menu again. "Decisions, decisions."

"If you're not sure what you want we can order appetizers while you choose."

His thoughtfulness made her smile. "Sounds like a perfect idea."

When their waitress returned, Vaughn's head came up over the menu. "Do you like spicy?"

Sienna grinned. "Bring it on."

After dinner, she made a beeline for the door. They went on the Bumper Boats and sprayed each other mercilessly with the built-in squirt guns. Vaughn suggested they play mini-golf while their clothes dried. "Okay, but I think it fair to warn you I'm a mini-golf connoisseur," Sienna boasted.

"I think I'll take my chances."

Sienna's golf victory was supreme. On the way to the Shamrock Slick Go-Kart track, she recounted her amazing shots. The slippery surface made racing the Go-Karts a blast. Sienna laughed so much she got hiccups.

"Come on, we'll get you a slushy."

Sienna ordered a Blue Raspberry Icee and Vaughn a Coke. They went back outside and he practically ran to the batting cage. Sienna frowned digging in her heels. "I don't think this is such a good idea, Vaughn."

He stopped and studied her. "Why not?"

Need I remind you that the last time we played baseball I almost wound up in the hospital?"

Vaughn snorted. "Sienna, this is a batting cage, not the Durham Bulls Athletic Park."

Sienna glared at him. "I'm glad my near death experience amuses you."

"Just how near death were you?" Vaughn asked as straight-faced as he could.

It wasn't good enough. Neither could contain their laughter.

"Sienna, I can show you all you need to know. You'll be fine."

She looked at the ball machine and then back at Vaughn. Skepticism was evident in her face.

He rubbed her shoulders in a comforting gesture. "This will be like coming full circle for us." His eyes never left hers. "Trust me."

Without hesitation Sienna nodded.

"Great. Vaughn grinned and set their drinks down. There was nobody around so he took his time coaching her. "I studied your swing while you were batting the last time."

Her expression relayed her surprise. "I didn't know that. It was pretty horrific, wasn't it?"

"It wasn't bad. There are just a few things I'd suggest you do differently."

He went to retrieve a bat for her. "Are you right or left handed?"

"Right."

Vaughn faced her. "Okay, the hand you write with goes on top." He handed her the bat. "Elbows up with the arm farthest from the pitcher angled higher."

He watched as she made the corrections. He got on the side of her. "Let me see you swing."

Sienna swung the bat and then looked at him. "How was that?"

"Watch the ball and swing. The key is to follow through with the bat and push your rear end out a bit." Vaughn sauntered over to the machine while Sienna lined up. "Are you ready?"

"As I'll ever be," she yelled back.

She missed the first ball and clipped the second. Vaughn came over and got behind her. "Here." He fit his body up against hers. "You need to work on the wait-watch-swing and follow through technique."

*Is he kidding?* Sienna was having an extremely hard time concentrating when he was spooning her like he was. She took a deep breath and willed herself to concentrate.

"Chin up," he whispered in her ear. "Watch the ball." Vaughn moved them to simulate a ball coming at her. He swung through the air with slow and precise movements taking her with him.

He retreated. "See how I did that? Okay, now you try."

She blinked several times while he ran across the space toward the ball machine. "Oh my," Sienna said, feeling disoriented.

"Push my tush back," she repeated his words. She stuck her butt out a smidgen. "How's that?" she yelled.

"More."

She tried it again. "Now?"

"Hang on," he bellowed, and then jogged over to her. Vaughn got behind her and grabbed her hips.

Sienna instantly stiffened.

"Relax," he coached. Vaughn adjusted her position bringing her back against his middle. "Your legs need to be farther apart, too." To demonstrate he wedged his right leg between the two of hers and pushed to widen her stance.

Sweat trickled down the small of Sienna's back. His touch was causing her body some serious distress. Her hands were moist so she sat the bat down and wiped them off on the front of her pants. After taking several deep breathes, she resumed her position.

Vaughn's voice sounded in her ear. It tickled her skin. "Sienna, head up. Always watch the ball."

She blinked. "What ball?"

"The ball that will be coming at you," he replied, with amusement. "Don't forget, your bat needs to be between a ninety and forty-five degree angle." He placed his arms around her and grabbed hold of the bat.

*Does Frankie's have a first-aid kit with an oxygen tank?* Sienna mused.  "I'm not going to survive this," she groaned.

"Sure you will," Vaughn replied.

Sienna blushed realizing she'd spoken aloud.

He tightened his hold. "Remember, your grip should be firm—and controlled."

"Firm and controlled," she repeated, hoarsely.

Without warning he released her. "You got it."

Sienna's knees buckled. Vaughn caught her immediately. "Doc, are you all right?"

"Uh-huh. Just fine," she smiled with considerable effort. *Rule number twelve: If you are being spooned and touched all over by a tall, sexy, crazy-good looking, breathing, single, heterosexual man and your knees buckle, play it off.* "I'm just not used to all this . . . sports stuff."

"You're doing great. Now, let's see how well I tutor," he joked before heading back to the machine.

She watched him the entire way. "Pretty damned well," she murmured.

*This is your chance, Sienna. Focus. Remember what he told you. Head up, elbows out, widen your stance, stick your butt out.* She went through all his suggestions like a check list. Confident that she was ready, Sienna nodded at Vaughn to proceed.

"Batter up," Vaughn warned.

Sienna lowered her head and said a silent prayer.

"Watch the ball."

She raised her head and waited. The ball raced toward her. She held her breath. The bat connected with a deafening thwack. She watched it sail across the cage. The only thing that stopped it was the net surrounding the area. "I did it," Sienna cried out, jumping around.

Vaughn raced over and picked her up. He spun her in his arms. "You were awesome, Sienna. Perfect swing," he said, proudly.

She giggled as he twirled her. When he set her feet on the ground his hands moved to her waist to steady her.

"Thanks for the lesson," she said, breathlessly.

"Thanks for being so teachable." They smiled at one another for a few seconds. Clearing his throat, Vaughn released her and went to retrieve their drinks, her stuffed animal, and tickets.

They went back into the arcade to cash in the large mound of tickets. Sienna couldn't choose what to get so they opted to redeem them another time.

Deciding to call it a night, Sienna and Vaughn walked back to his car. She secured her stuffed animal in the back seat with a seatbelt. He laughed at that.

"I'm not running the risk of my new buddy being hurt," she said, protectively.

He snickered. "I can see that."

They listened to music on the trip home. Sienna gazed at the stars overhead. Eventually, she turned to him. "Vaughn, I think it's time I admitted that I enjoyed myself at Frankie's—immensely."

His eyes didn't leave the road, but he grinned in reaction. "I'm glad you did."

"I know you had your doubts."

"Only in the five seconds it took to pass the car wash," he admitted.

They conversed on topics ranging from the economy and politics to their favorite cooking shows. By the time Vaughn pulled into Sienna's driveway, they were having a heated debate about the longevity of reality television shows.

Vaughn helped her and her prize out of the car.

"So, what are you going to name him or her?"

"It's a him, and I'm not sure yet. Maybe Curtis."

He made a face as his gaze roamed over the large bear. "Curtis?"

"Okay, maybe I'll go back to the drawing board."

"Good idea," he countered.

After she retrieved her house key they mounted the steps to the front door. Sienna turned to face him. "Would you like to come in for a drink, or some coffee? I don't drink coffee, but I have some. You know, in case company comes over and wants coffee. I try to be prepared."

The urge to tease her was too strong to ignore. "Yeah, I get that about you."

She wrinkled her nose at him. Vaughn pondered her invitation. He had to admit he enjoyed her company immensely and wasn't ready for their evening to end either. Decision made, he replied, "Actually, I'd love to come in."

Almost an hour later they were in another heated debate. "You can't put down a wild card and change the color if you already have that color in your hand."

"I can so."

"That's against the rules. You have to draw two cards."

"I do not. What kind of bootleg rules are you spouting?"

Sienna looked indignant. "I'm not making up rules. Just ask anyone that actually knows *how* to play Uno."

"Yeah, right. I want to see the rules. Where's your copy?"

"I don't have them anymore, but trust me, you can't do that."

"Trust you?" he snorted. "I don't think so." He batted the two cards she was shoving at him away.

She laughed and tried again. "Cheater."

"Yes, you are."

Reluctantly, Vaughn glanced at his watch. "It's getting late, I'd better get going."

Sienna looked upside down at the clock on the table behind her. "It was *late* an hour ago."

He helped her put the cards back in the metal tin. He got up off the floor in front of the couch and extended his hand. "Come on, cheater. I'll help you up."

Sienna accepted his help. "Thanks. You know for someone who cheats, you aren't so bad."

Sienna retrieved their glasses of water from off the floor as well. She placed them on the tray of snacks she'd brought out when they had first arrived. Vaughn took the tray from her and headed for the kitchen. She followed him. "I can take care of that," she told him after he opened the dishwasher.

"I've got it."

They tidied up and turned off the light. Sienna walked him back into the foyer.

"Thanks for such a wonderful evening, Vaughn. I had a great time."

He gazed down at her. "Me, too."

"Call me when you get home. Ring once so I know you got there safely."

"Ring once?" he chuckled. "My mother used to say that when we'd moved out on our own."

"My parents still do. So don't forget. Ring once," she warned.

This time Vaughn didn't resist the urge to tweak her nose. "Will do."

She opened the front door to let him out. She watched him until he had backed out of her driveway and drove down the quiet street. Slowly, she closed and locked the door. Turning out the lights, Sienna set the alarm, then went upstairs. Tired, she rushed through her night-time regimen. Once in the bed, she snuggled under the covers and stared at the ceiling.

Her day was simply fantastic. She smiled like a Cheshire cat when she recounted all the events. When the phone rang, she grabbed the receiver and hit the talk button. "Hello?"

"Why are you answering? I thought you just wanted me to ring once and hang up?"

She heard Vaughn's amused voice in her ear. She laughed. "Sorry, I forgot." Without warning, she hung up the telephone.

A few seconds later the phone rang again.

"Hello?"

"You are certifiably crazy."

She burst out laughing. "Glad to know you arrived safely."

"Yep, I did."

"What are you doing?"

"Watching the moon shine through the skylight above my bed. You?"

"The same—minus the skylight."

"So, which part of our outing was your favorite?"

Sienna was thoughtful for a moment. "Hmm . . . I'd have to say you winning me Rocco."

"Excuse me?"

"My stuffed animal. I named him Rocco."

"I see. So where is Rocco now?"

"Right next to me. I've got a king-sized bed so he's got an entire wing to himself."

Vaughn chuckled at that, but then grew silent. "I'd say he is one lucky bear."

Sienna's stomach lurched. Closing her eyes, she willed the lump forming in her throat to move. "You know, something tells me if we don't say goodnight now we'll be on this phone till dawn."

"Something tells me you're right. Goodnight," Vaughn said, quietly. "I'm glad we gave the friend thing another try."

She couldn't help the grin that stole across her face. "Me, too," she admitted before hanging up the phone.

# Chapter Ten

## And So It Begins

Sienna was checking in on her flight when her cell phone rang. "Sienna Lambert."

"Where are you?"

She smiled. "Chicago. You?"

"Seattle," Vaughn replied. "We had a skittish client that was thinking about going to another agency. Linda insisted I come out here immediately to keep that from happening."

"Did you convince them?"

"We'll find out shortly. Right now we're at Happy Hour going over how much more we're going to do for them—for less."

"Well, if anyone can blow sunshine up someone's—"

"Hey," he interrupted.

"I'm just saying—you're good at schmoozing."

"Is that supposed to be a compliment?"

"You know it is," Sienna countered. "Darn, I have to run. I'm heading to the security checkpoint. Dinner tomorrow night, okay? Does Michael Dean's Seafood work for you?"

"You're on. I'll call you when I land. Be safe, Doc."

"Ditto."

A day later, they were patiently waiting for the waiter to show them to their table. Once they were settled, Vaughn scanned the wine list and ordered a bottle of Merlot. He also ordered the most expensive oysters on the menu. Sienna glanced up from pondering her dinner selection.

"What's all this?"

"A celebration of sorts."

"You're still gainfully employed?"

"Yes, very much so. My client is staying with us. Seems a colleague of his overheard someone talking at lunch about the shoddy job the competition did on their last campaign. They screwed it up royally. Anyway, he decided that Chase & Burroughs was where his women's shoe line needed to be."

Sienna's eyes narrowed. "You wouldn't happen to have had anything to do with that, would you?"

Vaughn put his hand to his chest. "I'm shocked beyond words you suspect me of something nefarious. I emphatically deny any involvement and was nowhere near that restaurant at the time."

She looked at him skeptically. "Right," she drawled.

During dinner Vaughn said, "Hey, want to come over and watch a movie tonight?"

Sienna pondered his question. "On a school night?"

He leaned in conspiratorially. "Yes, on a school night. Come on, I'm too pumped up to go to bed any time soon."

Vivian's voice sounded in her head. *You'd better say yes or I'll say it for you. Yes, Vaughn. This crazy woman that hasn't had a date since Lord knows when would love to go out with you!* Pushing her friend's words aside she nodded. "Sure."

"Great. You want to follow me over, or drop your car at your house and ride with me?"

"Don't be silly, I'll follow you over."

"Okay."

When they had arrived at the house, Sienna followed Vaughn into his driveway. He parked in front of the garage and got out. By the time Sienna had turned off her engine, he was at her door opening it for her.

"Thanks, kind sir."

He bowed. "Right this way, milady."

"So, what are we watching?" she asked following him into the house.

"I don't know. It's your turn to pick."

They descended the basement stairs and went into what Sienna had now dubbed 'Vaughn's Playland'.

She sat on the couch and kicked off her heels while Vaughn turned the projection screen and sound system on. She grabbed a nearby Chenille throw.

"If you're cold I can adjust the temperature."

Sienna shook her head. "No need, this is fine."

She smiled over his concern. Every since their not-so-official date, they had spent a great deal of time together. Sienna admitted to herself that it had been fun getting to know him.

"So," Vaughn said, interrupting her inner musing, he plopped down on the couch next to her. "What movie would you like to watch?"

She sifted through choices in her head. After two minutes he moaned aloud, "Doc, we go through this every time. Just pick something."

"I know, I know. It's just that nothing is really standing out for me," she complained. "You pick."

"Fine, if I pick we're watching a UFC fight."

Sienna rolled her eyes. "I don't want to watch the Ultimate Fighter. I'm not in the mood for mixed martial arts tonight, but if we're going to watch regular TV, how about HGTV?"

"That'll work." Vaughn picked up the remote and flicked to the satellite guide.

Sienna tucked her feet under her and leaned her head on his shoulder.

When a door chime went off, Sienna looked at Vaughn curiously. "Who's that?"

He heard footsteps overhead and then rapidly hitting the basement stairs. "That would be Pierce."

Sienna sat up. "Great, I finally get to meet him," she said, excitedly.

"Don't look directly into his eyes." Vaughn warned. "He'll talk your head off."

"Hey, bro," Pierce called from the doorway. Pierce walked in and stopped short when he realized that Vaughn wasn't alone. When he saw Sienna, he grinned. "I see I finally get to meet the elusive Doc."

Vaughn frowned at his brother's use of what was now his nickname for Sienna. He stood up. "Pierce, I'd like to introduce you to Dr. Sienna Lambert. Sienna, this is my younger brother, Pierce."

Standing, Sienna extended her hand. Pierce raised it to his lips and kissed it. "The pleasure is all mine, Dr. Lambert."

"Sienna is fine," she corrected. "It's wonderful to finally meet you, Pierce."

Vaughn noticed he hadn't released Sienna's hand. He wrapped his arm around his brother's neck and squeezed. "So, what brings you by?"

"My guest spot on that cool new shopper's network on Satellite. I'm selling my new men's cologne, Dazzle," he turned to Sienna. "That's what they used to call me on the field. I dazzled them, baby," Pierce laughed. He waved a DVD in his hand."

"We're not watching that," Vaughn said, pointedly.

"Come on, man. It's definitely better than watching someone looking for a vacation home in Panama." Pierce turned to Sienna. He smiled his signature grin. "You wouldn't mind checking it out, would you, Sienna?"

"Of course not," she said, sitting down on the couch. *Rule number thirteen: Always be mindful of other's feelings.* "We'd love to. Right Vaughn?"

He did a double take. "No, we wouldn't."

"Very funny," Pierce said, taking the DVD out and popping it into the player.

Pierce sat next to Sienna. Vaughn returned to his original seat.

"Dim the lights," Pierce told his brother.

"Please."

"Yeah, that's what I said. Can you get me a beer while you're at it?"

"Pierce," Vaughn warned.

"Dude, I'm kidding," Pierce chuckled.

When they were finished watching the segment, Sienna turned to him. "That was great, Pierce."

"Thanks. I've got another spot coming up. This time I'll be marketing my ladies perfume, Be-Dazzled." Pierce winked at Sienna. "You know, it's all about the ladies."

"I don't doubt it," she replied.

"I've got another one in production now. "Dazzlicious." That one's got this pheromone thing going on. When it comes in contact with my men's cologne it's guaranteed to drive the ladies wild. If she's walking down the street and a man happens to be sporting my cologne, ooh, watch out." Pierce threw up his hands for effect. "Down for the count and the panties—"

Vaughn looked at his brother as if he'd lost his mind. "Say goodnight, Pierce."

"No, I'm the one that needs to be leaving," Sienna said, reaching for her shoes. "I've got a new client coming in tomorrow."

Vaughn glanced at her. "Really? Why didn't you tell me? We could've toasted your news earlier."

"It's not too late," Pierce spoke up. "I know where Vaughn keeps the good stuff."

Vaughn made a move toward his brother. Sienna's hand came up to Vaughn's chest. "Walk me out?" She turned to smile at his brother. "It was great meeting you, Pierce."

"Likewise, Sienna. We'll have to do this again."

"He was adopted." Vaughn quipped following Sienna up the stairs.

"That would be plausible if he didn't look like a younger, bulkier version of you."

Vaughn swatted her backside. "Are you trying to say I'm old and out of shape?"

When they were back upstairs, Sienna headed for the garage door. "Stop fishing for compliments, you know you're just as good looking as your brother—if not more."

She'd spoken without thinking. Before she could move, Vaughn's hand snaked out and stopped her in her tracks. "You think I'm good looking?" he grinned broadly.

*Rule number fourteen: If you say something too revealing act like you meant to do it.* "Vaughn, don't even try to act like you don't know how attractive you are. You know, I really think you've got a narcissistic thing going on."

"Hmm . . . maybe I do," he winked.

"Shameless."

When they got outside, Vaughn held her car door open. She slid behind the wheel, started the car, and then rolled the window down. Vaughn closed her door and lowered himself to her eye level. "Thanks for coming over tonight."

"Thanks for dinner," she countered. "Especially the oysters."

"Seafood addict," he joked as his hand grazed her cheek.

They stared at each other. Vaughn was the first to break their connection. He rose and stepped back. "I'd better let you go. Ring me once when you get home, okay?"

Sienna turned away. "'Night, Vaughn."

"Sweet dreams, Doc."

He remained there until her tail lights disappeared into the night.

"You still want to give credence to the fantasy that you two are just friends?"

Vaughn sighed, loudly. He didn't bother turning around to answer. "We've been over this before, Pierce."

"Yeah, and I still keep waiting for you to make sense."

"You're reading too much into this."

"Turn around and tell me I'm wrong."

He did and fixed his brother with a harsh glare. "Just let it go, okay? Sienna and I are just friends. That's all she wants to be."

Pierce shook his head. "If that's what you really think brother, I'd say you're definitely dumber than you are blind."

# Chapter Eleven

## The Getaway

Gordon slid another steak onto the grill. "Oh yeah, come to Poppa."

"Honey, do you have to say that for every piece of meat you put on the grill?" Cassandra asked.

"Or every time you grill?" Sienna piped in.

"Don't scoff at my ritual, ladies. You know you'll both be in line impatiently waiting with steak sauce drizzled on your plates," he laughed.

"That's true, darling," his wife said, kissing his cheek.

Gordon flipped his steak over and glanced at his daughter. "So, how's work, beauty queen?"

"Dad."

"What? Really sweetheart, I don't understand why the whole thing was such a mountain when it was nothing more than a mole hill."

A pained expression crossed her face. "It was a lot more than just a mole hill. Forget it. I don't want to talk about it," Sienna said curtly. "I am going to get the corn from the refrigerator."

Cassandra watched Sienna walk stiffly into the house. "Where'd that come from?"

"You're asking me? She gets upset when anyone mentions that damned pageant. Why that's the case leaves me just as bewildered as you are."

"It's been an area of contention between them for the last seventeen years." Cassandra shook her head. "I wish we could get out of them what really happened that night."

Their daughter returned before they had a chance to continue their conversation. "Here's the corn, Dad, and my apology," she kissed his forehead.

"Sweetheart, that's not necessary. I just wish you weren't still so hung up on something that happened so long ago."

She watched him work, but remained elusive. "Me, too."


Later that night, Sienna was home sitting on the couch with her feet up on an ottoman, her computer situated in the middle of her lap. She was working on the notes from the latest group of participants. Her latest client was a furniture company interested in expanding their product line. Thus far, their furniture was popular with middle-aged couples with children. Now they were looking to capture young, newly graduated, or recently married consumers. The company wanted to entice the buyers transitioning from dorms or rentals to their first homes.

Scanning her notes, she smiled when she recalled a specific line of questioning geared to discover just what consumers used their couches for. The answers ranged from pizza parties to butt-naked bingo. She laughed aloud. "One thing I can say is that my job is *never* boring."

Her telephone rang. Retrieving the cordless from her coffee table, she looked at the number. When she saw it, she frowned. *Sasha.* She stared at the phone until the ringing stopped, and then she placed it back on the table. After another minute, the message indicator light flashed. "Why do you even bother?" she said, in consternation.

Just then, Sienna's doorbell rang. She checked the time on her laptop and pondered who could be at her door. She placed the computer on her couch and padded across the living room to open it.

"Dr. Lambert?" a man inquired.

"Yes?"

"I have a package for you. I just need you to sign here."

Sienna signed the paper attached to a clipboard. "Here you go."

"Thank you," the man handed over her envelope. "Enjoy your evening."

"Wait, just a minute." She walked over to the table and retrieved her wallet out of her purse. She took out a few dollars and walked back to the door. "Here you are."

The courier thanked her with a smile and left.

She stared down at the manila envelope with her name and address written elegantly across the front. There was no return address. She went to the couch, she sat down and put her feet under her. Breaking the seal on the envelope, Sienna eased the contents out of its holder.

There was a smaller envelope with her name on it and another one that said, "Open Me Last." Her curiosity piqued, she opened the first envelope and slid a thick piece of ecru colored stationary out. She unfolded the letter and read it.

*"Sienna, by now I know you're wondering at all the cloak-and-dagger mystique going on here. Actually, I just wanted to surprise you and this was much more fun than a phone call.*

*By the time you read this, a few members of my creative team, and others from my office working on Best Kept Secrets, will be in Arizona on-location for one of the commercials. Right now, I want you to stop reading this and open the other envelope. After you open it, come back and finish the letter. Come on, Doc, quit frowning and humor me . . ."*

Sienna immediately smoothed her expression out. Perplexed, she set the letter aside and grabbed the other envelope. Flipping it over, she slid her finger along the inside to open it, then took the contents out. "Airline tickets?" she said, astonished. There was a yellow sticky on the front that said, *"Go finish the letter."*

"Okay," she huffed as if Vaughn were right beside her.

*"By now you've seen the rest of my surprise. I want you to join me here in Arizona for the weekend. You can work on that already amazing tan of yours, and I can have a much needed, highly anticipated diversion from the chaos that I'm surrounded by. So far today, one model quit, another threatened to walk out because we refused to re-shoot his scenes and focus on his 'best side,' oh yeah, and Sherry Bradshaw*

*and I are butting heads about the commercial's
'creative direction.' Please come, Sienna. I really
need you! By the way, you'll LOVE Sedona!!"*

Sienna read over Vaughn's letter three times.
She was torn between elation at being invited,
and the underlying meaning of his invitation.
After she mulled it over some more, she knew it
was time to call in a professional. Picking up the
phone, she hit a speed dial number and waited.

"Hello?"

"Hey, I need to run something by you. It's big.
Um, Vaughn invited me to Sedona to come visit
him for the weekend while he's on location. I
don't know if—"

"I'm on my way."

The next thing Sienna heard was a dial tone.
Shaking her head, she pressed the end button on
her phone and threw it next to her on the couch.
Setting all the correspondence aside, she went
to the kitchen. She retrieved two wine glasses
from the cabinet and a bottle of Chardonnay
from her wine cooler. By the time she crossed her
living room again Vivian was walking through
the front door. Immediately, Vivian grasped the
proffered glass and sat sideways in the closest
chair. "Details."

Sienna read Vaughn's letter aloud. After she finished, she set it down and glanced worriedly at her best friend. "What the heck does this mean, Viv?"

Taking a sip of wine, Vivian leaned her head back over the arm of the chair. "Hmm . . . my guess is he may be ready to take your relationship to the next level."

"What?" Sienna choked out. "What does the next level mean? We're friends, what other level is there?"

Vivian looked at her incredulously. "You can't be serious. Girl, I told you from day one the man wanted to jump your bones. I don't know why you thought I was kidding."

"He's never once talked about . . . my bones. Jumping them or doing anything else to them. You should've seen him at Frankie's. He had me right up against him when he was showing me how to bat. I swear I could've been wearing his shirt we were so close."

"And?" Vivian said, excitedly.

"And nothing," Sienna murmured. "He was as cool as chilled grapes. I on the other hand, was about ready to pass out from heat stroke. What in the world makes you think there's more to this than just a platonic weekend?"

"The fact that you froze like a deer in head-lights, and then called me speaks volumes."

"Will you be serious," Sienna hissed. "I don't know what to do. What if this invitation has some double entendre?"

"What if it doesn't?"

"How will I know?"

"You won't," Vivian countered, "unless you ask him."

"Uh-uh. Rule number . . . fifteen: Men don't like to be put on the spot. I'm most definitely *not* going to ask him," Sienna was up and pacing at this point. "I'll look like a fool if he's only inter-ested in us being friends and I hint at something more. Do you know what a disaster that would turn out to be?"

"So, what are you going to pack? Trust me; you most definitely better lose that horrific bun."

Sienna stopped short. "I haven't said I was going."

Vivian snorted loudly. "Oh, you most certainly are going."

Sienna's plane landed at the airport in Flag-staff, Arizona without incident. Vaughn had done a thorough job at planning her trip. By the time she made it off the plane and down to

Baggage Claim, a man sporting a black suit and small board with her name on it was waiting for her.

"I'm Sienna Lambert," she said, pleasantly.

"Good afternoon, Dr. Lambert. My name is Charles and I'll be your driver today. Welcome to Flagstaff. Let me retrieve your bags and then we'll be on our way to Sedona."

After getting her luggage, Charles escorted her to his car. His "car" turned out to be a black stretch Cadillac limousine.

"It will be just under an hour for us to arrive in Sedona so sit back and relax. There is water back there, soda, champagne, and plenty of ice. There are tea sandwiches in the fridge—if you wish."

"Oh no, I'm fine. Thanks, Charles."

"My pleasure, Dr. Lambert."

"Sienna is fine."

"Of course, Miss Sienna. If you want some privacy I'll put the glass up."

"No need, Charles."

As they sped by, Sienna found herself gazing out the window at the terrain. Vaughn was right. She liked what she saw. Though she'd never traveled to Sedona, Sienna knew by the pictures she'd fall in love with it. Charles informed her that Vaughn had booked her a room at L'Auberge de Sedona.

"It's a very swanky resort and they even have a spa there."

She closed her eyes and pondered her decision to hop a plane and join Vaughn on location. It was crazy. It was reckless. It was completely unlike her. Truthfully, that's why she did it.

"Miss Sienna, we're here."

"Hmm? Oh." Opening her eyes, she yawned. "I'm sorry, I fell asleep," she said groggily.

"No problem, I'll just get your bags. You take all the time you need."

Sienna had snuggled down into the plush seat to nap. Sitting up, she grabbed her purse and yanked out her make-up case. "I can't believe I fell asleep that fast." She tried to recall the last thing she'd seen, but she was drawing a blank. Shrugging, she opened her M•A•C compact and ran the small circular pad over the pressed powder, and then her face. She re-applied her lip color and smoothed her hair. Vivian would be livid if she knew her hair was still pulled back into the tight knot. Maybe after a much needed shower she'd contemplate putting it in a ponytail.

Her car door was opened and Charles stepped aside. "Ready, miss?"

"Yes, thank you." Sienna took the proffered hand and got out.

She glanced around. They were out front of what she figured was check-in. There was a large fountain across from the covered portico. The trickling water made her smile.

"You enjoy your stay and have a great time in Sedona. It's a great city."

Sienna went into her purse to get her wallet for a tip.

"No, no that's not necessary. Mr. Deveraux has taken care of everything."

*He truly thought of everything.* She mused. "Great meeting you, Charles."

"My pleasure." He waved before getting into the limo.

She watched him drive off. Facing the entrance again, Sienna took a deep breath. *And the adventure begins.* With her hand wrapped around the handle on her luggage, Sienna walked confidently toward the door.

# Chapter Twelve

## Natural Splendor

"Welcome to L'Auberge," a woman greeted her in the lobby.

Sienna eyed several people curiously as they stood around a table, sipping wine and snacking on cheese.

The greeter followed Sienna's line of sight. "You're right on time," she said, cheerfully. "This is our welcome, mixer. Feel free to stay and get acquainted with fellow guests."

*I'm not getting acquainted with anyone before I've had a chance to shower and change.* Sienna thought. "Oh, I'd love to, but actually I'm meeting a friend."

"No problem, the woman smiled. "You're coming at a very exciting time at L'Auberge. We've expanded our resort to offer our guests even more unparalleled luxury."

By the time she had finished listing their improvements, Sienna was in awe. "It sounds spectacular."

"We hope you'll enjoy your stay with us. Now let's get you checked in and then we'll have someone escort you to your room."

As she read over information on the resort, and nearby excursions, a young man greeted Sienna with a hearty handshake. He scooped up her luggage and took it out to a GEM car.

"That's cute," Sienna gushed eyeing the tiny vehicle.

"It's electric too, so we're doing our part for our environment. We offer our guests rides to shopping, restaurants, and other places so you let us know when you're ready to check out Sedona."

"Absolutely," Sienna had to laugh. His excitement was contagious.

"Here we are," he said, pulling into a space. He hopped out and got her bags off the back seat. She looked around the log cabin-type cottages as she followed him down a pathway.

"Do I hear water?"

"Yes, ma'am. You're creek side which means you're right next to Oak Creek."

"I'm staying creek side," she mouthed.

"Here we are." He walked up the stairs onto a porch.

The bellman opened the door, allowing her to enter first. Sienna's eyes widened when she realized the "room" Vaughn got for her was actually a cottage. It reminded her of a quaint ski chalet, or at least what a ski chalet would look like if she'd ever gone skiing. The floors were hardwood and there was a fireplace. There was an armoire for her clothes and an entertainment center across from a brown leather sofa. The pièce de résistance was the king-size bed. It had an intricately carved head and foot board in a dark, rich color. It looked elegant and stately. She loved it.

"If you'd like your fireplace lit for you, just call the desk."

"Huh?" She'd been drooling over the room so long she'd forgotten she wasn't alone.

"We offer a fire lighting service. On cool desert nights it comes in handy."

"Are you serious?"

He nodded. "The wood is right outside on your porch. Don't hesitate to call if you need anything."

"I will," she promised.

Once she was alone, Sienna leisurely explored her small piece of luxury. The bathroom would easily rival any spa. Thick waffle-patterned towels were stacked neatly on shelves. She peeked in a small container to find cotton balls. "They thought of every comfort." Next were Q-Tips and spa quality toiletries. There was even an aroma-therapy diffuser. She sniffed the wooden sticks sitting in scented oil. "This is unbelievable. Vivian is going to flip."

Strolling into the main room, Sienna unpacked before she freshened up. While she was walking to the armoire, she noticed a bouquet of flowers on a small table. She set her armful of stuff on the couch and walked closer. Lowering her head, she sniffed the fragrant petals. That's when she noticed the card. Easing the small square envelope off its holder, Sienna opened it.

*I am thrilled you came, Doc. I'll pick you up at seven o'clock sharp. Can't wait to see you. Vaughn.*

Sienna glanced at her watch. It was ten minutes to six. She did a double take. That barely gave her an hour to put her things away and get ready. She kicked herself into high gear. Her clothes and toiletries were put away in no time. She had chosen a red wrap-around dress with matching sandals. She wore tiny diamonds on her wrist, neck and ears. Her hair was in a chic pony tail. She'd left the bathroom after fixing her hair, not bothering to give herself a once over. A knock sounded at her front door. *Vaughn.*

Sienna ran her hands nervously over her outfit. Her tongue flicked over her front teeth. Confident that she was ready, she walked gracefully to the door and opened it.

They stood staring at one another.

Sienna immediately noticed he was wearing his glasses. She loved when he wore them, which wasn't often. The dark frames made him look more stud than studious.

"You don't wear those enough," she blurted out.

Vaughn grinned, boyishly. Taking her in his arms, he hugged her tightly. "Hello to you, too. We just finished up work for the day. Usually, I only wear them when I have reading to do, but I was so eager to get here I forgot to take them off." A few seconds later, he let her go. His eyes scanned over her appreciatively. "Doc, that red on you is—you look—truly amazing."

"Thank you." She shyly stepped aside. "Vaughn, why do you call me that all the time?"

He followed her into the room and shut the door. "I don't know. I just like it. I guess it's a term of endearment or something. Why?" He studied her closely. "You don't like when I call you Doc?"

This time the tone he used when the nickname rolled off his tongue made her throat tighten. Truthfully, she didn't care what Vaughn called her so long as he said it like that. It took her a moment to realize he was waiting for an answer. "Uh, no, it's fine. I don't mind at all."

"Good. I'd hate to have to figure out another name this late in the game," he mocked.

Without warning, Sienna closed the distance between them. This time she initiated the embrace. Her arms snaked around his neck. His arms encircled her waist.

"Vaughn, this was a wonderful surprise." She blinked back the moisture forming in her eyes. "One I'll treasure forever."

He tilted her face up to meet his. He rubbed her tears away with his thumb. "It was my pleasure. I'm very glad you came. I'll be the envy of every man we see tonight."

"Oh, please." Sienna looked away, sniffing. "I'm not that big a deal."

"You have to know how hot you look in that dress. A man would have to be in a coma not to notice you."

"Now, you're just exaggerating," she protested.

"Exaggerating?" Vaughn repeated in a shocked tone. "Come with me."

When she didn't move Vaughn took her hand and tugged her along behind him. He guided her into the bathroom and positioned her in front of the mirror. "If you don't believe me, see for yourself."

Sienna gazed at her reflection. It was an exercise that she didn't like at all. She never spent too much time pondering how she looked—at least not anymore. Years ago she had been all-consumed with her image and how others saw her. One dark and terrifying night had changed that forever. Shaking off old torments, Sienna glanced up at Vaughn's reflection in the mirror. If anyone was causing heart palpitations it was *him*. He wore a pair of black slacks with black leather shoes. The shirt was a long-sleeved midnight blue that buttoned down the front. Vaughn looked sexy.

*Sexy*. That was an understatement. Vivian's voice echoed in her head. *Girl, the man would have to drop that magnetism down a few levels to be considered just sexy*. Lately, Sienna was having all sorts of trouble keeping her mind from conjuring up thoughts that were off limits. *Who said they were off limits?* Her inner voice questioned. "I thought we did."

"You thought we did what?"

Sienna pinned Vaughn with a shocked stare. She'd sworn she'd said that to herself. *Rule number fifteen: Men don't like to be put on the spot.* "Brought a camera," she lied. "I thought I brought a camera is what I meant."

He laughed and tweaked her nose. "I'm sure I've got one. So, are you ready for dinner?"

***

They dined on the terrace at the Oak Creek restaurant. White lights were woven around the trees near their table. Vaughn chose the Filet Mignon while Sienna couldn't resist the Rack of Lamb. While sipping her wine, she observed the water rushing over the various rocks that sprinkled throughout the creek. There weren't many diners about so it was almost as if they had their own private spot. She felt enveloped in the serene beauty surrounding her. After they had finished their meal, her eyes settled on Vaughn. Sensing her scrutiny, his head lifted. "I can't imagine this weekend getting any better than this," she sighed, contentedly.

"I wouldn't make that claim just yet. You know how I love challenges," he countered. "How about a walk?"

"Sure, but I warn you. I'm so relaxed you may have to pour me out of this chair."

Calling their waiter over, Vaughn asked for the check. After he'd settled the bill, he and Sienna walked around. "You can't see it now, but we'll check out the Snoopy Rock tomorrow."

Her face lit up. "Oh, I heard about that rock. It looks just like Snoopy lying down. They said the rock just behind it looks like Linus playing on his piano with Lucy sitting on top of it."

They chatted amiably for several minutes. "So, how is work going? You haven't mentioned anything about it since you got here."

"And I'm not going to," Vaughn clarified. "Tonight, I want to focus on spending time with my best friend in one of the most beautiful places in America."

Sienna skidded to a halt staring at Vaughn curiously. "I'm one of your best friends?"

Vaughn turned. "Of course you are, Sienna. How could you doubt it?"

*Oh, I don't know, maybe because I'd like to do a lot more with you than be best buddies.* She said to herself. As they walked, Sienna studied his profile and continued to carry on a full blown conversation with herself. *I can't believe you brought your "buddy" to what is hands down one of the most romantic places on the planet. It is also astounding that I could barely salivate over the best lamb I've ever had because I was sitting there going gaga over how good you look. And how's this for irony? It was the best evening I have ever spent with a man—fully dressed. This was by far the most perfect date I've ever been on with someone that isn't interested in getting my clothes off.* The more she talked to herself the more distressed she became. *Rule number sixteen: Never ask a man why he wants to be your best friend instead of your boyfriend.*

Before she could stop herself, Sienna turned and blurted out, "Vaughn, what's wrong with me?"

He gave her the once over. "How do you mean?"

Seconds ticked by without a response from her. Sienna prided herself on her ability to think fast; to be able to assess a situation with clarity and respond accordingly. She did it every day in her profession, and yet she was standing in front of Vaughn like she had forgotten the mechanics of the English language. *Tell him,* her inner voice coached. *Tell him how you feel.*

"Sienna? Are you okay?"

She stared into Vaughn's concerned face. It was amazing how he became more attractive the longer she was around him. "I'm cold," she lied—again.

He studied her. "Cold?"

"Yes, isn't it crazy? Here we are enjoying this wonderful view and I'm freezing." She shivered for effect.

"Oh. Let's get you back then," he replied, draping his arm around her. "I'm sorry I didn't think to bring my jacket, or to suggest you grab something before we left your cottage."

"It's not your fault. I should've remembered. It's the desert, right? Deserts are chilly at night."

By the time they'd reached her residence she didn't have to fake the chills running over her. Vaughn's arm draped around her shoulder was wreaking all sorts of havoc.

# Chapter Thirteen

## Conversations

The insistent ring of a telephone roused Sienna from a deep sleep and an incredible dream. She sat up and glanced around the room. *Sedona.* Leaning over, Sienna picked up the telephone receiver. "Hello?"

"Did you sleep well?"

"Well? That would be an understatement. I slept the entire night in one spot. That's unheard of for me."

Vaughn chuckled. "I'm going to have to take your word for it. Are you hungry?"

She took a second to think about it. "Oddly, not yet."

"Good. There's a surprise waiting for you by the creek in thirty minutes."

"Thirty?" she glanced frantically at the clock. "Vaughn, women don't get ready in thirty minutes."

"Then you'd better be the exception," he joked.

"Seriously, what should I wear? What are we doing?"

"You'll see. Just wear something comfortable."

Vaughn hung up the phone.

Sienna glared at the receiver. "You aren't funny, Mr. Deveraux." Throwing the covers back, she jumped out of bed and ran into the bathroom to shower.

Twenty minutes later, Sienna was twisting her hair into a knot on top of her head. Dressed and ready to go, she was searching for her glasses when a knock sounded at her door. "Coming," she yelled running to open the door.

Vaughn was standing there with a small bag and cup in his hand. "Good morning."

"What's this?" Sienna asked when he handed them to her.

"A Chai latte and bran muffin. I figure we can have a real meal afterwards."

She tilted her head to the side curiously. "Okay, what are you up to?"

"You'll see."

"I'm sorry. Where are my manners?" She stepped aside. "Come in."

Vaughn stepped in and shut the door behind him. They sat at the small table. Sienna popped the lid off her tea and blew gently. Vaughn stared at her. So much so that Sienna looked up. "Why are you looking at me like that?"

"It's rare I get to see you with your glasses off. You look good with them on, but without them . . ."

"Isn't that funny? You like me with mine off, I like you with yours on."

He smiled at her. "I guess we're an odd couple."

Now she was the one staring. It was strange, but the more she tried to turn away, the harder it got. "Where are you staying?" *Oh, that sounded lame,* she told herself.

Vaughn ran a hand over his jaw. "My team is staying in a house by the creek. It's big enough that we can stretch out and not have to go searching for people when we need to do a group huddle. We'll stop by later today so you can see it."

"The resort has a house you can rent, too? It figures. Nothing about this place is ordinary," she observed.

"Hey, we'd better get going. I don't want you to be late," Vaughn remarked, edging toward the door.

She wished Vivian were here to give her some insight on how to get things moving. Vaughn wasn't making any moves and she'd done just about everything except parade naked in front of him. *Hmm . . .*

"Sienna?"

"Yep, coming," she said, quickly. She took her tea, but left the muffin. Vaughn told her she wouldn't need her purse. She opted for her prescription sunglasses and they were out the door.

As they walked down the path, Sienna told Vaughn about her parents. "You've got to meet them soon. My father is a retired Army Colonel. My stepmother, Cassandra owns a dance studio. She has a lot of wonderful programs."

"Your stepmother?"

"Yes. My real mother died when . . . I was six."

"I'm sorry to hear that. I've seen with Angella just how difficult it can be when your mother dies. Maybe Angella would benefit from taking dance lessons. Right now she's into golf, baseball, and soccer. I suppose a little variation might be a good thing."

"Sure. Talk to her about it and see if she's interested. You can bring her to Cassie's studio and she can check it out for herself."

They walked up to a portable cabana next to the creek. A woman was standing waiting for them. "Good morning, I'm Victoria. You must be Sienna."

"Uh yes, I am," Sienna replied looking questioningly toward Vaughn. He was the picture of serenity. Sienna's eyes narrowed. "This is the surprise?"

He nodded. I figured an hour-long massage by the water would be just what the Doctor needed."

Sienna was flabbergasted. "Vaughn. You are unbelievable."

"I try," he winked. "So, you get going on the nature thing and I'm going to check back in with the troops. I'll come back and get you and we can go explore Sedona together. Will that work?"

"Sounds wonderful. Only make it my place. I want to change after this is done."

After Vaughn bid the two ladies good-bye, he strolled back to the house. His thoughts drifted to Sienna. He retrieved his cell phone from his pocket. He dialed Carlton.

"You got a minute?"

"Sure, Angella's aunt just picked her up for a sleepover. What's up?"

"A lot. I swear, the more I'm around her, the more difficult it is to think about anything but kissing her."

"We must be talking about Sienna."

"Will you be serious? Who else would I be talking about? I'm telling you Carl, last night would've been the perfect opportunity; either on our walk back to her place or when we were sitting in front of the roaring fire at her cottage."

"Perfect time for what?"

"To make a move. Will you keep up? We've grown close since I crashed and burned when we met in Catawba. She's one of my best friends now. Sienna adds meaning to my life, you know? She fills a space I didn't even know was empty. She's witty, smart, sensitive, and beautiful—inside and out."

"From what you've told me she's also feisty enough to put you in your place."

"Which of course makes her that much more appealing."

"Of course," Carlton retorted.

"Despite the bizarre bun she wears more times than not, she's sexy as hell."

"Do you want my advice?"

"Carlton, that's what I called you for."

"Good. Here it is. You need to get off the fence and make a move. Find out how she feels about you."

Pierce's voice echoed in his head. *You need to dazzle her, baby.*

"Vaughn? Are you there?"

"Yes, sorry. I was just thinking."

"Wasn't that the whole point of this trip? Wasn't it because you were missing her like crazy and you wanted to see where things stood?"

"Yes. If I tell Pierce this I'll never hear the end of it, but I guess I did bring her here to . . . dazzle her."

"So what's with all the indecision?"

"I don't know if she's even ready to be in a committed relationship—with me."

"How about asking? Vaughn, you've told me how much it kills you to listen to her chat about the men that hit on her at almost every focus group. It's obvious you care about her. Stop being a baby about it and just tell her you want to see her naked."

"Will you be serious?"

"Well, isn't that what Pierce would tell you?"

"That's why I didn't call Pierce," Vaughn complained. "We already know I want to see her naked—that's a given. The question is when do I tell her and how?"

"Going from friends to lovers isn't always a smooth transition," his friend cautioned. "Things could backfire and then you're stuck with it being awkward if it doesn't work out."

"That won't happen," Vaughn dismissed.

"How do you know?"

"Because I won't let it."

"You're that sure of her feelings?"

"I'm that sure of mine. I can't imagine my life without Sienna Lambert in it. I also know that once we cross that line, and we most definitely will be crossing it, we won't be going back to just friends. She's everywhere, Carlton," Vaughn said, with a touch of awe. "My heart, mind, soul, and Lord knows my body. I can't escape her."

"Then I guess you know what you need to do, buddy."


Sienna had just pulled on a pair of shorts when her cell phone rang. Walking over to the night stand, she picked it up and hit the talk button. "Hello?"

"Did you do it, yet?"

"Viv?"

"Who else would it be . . . Cassie?" Vivian said sarcastically. "Did you sleep with him?"

Sienna collapsed against the bed. She sighed loudly. "No, nothing like that, but last night . . . I thought for sure it was going to happen."

"Well, why didn't it?"

Sienna stared at the ceiling. "I don't know, Viv. Something is holding both of us back. It's like neither one of us wants to make the first move."

"That's just crazy. One of you better get to it before you die of terminal sexual build-up."

"Vivian, that's silly."

"No, it isn't. I was watching the discovery channel and I—"

"You saw no such thing. Look, maybe he doesn't want anything more. I wore the *red dress* last night. The girls were front and center," she said, referring to her cleavage. "I had the sexy heels on, make up—the whole nine, Viv. Nothing. Not even a kiss. I can't force him to want to sleep with me."

"Are you insane? Women have been doing that since the freaking dawn of time. Heck, pick a civilization. Egypt, Africa, Asia, India. Does the Kama Sutra ring a bell?"

Vivian was silent for a moment. "Tell me you wore your hair down last night."

Sienna hesitated.

"Sienna Elizabeth Lambert. This has got to stop."

"I don't know what you mean," she evaded.

"You darn well do. Look, I hate to burst your bubble, but you are a beautiful woman. You hiding behind glasses and wearing your hair straight out of a magazine you borrowed from the Library of Congress doesn't matter. One jealous woman's ranting at you for a beauty pageant disaster doesn't alter that fact."

"Please . . . don't go there," Sienna ground out.

"Oh, I'm going there. Sienna, it's time to move on. That drama happened when you were a teenager. It doesn't change who you are."

Suddenly the well-erected wall she'd constructed cracked. "Yes, it does, Vivian," she said, tearfully. "Can't you understand how I felt? He practically raped me. He would have if someone hadn't come along. You know he had the nerve to tell me he'd never met a girl as beautiful as me? How ironic. You know she actually blamed me for it? He almost ruined me and it's *my* fault? That's what I can't forgive."

The line went silent. Eventually, Vivian spoke. "Sienna, listen to me. You weren't to blame. Not for any of it. What happened was not your fault. You shouldn't let it compromise your self-esteem. He wasn't worth it. Do you hear me? He wasn't and still isn't worth the pain and torture you are putting yourself through. That horrible night doesn't define you as a person. I know deep down you want it to. You think it should, but it doesn't. You are still going to be beautiful, talented, and smart. Not wearing make-up and all the props you put on are not going to change any of that. It's time to move on," she said, gently. "Let it go."

Sienna blew her nose. "So what do you suggest I do? She took his side, Viv. Despite what we were supposed to mean to each other she believed *him*. Am I supposed to forgive her after all these years of animosity between us?"

"I won't even begin to counsel you on that. Whether you forgive her is completely up to you. What I will suggest is that you live, Sienna—for you. That's how you get past that dark moment in time. You live your life, and you start now. I don't know Vaughn that well, but from what I can see you care about him. Truly care. You can't trivialize that. So get those contacts you've been wanting, lose the Princess-Leia-wannabe hairdo, get a new wardrobe, and go seduce your man."

# Chapter Fourteen

## Excursions

Vaughn came to Sienna's room about fifteen minutes after her phone call with Vivian. When she saw him, a blush immediately splashed across her face. "I'm not exactly ready yet," she apologized, glancing down at her plush terry bathrobe. His gaze followed hers. Tension crackled in the air like a well-established log fire. Vaughn stepped back slightly. "I can see that. I uh, can come back shortly if you'd prefer?"

"No, just give me a few minutes," Sienna walked quickly back into the bathroom and shut the door.

Vaughn practically stood rooted to his spot. The visuals roaming through his mind's eye were killing him.

Several minutes later, Sienna re-emerged dressed and ready to go. He escorted her out.

Vaughn rented a jeep with a GPS system. When Sienna saw it she couldn't help but name it. "I think we'll call it Liesl."

Vaughn snickered. "Liesl? Been watching the Sound of Music lately?"

"Not recently," she clarified.

"Recently being in the last month?"

She rolled her eyes. "Anyway, where are we going for breakfast?"

"The Coffee Pot. I have it on good authority that they have the most extensive list of omelets you're ever going to find."

"How many do they have?"

"One hundred and one."

"Wow, that's quite a list."

"The team says it's quite a restaurant."

"It's going to be a challenge trying to pick one."

A snicker escaped his lips. "You forget, I'm well acquainted with your indecisiveness."

Sienna turned sideways in the seat. "What's that supposed to mean?"

"It takes you forever to order," he said, dryly. "I don't know what I want, you go first, I'll order last," he mimicked.

"I can't help it if everything looks good."

"Just remember our flight leaves for North Carolina tomorrow afternoon."

"Shut up." She hit him in the arm.

When they arrived at the restaurant there was only a few minutes wait. Vaughn passed Sienna a menu. "Here, start reading," he teased. "Maybe by the time we're seated you'll have picked something."

"Oh come on, like you already know what you want."

"I'm a simple man, Doc. I always know what I want."

She scrutinized him closely. "Not always."

Before Vaughn could comment, the waitress escorted them to their table. He waited until Sienna was situated before he sat down across from her. He laughed when she resumed studying the menu with quiet fervor.

"So, I was thinking we could go out with the team tonight. It would give you a chance to meet them."

"Mmm hmm." Sienna nodded distractedly.

Vaughn reached for her hand. That got her attention. She looked over at him.

"You know it's not that serious."

"Easy for you to say," she grumbled. "You already know what you're ordering. I'm only on the sixty-second omelet."

The waitress came back to their table and asked if they were ready to order. Surprisingly,

Sienna confirmed that they were. She closed her menu and handed it to the woman. "I'm going to go with number forty-one."

"The zucchini, mushroom, spinach, tomato, and cheese." The woman told Sienna what sides it came with.

"Do you mind if I get the banana pancakes instead?"

The woman wrote it down. "No problem. Will that be all, ma'am?"

"Oh, and a large glass of milk. That's it."

Vaughn was staring at her in surprise. "That was fast."

"Don't get excited," she joked. "It may never happen again."

He ordered the number twenty-seven omelet which was sausage, bacon, tomato, mushroom, and cheese. He also ordered green peppers, potatoes, and homemade biscuits. When the waitress had taken his order and their menus she left. Satisfied, Vaughn turned to Sienna. It was her turn to stare in astonishment.

"What?"

"You're going to eat all that?"

"Like there was any doubt?" he laughed. "I'm more worried about you, though."

"Oh, I'll have room."

After eating, they drove around Sedona while their food settled.

"I'm going to pop," Sienna moaned rubbing her stomach.

"Nonsense, you didn't eat that much."

"By whose standards?" She rubbed her stomach again. "So, where are we headed?"

"We're going to Cave Creek. There's a place called Extreme Arizona that does ATV tours. It's just over one hundred miles from here."

"Good. It'll give my body a chance to digest all this food."

Vaughn chuckled. "Have you ever been ATV'ing before?"

"Yes."

He turned to face her.

She rolled her eyes. "I know it's shocking, but I've actually done a few things you may not believe."

"Is that so?" he said, intrigued.

"I'm not a pro, but I've gone out a few times."

"With?"

"My dad, and on other occasions, a few friends."

He laughed but refused to elaborate when she asked him what he found amusing.

It took them two hours to get to reach their destination. After they were registered, Vaughn and Sienna were outfitted in pants, gloves, a riding jersey, boots, socks, and safety gear. "I feel like a stuffed sausage," Sienna giggled sliding her helmet down over her head.

"Trust me you're too hot to look like a sausage."

"I feel kind of hot," she said, sitting on her all-terrain vehicle.

Vaughn's eyes raked over the yellow and black riding outfit she wore. From her helmet down to her boots his gaze missed nothing. "Doc, that definitely was not the hot I was referring to."

Sienna couldn't contain the silly grin splattered across her face.

The guides had other riders to bring over from the shop so their vehicles were loaded up on the trailer. Vaughn and Sienna followed behind in their jeep.

Arriving at the trailhead, the employees backed the various ATV's and dirt bikes out of the trailer while the riders stood off to the side. Sienna took that time to take in the scenery. There were power lines that ran overhead as far as her eye could see. The mountains and hills in the distance kissed the cloud-filled sky. The sandy trails stretched out ahead of them. Succulents, cacti and other plant life took her breath away with their natural beauty.

Sienna went back to the car and grabbed Vaughn's digital camera and a guide book for all the indigenous plant life. She snapped a few photos and tried to put a name to some of the shrubs and bushes she saw. *Desert Broom*, *Shrubby Coldenia* and *Feather Dalea* were in abundance. Vaughn came up behind her. "We're ready."

She turned. "Sedona is so beautiful, Vaughn. I am so glad you brought me here."

He looked into her face. It was hard considering she still had a helmet on. "Sienna, there is nobody I'd rather share such an amazing place with besides you."

A fellow rider offered to snap their picture. Vaughn wrapped his arm around her waist and they took the picture, sans helmets.

Some of the riders were on guided tours while others explored the trails on their own. Vaughn and Sienna decided to go at their own pace. The driver would come back to get them in a few hours. They all synched their watches and hit the road.

She was hot when they were standing around waiting to leave, but the moment they got their ATV's, Sienna cooled off. It took her a while to get acclimated to shifting the gears of her quad, but she eventually mastered the task. Vaughn stayed close by. Sometimes he took the lead, other times Sienna was out front. They stayed to the right of the trails so that riders on the faster dirt bikes, quads, or in multi-passenger off-road vehicles could get by.

There were respectful of the land and never strayed from the marked trail. A few times they pulled over to drink some water or take a break. The last time they did Sienna took her helmet off.

"Are you tired?" Vaughn inquired.

"A little," she admitted. "I'm not ready to call it quits, though. It's too spectacular out here."

"As much as I'd love to stay out here I think we'd better start heading back. Those are storm clouds on the horizon and the last thing I want to do is have us out here when it hits."

Sienna followed his gaze. "My gosh, I didn't even notice," she placed her helmet back in place and started her ATV up. "Ready when you are," she said, loudly.

"Let's pick up the pace, okay?"

She nodded and let him lead. They heard the first clap of thunder. A storm was definitely headed their way. A few minutes later, the clouds opened up and it began to pour. The rain was making it extremely difficult to see. She slowed down to keep from being pelted so severely by the wind and water. As they were coming down a steep hill Sienna wiped her goggles. When her vision cleared she realized she was about to drive into a jagged stretch of the trail. She swerved to the right to avoid driving on uneven terrain. The second she realized she'd overcompensated it was too late. Her right wheel hit a crater and her ATV pitched severely. It rolled over taking her with it.

Vaughn made it down the hill and was heading down a flat stretch of trail. When he turned around to check on Sienna the yellow ATV was no longer behind him. He pulled over to the side and waited for a few moments. When there was no sign of Sienna his face creased with worry. *This isn't good.* Vaughn wheeled around and accelerated back up the steep incline. Eventually, he spotted the ATV. It was lying upside down with Sienna's legs protruding out from under it. His heart stopped. "Sienna," Vaughn yelled, loudly. It was futile. His voice couldn't be heard over his helmet, or the raging storm.

His vehicle skidded to a halt. He cut the engine and was off the machine in one seamless motion. "Sienna," he shouted again. "Hang on, Sienna, do you hear me? Hang on."

# Chapter Fifteen

## Turning Point

It had happened in an instant. One minute she was riding along the flooding trail, the next she was on the ground with an ATV on top of her. Adrenaline rushed through her veins. The vehicle didn't feel as heavy as she would have expected. *Focus. Rule number seventeen: Don't panic, there's a way out of everything,* she told herself. The first order of business was to get out from under the vehicle. With as much strength as she could muster Sienna sat up and pushed with all her weight. She flipped the quad over. It cleared her and came to rest right side up and on all four wheels. *Thank God it isn't as heavy as it looked,* she told herself.

Vaughn rushed over to her side and dropped to his knees. Cautiously, he removed her helmet and gloves. His hands roamed over her body. As he fired off a barrage of questions, Sienna had to wonder if he had any medical training. "Sienna, can you tell me where it hurts? Are you dizzy or nauseous? How many fingers am I holding up?"

"Not sure at the moment, no, no, and one," she answered dutifully.

She saw relief in his eyes, but worry too. His hands were shaking slightly as they traversed her limbs to look for injuries. She tried her best to waylay his fears. "Vaughn," she said, loudly over the deafening storm. Her hands sought his out and stilled them. "I'm all right."

An expression crossed his face that she couldn't decipher. She simply stared at him. Vaughn was motionless for a moment longer before guiding her head to his.

Vaughn crushed his lips to hers. He kissed her with a single-minded purpose. It was meant to dispel any chance that Sienna was thinking he was just happy she was safe. He was, but he wanted his intent to be crystal clear. Right now Vaughn was trying his damndest to kiss the taste out of her mouth.

He eased her onto his lap. When Sienna wrapped her arms around his neck, relief coursed through him like an intravenous drug. His arms locked around her waist to hold her in place. Her legs clamped around his middle. A second later her tongue dueled boldly with his. It was like an aphrodisiac to him. The more Vaughn tasted her, the more he wanted.

The rain beating down on them was irrelevant. The clumpy sand they were sitting in inconsequential. The only thing that mattered to Vaughn was that he didn't break contact with some part of Sienna's body. He rolled her over and under him. A second later, Sienna yelped. He released her immediately and reared back. He searched her face. "What's wrong?"

"I don't know I—ow," she cried out, bolting upright. "It burns."

"What burns? Where?" Vaughn was back in medical mode.

"On my back."

He got behind her. He ran his hand lightly over her wet jersey. He yanked it back half way down. It was dark, but his eyes scanned over the ground. He studied the area and then declared, "I know what it is."

"Great, what is it because it's driving me crazy."

"It's cactus needles. We rolled you into cacti."

"Well get them out."

"We need some light. Come on," he helped her to her feet, and then over to her ATV. He started the engine and turned the headlights on. They kneeled down in front of the bright beam. Vaughn got behind her again. Despite the rain he worked carefully to pull out the needles stuck in her shirt. After a few moments he asked, "Can you raise your shirt up?"

Sienna eased the jersey higher.

"Okay, that's far enough."

Sienna bit her lip while Vaughn worked on her.

"Done," he finally announced. She slid her top down. Vaughn got to his feet, and then helped her up. "We've got to get going, Doc." He walked over to retrieve her helmet. Shaking it a few times, he secured it to her head. He swung his leg over her ATV and revved the engine.

"Is it okay?"

"It should be fine. Hop on and hold on to me as tight as you can."

Sienna's arms went around his waist as he directed. Turning around, he gunned the engine and took off toward the steep hill driving back the way he'd come. Sienna closed her eyes and molded herself to his back. They drove up the incline without incident. He pulled in next to his ATV. "Are you going to be able to drive back to the Jeep?"

Sienna nodded into his back. Vaughn got off and she slid up to the front.

"The trail's wide enough here where we can ride side-by-side. We'll be back in no time," he said, squeezing her arm reassuringly.

He jogged over to his ATV and jumped on. He started the engine. Sienna drove up to his side and waited. He gave her the thumbs up sign and they started down the path. It wasn't long before they reached the beginning of the trailhead. By the time they came to a stop, it was done raining. Vaughn was glad to see that everyone had made it back without serious incident. The guides loaded the vehicles back on the truck. Sienna waited while Vaughn spoke to the driver. After he was done he came back and escorted Sienna to the car.

The top was up, but all the windows had been down so the seats were wet from the storm. Neither one paid much attention since they were already wet and uncomfortable. They drove in companionable silence for a while. Eventually, Vaughn reached over and clasped Sienna's hand in his. "Are you okay?"

"I'm fine, Vaughn. Nothing a good meal, hot shower, and dry clothes won't cure," she said, tiredly.

His eyes roamed over her. "You sure you don't want to go to the hospital and get checked out?"

Sienna was shaking her head before he'd finished his sentence. "No. I will be all right. I just want to go home."

Vaughn nodded. "If you feel any pain—"

"I promise I'll let you know."

"Fair enough, but we're going to stop on the way home to get something for your back."

When they arrived at the tour shop the woman working there gave them towels to dry off with before getting re-dressed. They were still a bit dirty, but elated to be in dry clothes again. On the drive back to Sedona, Vaughn stopped to get something hot to drink and some first aid supplies. He bought tea for Sienna and coffee for himself. She thanked him profusely while sipping her steaming beverage.

It was almost ten minutes before Sienna broke the silence. "So is one of us going to talk about the gray elephant in the car?"

Vaughn glanced over. "I suppose we need to, don't we?"

"That's a big yes."

"Okay Doc, you want to start or will I?"

"You can."

Vaughn's grip on the steering wheel tightened and then relaxed. "First off, I want to apologize for putting you in harm's way this afternoon."

"Vaughn, you couldn't have anticipated a freak storm blowing in."

"I know. Up until that point we were having a great time. Weren't we?"

"Of course we were," Sienna said, stifling a yawn.

"You're exhausted."

"No, I'm not."

"Why don't you try to close your eyes and take a nap? We'll have our heart-to-heart when you get up."

Sienna looked over at him. "Vaughn, I'm fine."

Vaughn's gaze raked over her. She looked like a bedraggled kitten with her hair plastered to her face and dirt streaked over her skin. He smiled a lopsided grin. "That you are, but humor me and close your eyes."

Sienna sat back and sighed loudly. Her eyes drifted shut. "See? Nothing."

Vaughn remained silent. When her breathing evened out and her head rolled to the side he couldn't contain the low chuckle that escaped his lips.

Sienna slept the entire ride back to Sedona. Vaughn was able to find a parking space close to her cottage. Before he got out of the Jeep, he retrieved her key from her jacket pocket. He walked around the car and opened her door. He unbuckled her seatbelt and gently retracted it back from across her body. Vaughn put her purse in his hand before scooping her up into his arms.

After he cleared the door he used his back to shut it. Sienna stirred, but didn't wake up.

At the door he had to stand her up while he opened it. Her eyes fluttered open. "Oh, we're home," she said, yawning.

"Sorry I woke you up," he replied, softly. He opened the door and helped her inside.

"I've got to take a shower. I feel like things are crawling on me."

"Good idea. I should probably go. I'm definitely in need of a shower myself."

"No," Sienna said, quickly.

He arched an eyebrow. "No, you don't want me to take a shower?"

"No, I don't want you to leave."

Vaughn's eyes darkened. Slowly, he walked up to her. Putting his hands on either side of her face, he lowered his head and kissed her with a thoroughness that made Sienna lean toward him. When he ended the kiss, his thumb glided over her moistened lips. "I'll be back, Doc."

"Promise?"

He kissed her again. "I promise."


After Vaughn left, Sienna went straight to the bathroom to strip out of her soiled clothes. Before she climbed into the shower she found a bag to put them in. When the steaming water hit her body, she sighed languorously. Many things had transpired over a short period of time. A sudden storm had thrown a myriad of events into motion that from she was still reeling. Her accident, Vaughn's protectiveness, that incredible, stomach-knotting-toe-curling kiss he'd given her. *Correction, kisses,* she mused. She ran a wet hand over her face. She wasn't dreaming. He had *finally* kissed her, and that kiss left no ambiguity as to what their status was. *Did it?* Her conviction wavered slightly. *No, he wanted more.* They both did.

The soap she was holding hit the shower floor. Snapped out of her reverie, Sienna bent down to retrieve it. A pain shot up her rib cage. She cringed and leaned against the tiled wall. Sienna cautiously breathed in and out a few times assessing the severity of her possible injury. Determined to wash her hair, she cautiously tested her range of motion before commencing. A few minutes later, Sienna was finished and drying off. She towel dried her hair for a while before applying hair-styling mousse and blow drying it straight. She twisted it into a bun before brushing her teeth and finishing the rest of her nightly routine.

Sienna chose a comfortable pair of purple and white cotton pajama bottoms and a white sleeveless camisole with a built-in shelf bra. By the time she was looking for her slippers Vaughn knocked on the door. She went to let him in.

Seeing him on the other side of the door did weird things to her system. He was carrying a bag in one hand. "What's that?" she asked after closing the door.

"I didn't know if you were hungry or not so I brought us some sandwiches."

Sienna took the bag and looked in. "Vaughn, this is a lot more than sandwiches," she laughed. She sat cross-legged on her bed and motioned for him to join her.

"In a minute," he proclaimed. He walked over to the fireplace and made a fire. After he was satisfied that it was well established, Vaughn returned to the bed. "Now let's take a look at your back."

"It's fine," Sienna told him.

"I'm looking at it anyway," he said sitting down behind her.

She lifted her top to give him better access. Vaughn looked over her back.

"See? Nothing but a few scratches," she replied.

"I'll feel better if we put some antibiotic on it anyway," he told her as he got up and went into the bathroom.

When he returned he was carrying Neosporin and a large Band-Aid. Vaughn made quick work of administering to the abrasions on her back. Satisfied, he kicked his shoes off and joined her on the bed.

Sienna laid the food he brought between them. Vaughn had made a roast beef and Swiss cheese sandwich and a turkey club. There were also two bags of Sun Chips, grapes, bottles of green tea, and bottled water. There was also two Rice Crispy Treats.

"You made Rice Crispy Treats?" she hid a smile.

"Actually, I can't take credit for those. Two of my team members had a bake off."

"Lucky me," Sienna said, eagerly.

They delved into the makeshift picnic with gusto. They talked about work and recreational activities while they ate. While they were cleaning up the remnants of dinner, Vaughn handed her a plastic wrapped Rice Crispy Treat. After she'd removed the plastic, Sienna reverently sank her teeth into it. Vaughn followed each bite with rapt interest.

"Is it better than the cheesecake at the picnic?"

She smiled in recollection. Her eyes closed while she chewed. "Close, but not quite."

"You know, there's something I've wanted to do since that day," he confessed.

"What?"

Reaching over, Vaughn's hands went up to either side of her head. Sienna's eyes fluttered open. He undid the knot and arranged her hair around her shoulders.

Sienna bit her lower lip nervously.

"Hey," he lifted her face up to meet his eyes. "You are a gorgeous woman, Dr. Sienna Lambert—inside and out. I'm sorry to tell you, but that bun doesn't detract from how pretty you are."

"So I've heard."

"I'm certain it hasn't kept any man from wanting to approach you, and it sure isn't going to keep me at bay." His hand stroked her hair. "Personally, I think you can lose that awful thing."

Sienna laughed when his lips curled in distaste. "When I'm with you, or all the time?"

"All," he clarified.

An uncomfortable look crossed her face. "I don't think I can do that."

He regarded her. "Why? What's so important about it?"

"I . . . it just makes me feel . . . I don't know. I can't even explain it. I just know that I'm not ready to change it. Please try to understand."

"Sweetheart, I'm not going to pressure you. If you want to wear that thing by all means . . . I just don't get why it's so important."

"I'll explain it to you one day."

"Whatever you want," Vaughn kissed her lips. "We have all the time in the world, but for tonight it stays down—deal?"

She nodded. "Fair enough."

"You know, if it's supposed to be keeping me at bay, I'm telling you right now it ain't gonna work," he grinned. When he would've retreated, Sienna wrapped her arms around his neck to keep him there. She returned his kiss with an ardor that left them both breathless.

He leaned his forehead against hers. "Sienna, you could've been hurt badly today."

"But I wasn't."

He ran his hand through her hair. "Just seeing you lying under that ATV . . . it almost drove me insane with worry. I can't—Sienna, I can't pretend any more that you don't mean the world to me."

She let out a small gasp. After a few seconds she shook her head. "Neither can I."

He expelled a breath, and then leaned back to study her face. "This is beyond friendship. You know that, right? You're in my heart Sienna, and I most definitely want you in my bed."

"Vaughn," she said his name as if it were the key that unlocked all the pent-up emotions she'd been trying hard to suppress.

He ran a thumb over her lips, and then his hand trailed down her chest to rest just above her heart. Desire was more than evident when his eyes sought hers. He kissed her neck, her cheek, and then devoured her lips. Vaughn's eyes traveled over her body, and returned to her eyes. His expression was serious, but also held a touch of awe. "I want you, Sienna. I can't begin to put into words how much I want to make love to you." His hand traveled up her chest to rest on her heart. This time his touch was unsteady. "You're killing me," he whispered before his lips reverently met hers.

# Chapter Sixteen

## The Sleepover

This was what she'd been waiting to hear for weeks. She couldn't contain the staccato beat of her heart at hearing his affirmation. There were two things that Sienna was absolutely certain about. The first was that Vaughn made her feel completely beautiful and utterly desirable. The second was that if he didn't make love to her before the night was over she'd implode. Sienna arms went around his neck. Slowly, she leaned back toward the pillows taking him with her.

Vaughn's left hand ran lightly down her side. His fingers closed around her thigh. He gently eased her leg up and positioned it around his waist. Sienna needed no further coaching. She wrapped both legs around his middle. He sat back and brought her up with him. He buried his face in her neck. "You're so beautiful."

Her hands moved to his waist. She grabbed his shirt and slid it up his chest. He took the hint and removed it.

She allowed herself a moment to run her fingers across the chiseled muscles. "I've got a request of my own," her voice came out in a hoarse whisper.

"Baby, you name it," he replied between kisses.

She met his intense gaze. "I want you to make love to me."

Vaughn's smile was blinding. "That was a given, Doc."

"You weren't planning to stop?" her voice held a note of relief.

He placed a hand lightly on one of the straps on her camisole. He moved it out of the way and put his lips in its place. He kissed her lightly on her shoulder. Next, he slid his hand under her top to tease the underside of her breast. Lowering his head, Vaughn feathered soft kisses down her stomach. Eventually, his gaze returned to her face. "Why? Did you want me to stop?"

*Rule number eighteen: If a man you've wanted since you regained consciousness wants to take you to bed, try not to ruin it by being too gaga over him. Wait, that's a stupid rule.* She scolded herself. She felt him watching her. He was giving her a chance to say no. To stop them before things progressed too far. It was her choice. Sienna made her decision without hesitation. "Even if this place was being demolished, I wouldn't want you to stop."

"Good to know."

Their hands continued to roam over each other's bodies. Vaughn kissed her neck causing Sienna to shiver from excitement. "I'm curious."

Sienna's fingers grazed his jaw. "About what?"

"Whether you're wearing a pair of Best Kept Secrets under those pajama bottoms?"

She raised her hips several inches off the bed. "Well Mr. Creative Director," she said, seductively. "I think you'd better find out."

Vaughn's eyes darkened in response to her open invitation. He looped his fingers around the waistband and eased the pants down her legs. He gathered the pajamas in his hand and ceremoniously dropped them on the floor. He perused her body. He ached to have her long legs wrapped around him. He almost moaned aloud at the image his mind created. "No men's underwear? I'm shocked."

"If I knew when I got dressed earlier we'd end up here, I would've planned accordingly."

Vaughn kissed her leg, and then tickled the back of her knee with his tongue. Sienna giggled in response.

"Ticklish, huh?" That was all the incentive he needed. Vaughn trailed kisses up the length of her body. He gave prolonged attention to spots that were sensitive for her. He didn't stop until he was poised at her lips. "I think you're sexy as hell regardless of what you're wearing."

She blushed at his compliment. "How do you always know the perfect thing to say?"

"I guess it comes naturally when I'm with you."

"You have too many clothes on," Sienna stated pointing to his pants. "It's your turn."

His eyes never broke contact with hers as he eased off the bed. Standing, Vaughn lowered his pants and stepped out of them.

Sienna looked him over appreciatively. "Hmm . . . looks like I'm not the only one not keeping secrets tonight. You aren't wearing them either."

"Pity," he told her returning back to the bed. He covered her body lightly with his.

Sienna moaned aloud when they made contact. When Vaughn wedged his knee between her legs, she shuddered. "Now you're killing me."

"With pleasure?"

"Always."

Vaughn placed both of her wrists in his hand and raised them over her head. Sienna gasped.

He let go and was off her in an instant. "What's the matter? Sweetheart, did I hurt you?"

"No, you didn't. I guess I just hurt my side earlier."

He searched her face. "Sienna, when were you going to tell me? How long has it been bothering you?"

"Vaughn, I just noticed it in the shower. I reached for something and felt it. I'm sure it's just a bruise."

He glared at her. "You don't know that for sure. We should go get it x-rayed to rule out a broken rib or something."

"Vaughn, it's not major. The ATV rolled over on me. I'm bound to have some soreness over the next few days. I promise if it feels worse I'll go get it checked out," she soothed reaching for him.

He was still tense. "If it's not better tomorrow, we're going in," he clarified.

"Okay, okay."

"Where does it hurt?"

She lifted up her top and pointed to her rib-cage on her right side. Vaughn leaned in to examine it. He ran his fingers lightly over her skin. Sienna tried to remain on an even keel, but it was difficult. His warm touch was causing her breathing to accelerate.

When she felt his lips on her skin, her eyes fluttered closed. "Vaughn," she pleaded.

"I'm right here, baby," he returned to the attention he was giving her body.

This time when he leaned over her he supported most of his weight with his forearms. Sienna wanted to feel him against her, but it was clear Vaughn was being overly cautious. Wanting him closer, she wrapped her legs around his middle to pull him in. She almost saw stars.

She wasn't fast enough to hide the pained expression. He took her legs in each of his hands and gently eased them back onto the bed.

He took a deep breath and expelled it raggedly.

When the pain subsided, Sienna eyed him quizzically. "Vaughn?"

"Doc, I want you so badly, but—"

"If you want me, why do you look so tortured?"

He closed his eyes. "Sweetheart, we can't—"

Sienna's mouth dropped open. "Oh my God," she murmured. Her face drained of color and she leaned as far away from him as she could manage. "I can't believe this," she cried out.

"Sienna—"

"You don't want me."

Vaughn looked incredulous. "Huh? What are you talking about?

"Then what is it you're not telling me? I . . . I didn't think you had a girlfriend, but—"

"Whoa, slow down," he cut her off. "There is no other woman, nor am I a priest."

Her face crinkled with confusion. "Then I don't understand. Why don't you want to sleep with me?"

"Are you crazy? Sienna, I want to—very much." He slid his hand under her top and raised it past the now reddened area above her ribcage. He lowered his head and feathered a soft kiss on her bruised skin before returning his gaze to her face. "I just don't think we should make love until we get your side checked out by a doctor."

She searched his face. "That's all?"

He took her face in his hands. "Believe me that is the only reason why I stopped."

Sienna released the breath she was holding. "It's not that bad, Vaughn. I can handle this."

Vaughn smiled. "Sienna, our lovemaking is supposed to be bringing us pleasure, not pain."

She averted her eyes.

He tilted her face toward him. "Hey, this isn't easy for me, either."

She snorted, "Could've fooled me."

He placed a finger under her chin and tilted her face to meet his. "Sleeping next to you and not being able to make you mine is going to be one of the hardest things I've ever had to do. Trust me when I tell you it poses a serious challenge. I may not even sleep tonight."

Her face lit up. "You're going to spend the night?"

"Where did you think I'd be? I'm sure as heck not leaving you alone. You may take a turn for the worse and need to go to the hospital. Besides, I couldn't stay away from you if I tried," he admitted. He studied her face. "You don't want me to stay?"

"Vaughn, of course I want you to stay," she assured him.

"Good to know. I'll take the couch."

"No. I want you here—right here," she pointed next to her. "You may not be *sleeping* with me tonight, but I want you sleeping in this bed," her eyes sought his out. "You aren't the only one that can't stay away."

"I don't want to run the risk of hurting you during the night."

"You won't," she said, confidently.

He kissed the bridge of her nose. "All right, Doc." Vaughn got up and went to throw another log on the fire. He went to the bathroom while he was up. When he returned, he helped Sienna get comfortable in bed before sliding in next to her.

He gathered her carefully in his arms. "Can I get you anything, or do you want to watch television?"

"Nope," Sienna replied trying hard to lose the visual in her head of him in nothing but boxer briefs. "I'm fine right here."

Silently, they gazed at the fire blazing in the hearth. Occasionally, Vaughn would rub her shoulder or kiss the top of her head. Sienna was perfectly happy spending this intimate time with him. Their tumultuous beginning made the recent declarations between them even more special. They were best friends now, and soon would be lovers. Just anticipating their union made her antsy. *This is how it should be.* She let out a contented sigh. Her last thought before she drifted into unconsciousness was of Vaughn wearing nothing but a devilish smile.

# Chapter Seventeen

## A Second Opinion

Vaughn heard Sienna's breathing even out. She was finally asleep. He gazed at the ceiling. Beads of perspiration were forming at his brow. If he slept at all tonight it would be a miracle. The effort to keep his body in check this close to Sienna was herculean. The only thing prohibiting him from burying himself deep within her honeyed walls was her injuries. At this point they didn't know how extensive they were. Not being able to get her looked at that night made him more on edge.

Suddenly, Sienna shifted in her sleep. Her hand was centimeters from his groin. *Lord, I'm going to lose my mind,* he lamented. Slowly so not to wake her, Vaughn raised her hand back to his chest. He kept his fingers at her wrist. A breathe escaped his mouth in a loud shudder. *You can do this.* No matter what the personal sacrifice to his mind—or body—Vaughn refused to knowingly cause Sienna pain. If that meant being tortured all night with fantasies of making love to her, and that intoxicating scent of hers overwhelming his senses, so be it.


The next morning, Sienna woke up to find herself stretched across Vaughn's expansive chest. She blinked a few times to be sure she wasn't dreaming. *Nope. It's real all right.* The silly grin plastered on her face was spreading by the second. Vivian wouldn't believe the turn of events her life had taken in two short days.

"Good morning, sweetheart," Vaughn's deep voice rumbled in the ear she had lying on his chest.

The vibration tickled. Sienna lifted her head. Her hair splayed across his chest. "Morning," she leaned in and kissed him.

When she pulled back she got a good look at his face. Her smile vanished. "Vaughn, you look like warmed over crap."

"Thank you, I feel like it, too."

"You didn't get any sleep?"

He rubbed his hand over her back. "A certain sex goddess kept me up all night with erotic images dancing through my head."

Sienna cautiously raised herself up. "Vaughn, I'm sorry. I didn't mean for you to be up all night."

"Baby, it's okay. It wasn't all night, just some of it. I'm fine, really."

She kissed him lingeringly on the lips. Vaughn's smile could have rivaled the silly grin on her face moments earlier. "This is how I want to wake up every time we're together."

Her hand drifted over his abdomen. "I think that can be arranged," she said, teasingly. When it went lower, he lightly grabbed her wrist. "Doc, you're playing with fire. My defenses are weakest in the morning."

"Ooh, good to know."

Her suggestive tone got to him. In one swift motion, Vaughn turned her over and under him. Sienna cried out in pain. He was off her in an instant. "Damn, I'm sorry. I forgot."

"I'm fine," her hand instinctively went to her side.

He moved her hand out of the way and raised her shirt. Her bruise was deep purple. "That's it. We're going to the hospital. I'll help you into the bathroom and when you're ready we'll get you dressed."

He got up off the bed and went to retrieve his clothes. "We'll stop at a coffee shop on the way."

"This is crazy, Vaughn. It's just a bruise. All bruises hurt worse on the second day. Everyone knows that."

Vaughn ran a thumb lightly over her lips. "Humor me, Doc."

Her stomach fluttered. There was no way she could refuse him when he looked at her like that or called her pet names. "Fine," she said, grudgingly, "But I'm telling you the doctor is going to say the same thing I did. That it isn't serious."

Vaughn kissed the tip of her nose. "I have no problem with that."

"Good. I'm glad you won't have a problem when we find out it's nothing and I say 'I told you so.'

With Vaughn helping her it didn't take Sienna long to get ready. They were on the road with Vaughn driving her to Verde Valley Medical Center in no time. Their wait in the emergency room waiting area was negligible. Vaughn remained seated while Sienna was escorted back to get her temperature and blood pressure taken.

When she was accompanied back to a trauma room Vaughn went with her. She answered various questions from the nurse regarding her symptoms. The woman gave Sienna a gown to wear and other instructions before the doctor came in to see her. Vaughn averted his eyes while she changed. He swallowed hard. Just thinking about her naked made his imagination run wild. *Get a grip, man,* he scolded himself. This wasn't the time for fantasizing. With a deep breath, Vaughn turned his attention to the patterned cotton curtain in front of him.

Sienna gingerly removed her clothing, but had difficulty unhooking her bra.

"Vaughn, I'm going to need some help with this," she called over her shoulder.

"Sure," he tried sounding calm and nonchalant. Turning, Vaughn walked over to stand behind her. He released the hooks one at a time. His fingers lightly grazed her skin. *We're in a hospital,* he admonished, *not exactly an ideal spot to see your girlfriend's breasts for the first time.* His thoughts turned to his brother. He could almost hear his voice. *"Are you crazy? Any time is the right time to take the girls out for a spin."*

"All done," he said, slightly louder than necessary.

"Thanks." She eased back into her gown.

Vaughn assisted Sienna with tying it at the nape of her neck, in the middle and at the small of her back. Gathering her clothes, Vaughn folded them neatly and placed them on a nearby table before helping her into the hospital bed. He adjusted the blanket over her.

"How do you feel?"

"A little wiped out to be honest."

"Why don't you close your eyes and try to nap? It always takes a while for the doctor to get here."

"I'm not too sleepy. Vaughn, tell me about your family? Do your parents live in the area?"

"No, they live in Michigan. They have a place in Florida, too. They drive down during the winter months like the majority of retirees their age. I have two brothers. You've already met Pierce, and I have a brother, Chase."

She looked shocked. "Chase? Vaughn, I've never heard you mention him before."

"He travels all the time. He's in the Army. The next time he's home on leave I promise we'll go up to my parent's house so you can meet everyone."

The silly smile was back and plastered securely on her face.

Just then the curtain was pulled back and a tall, well-built man walked in.

"Good morning. I'm Dr. Ivan Weissman. You must be Dr. Sienna Lambert."

"I am," she replied.

"It's a pleasure to meet you." The doctor shook Sienna's hand. He glanced over at Vaughn. "Are you Dr. Lambert's husband?"

Vaughn winked at Sienna. "I'm her boyfriend."

Sienna couldn't contain her smirk. When asked, she recounted her accident and the symptoms she'd reported. Dr. Weissman took rapid notes.

"How long has the pain persisted?"

"Since the accident yesterday."

"Any difficulty breathing, Doctor?"

"Some," she admitted looking away from Vaughn.

Dr. Weissman asked a few more questions before he began Sienna's physical exam. He carefully prodded her side with his gloved fingers, listened to her breathing with a stethoscope and made more notes in her file.

"There's some definite blunt force trauma to your ribcage, Dr. Lambert, but we're going to take a chest x-ray to determine whether you have any broken ribs or fractures. This is just a precaution. The good news is we aren't too busy this morning, so we'll know what we're dealing with shortly."

He stepped out to go write up the order. Sienna leaned back against the pillows. Vaughn came over and gently sat on the side of her bed. "I should have insisted we come here last night. I suppose telling me you were having difficulty breathing was an oversight?"

Sienna could tell by his expression he wasn't pleased to hear her admission. She touched his arm. "Vaughn, I didn't want you to worry. I honestly think it's just something that will have to wear off."

"Yes, but it's better to know that for sure instead of guessing, don't you think?"

The nurse arrived interrupting any further conversation between them. Minutes later, Sienna was being wheeled out to go get her x-ray.

It was almost an hour later when Dr. Weissman parted the curtain and came in. He stood at the end of Sienna's bed. "Good news, Dr. Lambert, there were no broken or fractured ribs, just some bruising. There is really no treatment for this kind of injury other than to manage the pain you'll have while your ribs heal. So, I'm recommending plenty of rest, I'm going to give you a prescription for the pain and an anti-inflammatory. I'd like for you to use ice packs to reduce the swelling as needed."

"So what can't she do, Doctor?"

"She'll have to avoid anything that will aggravate the injury. No sports of any kind, and no sudden, jarring movements. You will experience pain when breathing, Dr. Lambert, but I want you to continue to breathe regularly. I can't stress that enough, okay? If you don't, you run the risk of developing pneumonia. That would be bad."

"Got it."

"If your condition worsens, I want you to go see your primary physician immediately."

"She will," Vaughn assured him. "Oh, we're scheduled to fly back to North Carolina today. Will she be okay to travel?"

"Yes, she'll be fine. Just make sure she takes the medication I've prescribed before then." He handed Sienna the prescriptions.

"Thank you. It was nice meeting you, Dr. Weissman."

"You too, Dr. Lambert. Your nurse will be in with your discharge instructions shortly. You can get dressed whenever you're ready. A wheel chair will be here soon. Take care." He smiled and left the room.

Vaughn looked down at Sienna. "You look tired. You'll feel better when we get some pain killers in you. You want me to help you get dressed?"

"That would be great."

By the time Sienna was dressed the nurse had returned with her discharge instructions. The nurse pushed Sienna in a wheel chair to the main entrance while Vaughn got the car. When he returned, they both assisted Sienna in on the passenger side.

Once she was secure, he walked around the car and slid into the driver's side. He found a pharmacy nearby, and ran in to get her prescription filled while Sienna closed her eyes to rest. By the time he returned, she was asleep. He didn't wake her until they were back at L'Auberge. Helping her inside, Vaughn got her situated in bed. He gave her a bottled water so she could take her medication. "You should try and catnap. I've got some calls to make and packing to do."

"Vaughn, I'm not an invalid. I can pack myself."

"Tell you what; if you take a snooze, I'll let you help when you wake up."

She yawned loudly. "Tyrant."

While Sienna slept Vaughn made several calls. He changed his flight, booked himself on Sienna's plane and moved their departure to late afternoon. He phoned Pierce to make arrangements for him to retrieve his car from the airport and drop it at Sienna's house.

"Is she going to be okay?" Pierce asked after Vaughn filled him in on the accident.

"She'll need to take it easy the next few weeks, but she's on the mend."

"There's something different in your voice, big brother. Did you and Sienna—"

"Pierce," Vaughn said, in a clipped tone.

"You dazzled her didn't you?"

"We're not having this conversation."

"Okay, okay," Pierce chuckled before hanging up.

Vaughn called his assistant next to let her know he'd be working from home for the next few days. While Sienna was napping, Vaughn went back to the Creek House to pack. He informed his team of his plans and contact information in case they needed to reach him.

"We're sorry we didn't get to meet her," one of his associates replied.

"You will, soon," he assured her before heading to his room to pack.

Several hours later, Vaughn sat on the side of Sienna's bed, handing her a pill to swallow. She took it and washed it down with water. He filled her in on the arrangements. "I can't believe everything you've done today," she said, in disbelief.

He brushed an errant lock of hair out of her face. "All in a day's work, sweetheart."

Most of the day had been a blur for Sienna. Vaughn hired a limousine to take them to the airport, and had insisted she be transported by wheelchair to the gate. He'd upgraded their tickets to first class to ensure she was as comfortable as possible. The moment she was settled in her seat, Sienna promptly fell asleep. She didn't stir until Vaughn kissed her cheek and whispered in her ear, "We're landing."

A driver met them at baggage claim. While Vaughn waited for Sienna outside the ladies room, the man went to pull the car around. At the curb, he took their luggage and loaded it into the trunk while Vaughn assisted Sienna into the back seat.

As they were heading onto the interstate on-ramp Sienna turned toward Vaughn. "Thank you—for everything," she said, tearfully.

"Hey, what's all this about?" he wiped the tears from her cheeks.

"This weekend was amazing, crazy romantic, and more than I ever could have anticipated," she informed him. "To top it off you have a wonderful bedside manner."

"Doc, there isn't anything I wouldn't do for you. You should know that by now," he said, seriously.

She nodded. "I do."

# Chapter Eighteen

## Down Time

As soon as they arrived at her house, Vaughn ushered Sienna upstairs, helped her out of her clothes and into comfortable pajamas. He insisted she get in the bed and rest. Propped up with several pillows behind her, a book, and several magazines next to her, and the television remote, Sienna felt pampered.

"Hey, do you want me to call Vivian and tell her you're back or do you want to let her know?"

"I'll call her," Sienna sat up to kiss him. Vaughn met her half way.

Their kiss was chaste, but when both pulled away their eyes held a glint of something more.

"I don't think I'll ever get used to kissing you," Vaughn admitted.

Her cheeks reddened. "Nor I."

Vaughn went downstairs to make her some tea. Sienna glanced around her room. She was glad to be home, but part of her missed their desert paradise. She sighed, loudly, just thinking about the weekend. She picked up her cordless phone and dialed Vivian's number. Vivian answered on the first ring.

"So, what happened? Did you and Mr. Deveraux get down and dirty?"

Sienna blushed and melted against her pillows. "Vivi, I don't even know where to start," she gushed.

Vivian screamed excitedly into the phone. "You'd better start with the clothes, and don't stop till they're off."

"Well, we didn't exactly have sex."

"You didn't? Why not? I thought for sure you going to Sedona for the weekend would put the icing on the cake."

Sienna filled Vivian in on their outing and her subsequent accident. She recounted their amazing night together and her doctor mandated down time.

"I'm relieved you're okay, but that sort of puts a damper on your would-be sex life."

"Tell me about it," Sienna sighed. "Still, I'm just glad we've come to an understanding about it—about everything. Things are so good between us, Viv. Vaughn is incredible. He is attentive, he treats me like a queen, and he gets my temperature rising with just a look or the way he says my name—and his kisses—"

"Please tell me the bun's gone," Vivian interrupted.

Sienna laughed and then winced at the stitch in her side. "Don't make me laugh, it hurts, and no, my choice of hairdo hasn't changed."

Vivian exclaimed, loudly into the phone. "I don't know why you insist on wearing that ridiculous style to begin with. It's a real buzz kill, you know."

"You've mentioned that."

"I'm sorry, but it's foolish to think a centuries-old, outdated hairstyle is going to keep your natural beauty from shining through or keep people from noticing you."

Sienna sighed, loudly. "Vivian . . ."

"We'll skip the lecture—for now. I want to know more about you and your new boyfriend."

*My boyfriend.* Sienna said the title in her head. It was strange, but at the same time perfectly normal to think of Vaughn in that capacity.

"How long will it be before you can sample the cookies?"

"Viv, how many slang words do you have for sex, anyway?"

"Girl, please. I could go on all night," Vivian retorted.

"Anyway," Sienna continued. "The doctor said no strenuous activity for the next few weeks."

"What about if you got on top?"

"Vivian," Sienna chided.

"You could stand up and—"

"Will you knock it off? You're making this more tortuous than it has to be. Besides, Vaughn has been beyond diligent ensuring that I don't injure myself. There's no way we're consummating this relationship until I get a clean bill of health from a medical doctor," Sienna said, wistfully.

"Suit yourself, but it seems like there are plenty of workarounds."

"We'll use the time to get to know each other better. I'm looking forward to discovering more about Vaughn. He's such an amazing guy."

"Amazing?" Vivian repeated. "Me thinks you've got it bad, milady."

Just then Vaughn walked back into the room. A smile lit up her face. "Viv, me thinks you're right."


The next few weeks became a well-established routine. Vaughn had worked from Sienna's house the first few days, but then had to return to the office to handle some key meetings. The Best Kept Secrets campaign was in full swing and the men's undergarments were in massive demand. Dexter Clothiers executives couldn't have been happier. They were spending millions on promoting the new line which made everyone at Chase & Burroughs ecstatic.

Sienna still wasn't able to travel for work so she concentrated her efforts on writing proposals for prospective clients and getting caught up on paperwork. Vaughn would call her several times throughout the day to check on her. When he got off work, he would come over to cook dinner or run errands for her. After dinner, they would play cards, watch a movie, or just talk about their day.

Every night Vaughn slept at her house. Most night's their sleeping together was chaste. On a few occasions, one or both of them would have difficulty adhering to the 'No Sex' rule. They would chalk up their momentary lack of will power to being human and end the night in each other's arms.

Sienna had a hard time keeping her parent's from fussing over her. They still hadn't officially met Vaughn yet, but had talked to him often on the telephone. Gordon and Cassandra kept her company most days and Vaughn was there at night.

One night when she and Vaughn were playing cards, she looked up from her hand. "After I'm cleared by my doctor, I want to have a dinner party."

"You do? What's the occasion?"

"It's two-fold, actually. I want to say thank you to everyone for taking such good care of me since my accident. The second is that it's high time I met Carlton and Angella and you met my parents face-to-face."

Vaughn grinned. "I see your point. Sounds like a plan. I'll set everything up."

"No, I can do it. You just let your family know and I'll tell my parents."

"Doc, you sure you're up to this?" he said, searching her face.

"Yes, I'm sure. I'm fine, Vaughn."

"You can have your party, but I will be helping."

There was no arguing with him when he used that tone. She simply smiled and resumed their game.

Later that night when they were in bed in each other's arms, Vaughn sat up. "Hey, I want you to close your eyes."

Sienna's eyebrow arched. "Why?"

"It's a surprise. Come on, no peeking."

Sienna sat back against the pillows and closed her eyes. Checking to make sure she wasn't peeking, Vaughn waved his hand in front of her face several times.

"I may not be able to see, but I can still sense things, you know."

He laughed at that. He reached over and retrieved a gift wrapped square box from the nightstand drawer. Vaughn placed it in her lap. "Open your eyes."

Sienna's eyes flew open and zeroed in on her legs. "Vaughn, it's beautiful."

"Sweetheart, the beautifulness is actually in the box," he teased.

*Rule number nineteen: If your man gives you an unexpected gift, don't embarrass yourself by ripping the paper asunder.* Her fingers gently tugged at one scotch taped side. Her face was a mask of concentration, her bottom teeth worrying her lower lip while she tried her best to coerce the tape to release the paper. When one side came free, Sienna almost whooped aloud with joy.

"Doc?" Vaughn said, suddenly.

Sienna looked up from her task. "Yes?"

He retrieved the box from her hand. "It's not that serious," he said, ripping the gift wrap from the box.

"Vaughn," she glowered at him. "I would've been done in a few minutes."

"Or never," he said, dryly. "Now we're done, so open it."

She rolled her eyes. Her false show of annoyance was forgotten when she opened the box. She opened the tissue paper and gasped. There was a framed picture of her and Vaughn from the restaurant by Oak Creek. Draped over the frame was a gold chain holding a small square covered in tiny diamonds. She ran a finger over the small pendant. "Our first picture together," she said, softly. "Vaughn, thank you."

She picked up the necklace and watched fascinated as the light danced off the brilliant gems. He couldn't contain a grin. "Are you going to ask me?"

She nodded, her laughter echoing around the room. "I give up. What is it?"

"It's where it all began."

Sienna leaned in to let Vaughn secure the clasp. She fingered the jeweled square, her face a mask of concentration. Finally, she figured it out. Tears brightened her eyes. "Third base."

He kissed her soundly. "Where the magic started."

"After I regained consciousness, of course."

He shook his head and smiled down at her. "Even incoherent, bloodied, and disheveled, I thought you were the most beautiful woman I'd ever seen."

"You're idea of beauty is slightly askew," she concluded.

"Hardly. You're unique, Doc, completely one-of-a-kind."

A shadow crossed her face. Her smile faded.

"Hey, what is it?" he caressed her cheek.

"Nothing," she said, pulling him into a tight embrace. "Thank you for my gift, Vaughn. I'll treasure it always."

She ran her hand down the front of his chest. Unable to stop herself, her hand continued around to his backside. When she squeezed, his arms tightened on her shoulders. "You're playing with fire again, sweetheart."

"Tonight, I'm going to be living dangerously Mr. Deveraux, so I suggest you get used to it. Maybe tonight we'll get past third base."

Vaughn's eyes darkened with desire. "Sienna, you know we can't—"

She kissed his neck and ran her tongue over his collar bone. "I know," she cut him off, "but I intend to have a real good time practicing."

# Chapter Nineteen

## Untimely Arrival

Sienna sat at her desk making last-minute corrections to her grocery list. She'd done the bulk of the shopping already and had just a few things to pick up on the way home.

"What are you doing here?" Vivian asked from the doorway.

"I left my To-Do list on my computer," Sienna replied, still typing.

"I could've saved it to my flash drive and dropped it by your house, you know."

"I brought mine. Besides, I had a doctor's appointment this morning, so I was out and about anyway."

"How did it go? Did you get a clean bill of health?"

"You bet I did. I even asked my doctor to put that I could resume all my activities in writing so that Vaughn would believe me. Trust me he's going to sulk when he finds out I went without him."

"So that means—"

"Absolutely," Sienna grinned. Standing, she retrieved her thumb drive and put it in her hand bag. "I've got to go. See you tonight around six?"

"Of course. Is tonight the big night?"

"Vivian, where have you been? Of course it's a big night. My family and Vaughn's are meeting for the first time. Everyone except his parents though. They couldn't make it this weekend."

"Uh, yes I know, but that wasn't the big night I was talking about. I was asking if you and Vaughn were going to . . . you know . . . tonight?"

"I'm so not answering that. You're bringing the wine, and that CD of yours I wanted to borrow, right? I want everything perfect," Sienna said, anxiously.

"Will you relax? Everything will be fine. Don't start thinking things to death."

Sienna rolled her eyes. "I wasn't doing anything of the sort."

"Uh-huh. How many cookies did you eat today?"

"None."

"Donut holes?"

"Zero."

Vivian was thoughtful for a moment. Suddenly her eyes narrowed. "Cream puffs?"

Sienna looked away guiltily. Not . . . many."

"Define not many."

"It's irrelevant," Sienna said, dismissively. "I'm fine."

"If you say so, but just remember, it's a dinner, not a wedding rehearsal."

The rest of the day went by without incident. By five fifteen, Sienna had the appetizers laid out on colorful plates in strategic locations, wine and other beverages were chilling in ice buckets and the candles around the first floor were ready to be lit. She took a deep breath and surveyed her handiwork. *Beautiful.*

She walked back to the kitchen and opened the refrigerator to retrieve the olive tray. On the way to the counter, Sienna tripped on the area rug. She righted herself before the tray hit the floor, but the olives weren't so lucky. Half of them went airborne flying off the plate and scattering onto the floor.

"Oh no," she exclaimed. She sat the tray down and bent down to pick up the wayward olives. She dumped them in the trash and went to the fridge to get more.

Upon inspection Sienna discovered she was fresh out. "Great," she said, moaning aloud.

She contemplated calling Vaughn or Vivian to ask them to get more. "No, I'll go myself. I'll get back and have everything set up before anyone arrives." With her plan of action in place she headed for the door. Before she got there her house phone rang. Pressed for time, Sienna chose to ignore it. She retrieved her purse off the table and headed out the door.

"Uncle Vaughn, are we almost there?"

"Yes Angella, we'll be there in about five minutes."

"Great. I can't wait to meet her," she replied, eagerly.

"Neither can I," Carlton agreed with his daughter.

Just then Vaughn's cell phone rang. He answered it on speaker. "Hello?"

"Hi, it's me. How close are you to the house?"

Vaughn heard the edgy tone in Sienna's voice and switched the call to his handset. "We're almost there. Why?"

"Oh, thank God. I'm running late. I had a mishap with the olives and had to go out to get some more. There was a ridiculous line at the grocery store, but I'm on my way home. I just wanted to ask if you wouldn't mind meeting my parents without me. You know, just in case you get there first."

"Sweetheart, it's no problem. I'm sure we'll be fine. Relax, and I'll see you shortly, okay?"

He heard her sigh. "Thank you, babe."

"You're welcome, Doc."

Vaughn hung up. Pierce gazed at him from the passenger seat. "What was that about? You sounded like a hostage negotiator trying to talk someone down."

"She's just nervous about this dinner party," he explained.

"I can see that. I should have brought her some Be-Dazzled. That would've helped. There's just a hint of lavender in my new fragrance. It calms and soothes them."

"If you needed something for Sienna, Vaughn, I could've brought something from work. I just created this new aromatherapy massage oil. It's got Lavender and German Chamomile mixed with just a hint of Vetiver essential oil. It will give her emotional stability and—"

"Well, my perfume works like that too. I mean it really gets them in the mood to get loose with the—"

"Pierce," Vaughn said, loudly.

"What?"

Vaughn tilted his head to the back seat. "Can we save the chemistry lesson for later?"

Pierce glanced over his shoulder at Angella and an annoyed looking Carlton. "Uh sure. Sorry about that. I figure if your girl's a basket case . . ."

"She's not a basket case," Vaughn said, slightly annoyed. "Sienna just wants this evening to go well. It's really important to her. So be on your best behavior, little brother."

"Aren't I always?"

There was a car in Sienna's driveway, so he parked at the curb. "Someone beat us here," Vaughn replied turning off the engine. Vaughn jumped out of his Ford Explorer and walked around to the trunk. Opening the tailgate, he sat the ice cooler on the ground in front of Pierce and handed another large bag to Carlton. He placed his laptop bag on his shoulder.

"Please don't tell me you plan on working this evening?" Carlton said, aghast.

"Just a few files I need to e-mail back to the office. Then that's it for the work stuff."

"Hey, don't I get to carry anything?"

"Of course, Angel. I saved the most important item for you." Vaughn winked. He handed her a cake box. "I thought you'd like to share your favorite with Sienna and her family."

Angella's face lit up. "Uncle Vaughn, you brought a coconut cake with strawberry preserves in the middle?"

"Yes, specially ordered for my two favorite ladies to share."

Angella turned to face her father. "You think she'll like it, daddy? Not everyone may like strawberry preserves in the middle of their cake. Most people like the icing there instead."

"Don't worry, darling. I'm sure Sienna will love it as much as you do," Carlton replied, tweaking his daughter's nose.

She laughed and followed the three men up the driveway.

Vaughn used the key Sienna had given him when they returned from Sedona. He opened the door and stood aside while everyone entered.

"It's pretty," Angella concluded.

"Yes, it is. I see the patio door is open. Why don't you guys take this stuff out there and get it set up. Angel, you make sure they do it right, okay?"

"Sure, Uncle Vaughn. Let's go guys," she commanded walking in front of them.

"A true Diva in the making," Vaughn teased her father.

"Tell me something I don't know," Carlton groused.

Vaughn went in the kitchen to check on Sienna.
She was standing on her tip toes trying to
reach a wine glass. He watched her struggle a
moment before she cursed the wineglass. Smiling, Vaughn walked silently across the room to
help her. "Here, let me get that," he said, leaning in from behind her. He raised his hand over
head effectively trapping her against him. He
lowered the glass and moved back an inch so
that she could turn around. When she did, she
looked him over thoroughly before slipping the
glass from his fingers. "Thanks," she replied with
amusement.

"All my pleasure," Vaughn said. Suddenly, he
noticed her hair was out. It was in a straight style
that framed her face. He also noticed she had
added golden highlights.

"Wow," he said, with surprise. He hugged her
to him and whispered in her ear. "I love the new
hairdo. It makes you look even hotter." Before
she could respond, Vaughn kissed her. It was a
deep thorough kiss meant to show her just how
much he admired her new look.

There was a loud crash behind them and the
sound of glass breaking.

"Vaughn?" A woman cried out.

Startled, Vaughn released her. He spun around.
There were several people standing in the door-

way with various expressions on their face. When he zeroed in on the person standing slightly in front of everyone with a look of utter shock the color drained from Vaughn's face.

"Sienna?" he mouthed.

Vaughn slowly turned to face the woman behind him. He blinked repeatedly then staggered back like she'd branded him. "What the hell is going on?" he said, hoarsely. He tore his gaze away from her to the crowd gathered at the doorway.

"Uncle Vaughn, isn't it obvious?" Angella spoke up. "Miss Sienna has a twin."

"A twin?" Vaughn repeated.

Still ashen, Sienna glanced over Vaughn's shoulder. Her sister returned her stare without wavering. "Yes, Vaughn, I have a twin. The woman behind you is my sister . . . Sasha."

She looked derisively at her sister. "It appears an introduction isn't necessary, but the man you were all snuggled up with a moment ago is my boyfriend, Vaughn Deveraux."

"I wouldn't exactly call it snuggling," her sister retorted. "Charmed to meet you, Mr. Deveraux."

"You're right. From where I was standing it looked more like your tongue was down his throat," Sienna snapped.

"Oh contraire, darling, if anyone's tongue was in places it shouldn't have been it was definitely your boyfriend here."

"That's because I thought you were Sienna," Vaughn said, icily. "A point you could have clarified immediately."

"You're right," Sasha replied, nonchalantly. "I could have."

Before anyone could respond Gordon moved further into the room. "Sasha, it's been a long time, kiddo." He hugged her to him. "I thought we'd have heard from you by now. What have you been doing with yourself?"

"You mean besides feeling up my boyfriend?"

"Sienna," her father chided.

"Don't you Sienna me, Dad. She breezes into town—unannounced—breaks into my home, she lets Vaughn think she's me, and you want to read *me* the riot act?"

"I didn't break into your home," Sasha clarified. "I used a key."

"A key you'd better be leaving on your way out," Sienna snapped. "Which still leaves me with the same nagging question, why are you here?"

"For a visit. Besides, I heard you had a new man in your life. Keeping him for over two months has to be some kind of record for you. I thought I'd fly in to see who had you so enamored."

Sienna turned to her father. "You did this," she said, accusingly. "Daddy, how could you?"

Her father didn't look the least repentant. "I simply mentioned that you'd invited us over to meet Vaughn and his family. I didn't know your sister would fly all the way from London just to meet him."

"Oh, she met him all right," Sienna sent a frosty look to her sister. "Is this what you had planned? To come over here and try to mess things up for me?"

Cassandra immediately put herself in the middle of the fray. She walked over and embraced her stepdaughter. "Hello, darling, it's good to see you."

"Hi, Mom."

"Look, I don't mean to ruin a family moment, but I think I'm going to need a few answers." Vaughn looked at Sienna sharply. "Like why I'm just now finding this out?"

"Gordon, it's obvious these three have some talking to do. Why don't we take everyone else out to get some dinner?" Cassandra said, looking at Pierce, Carlton and Angella still standing in the kitchen surveying the scene.

"You're right. I think we could all do with a change of venue," he concluded, regarding both daughters. "You two get this sorted out. This nonsense has got to stop. We're family," he chided. "It's time you two started acting like it."

"Dad—"

Gordon's stance was firm. "I mean it, Sienna, you too, Sasha. You two get this bad blood between you aired out. I'm not tolerating another family gathering or holiday with my two girls at odds with one another."

# Chapter Twenty

## Truth is Stranger than Fiction

When his daughters remained silent, Gordon faced his oldest daughter, Sasha. "Where are you staying?"

"Well, since I'm not welcome at my sister's house—"

"Gee, what tipped you off?"

Sasha looked back to her father. "I'll get a hotel."

"Nonsense," Cassandra chimed in. "You'll stay with us."

"Mom," Sienna choked out.

Sasha glanced at her sister. "Dad, I don't want to cause any trouble."

"You should've thought of that before you got off the plane."

Gordon gave Sienna a stern look. "Nonsense, it's all settled. We'll see you at home."

Gordon and Cassandra walked toward the doorway shuttling everyone out with them.

Without a word, Vaughn followed suit. He walked next to Gordon. "Mr. Lambert, if you wouldn't mind dropping everyone back here, I'll take them home."

"Nonsense. You stay here with those two. We'll see everyone home. Besides, I think they're going to need a referee," Gordon replied, grimly.

"I don't know if I'm the best person for that task, sir. Truthfully, I'm still reeling from all this."

"I understand. Don't go too hard on my daughter. She and her sister, Sasha, have been at odds every since that damned beauty pageant."

Vaughn looked over. "What beauty pageant?"

"I'll let Sienna fill you in on that one. Both of them are pigheaded. Lord knows where they got that from," Gordon chuckled. Suddenly, he grew serious. "Vaughn, though brief, it was good meeting you. It's nice to see Sienna so happy. Still, as a father I can't help but worry about her—about both my little girls."

"From what I've seen, you have just cause."

Gordon slapped him on the back. "Don't I know it? I've been running behind those two since the moment they learned how to walk."

Vaughn said good-bye to his brother and Carlton. He gave Angella a kiss on the forehead. "I'll see you later."

"Never a dull moment, huh?" she observed.

"Don't get fresh, young lady," He didn't want to, but Vaughn couldn't help but smile.

"I don't suppose you could call me later and tell me what happens?"

He playfully yanked on her ponytail. "Not a chance. Too much grown-up stuff for you, little Miss."

Cassandra came over and hugged Vaughn quickly. "I'm sorry we had to cut our evening short. It was wonderful to finally meet you, Vaughn."

"Likewise, Mrs. Lambert."

"None of that. You call me Cassandra or Cassie."

Grinning, he nodded. "Thank you, Cassie."

He stood at the door watching them all load up into Gordon's Chevy Tahoe. By the time Vaughn stepped aside to shut the door, a heated discussion could be heard from the kitchen.

"So why have you shown up, Sasha? Somehow, I doubt you came all this way for the little cumbayah moment we all just had. Mom and Dad are gone so you can come clean."

"Actually, I just came here to visit and to relax. Work has been crazy lately and I missed everyone."

"You missed us? You haven't been home in over a year and you expect me to believe you were so homesick you caught the first flight out of London to Raleigh just so you could see your long lost family? Give me a break. Our parents may buy that snow job, but I don't."

"If you recall I tried to call you—several times over the last few months. You haven't bothered returning my calls."

"That's because I have nothing to say to you."

"So," Vaughn called from across the room interrupting the mêlée. "Are there any more siblings or dark secrets I don't know about?"

Both sisters remained tight lipped. When Sienna glanced at him, she noticed the strain in his features. It was obvious that Vaughn was holding himself in check. She bit her lower lip. "I guess you and I have some things to talk about as well."

"Why don't the two of you sit down in the living room and talk? Going twenty rounds in the kitchen may not be the ideal place to sort things out."

Neither one moved.

"Okay," he went over and placed a hand at Sienna's back and guided her off to the side. "You and Sasha need to go hash this out. It doesn't take someone with a Ph.D. in Psychology to figure out you two have some serious baggage."

"I'm sorry," she said, quietly.

He looked down at her. "One thing at a time, Doc," he said, with resignation. "But make no mistake you and I will talk later."

She nodded, and then walked into the living room. Sasha remained where she was. Vaughn turned to face her. "You brought the match to this bonfire, now you go put it out."

"It's hardly that simple," Sasha swept past him and out the door.

Vaughn retrieved a beer from the refrigerator. He walked over and sat heavily on a nearby bar stool. "If they had metal chairs to throw around, we'd have a daytime talk show."

When Sasha entered the room, Sienna reeled around to face her. "Why did you do it? As if our relationship wasn't screwed up enough you felt the need to bring Vaughn into this?"

"I don't know what you mean."

"Bull. You just admitted you came here because curiosity got the better of you. You had to see for yourself who I was dating."

"I wonder if this relationship will last. Don't you find it odd that we both have such difficulty sustaining lasting relationships?"

"Not really. Sooner or later they all end with you trying to sabotage my relationship."

"It hurts doesn't it?"

Sienna laughed harshly. "You've got to be kidding me. This isn't the same and you know it. Your boyfriend was a trifling S.O.B. that didn't deserve the time and effort you spent claiming to love him."

"I did love him."

"Then those sentiments were sorely misplaced. He knew I wasn't you and yet he tried to sleep with me anyway. If he hadn't been so freaking drunk that night it would've ended a lot worse," she said, tearfully. "What he did to you—and me was reprehensible, but did you call him out for it? Did you kick him to the curb? No, you blamed me, like I'd ever purposefully entice that sorry excuse for a man. What's sad is that you stayed in that dysfunctional relationship after what happened. You chose him over your own sister. You knew he was unworthy of you, and yet you continually projected your dislike of him and his shortcomings onto me."

"Stop it," Sasha warned. "Don't you dare analyze me. You're no saint, Sienna. You're just as flawed as I am."

"I never said I wasn't."

"Since when? All I heard about growing up was how all this was my fault. The one thing I was good at, you took from me."

"I didn't take it from you, Sasha. You asked me to do it."

"Like I had a choice? I wasn't about to be booted out of the pageant because of a stupid broken leg, so I asked my twin sister to take my place. How did I know my very own sister would stab me in the back?"

"You call my winning stabbing you in the back?"

"It was my name. I won and I deserved that crown."

"What am I just a stunt double when it's convenient? I won that beauty contest on *my* merits Sasha, not yours."

"Without me you wouldn't even have been in the contest."

"And without me, dear sister, you wouldn't have won. You would've been disqualified. I can't believe you're so ungrateful. I gave you everything else: The title, the accolades, the prizes. You had it all. Why wasn't that enough for you? Why would you begrudge me that one tangible object that proved I'd done something for myself?"

"Correction, you did it for me."

Sienna threw up her hands. "You always were a narcissist, Sasha. Don't you find it sad we're still harboring grudges for things that happened seventeen years ago, and why? Because you can't stand that for one brief moment in time you weren't the center of everyone's universe?"

"Are you trying to call me shallow?"

"If the stilletos fit. . ."


Vaughn was texting Carlton on his BlackBerry while Sienna and her sister hurled salvos at one another.


"Coast clear?"

"Nope, they're still going strong. How's dinner?"

"Much better for us than for you."

We went to the Asian bistro on High House Road."

"Red Bowl? Man, that's one of my favorites."

"It's odd, though."

"What?"

"I can't believe you didn't know it wasn't Sienna."

"How the hell was I supposed to figure that one out? I just thought she'd done something different with her hair."

"Couldn't you tell by how she kissed or something? I know she's an identical twin, but aren't there some differences?"

"Remind me to punch you when I see you."

"So why didn't she tell you she had a sister?"

"That, my friend, is the question of the night."

"Pierce is in rare form. It's like he finds an entourage wherever he goes."

"Tell me about it."

"I'm serious, it's incredible to watch. Apparently, it's pheromones."

"Don't encourage him."

"Angella says I need to get Dazzled."

"No, you need to get Dating."

Suddenly, Vaughn heard Sasha call Sienna's name twice. After that, he heard a loud thud. He dropped his cell phone on the counter and raced from the room.

# Chapter Twenty-one

## Full Disclosure

When Vaughn entered the living room he found Sienna lying prostrate on the floor with her hands griping her temples. He dropped down beside her. "Sweetheart, what's wrong?" When she didn't reply, Vaughn turned on Sasha. "What in the hell did you do?"

"I didn't do anything," Sasha said, bitingly. "She collapsed."

He watched Sienna writhe in pain. Smoothing her hair out of her face, he didn't bother looking up when he ground out, "Start talking."

"Lower your voice," Sasha scolded. "She's suffering from a migraine headache."

"A migraine? I've never seen someone collapse from one."

"Really, and how many people do you know with this affliction?"

Vaughn remained silent.

"I'm going to be sick," Sienna announced, doubling over.

Running to the laundry room, Vaughn returned seconds later with an empty five-gallon bucket.

Sasha gawked at him. "What are you doing?"

"She said she was going to be sick."

"Could that bucket get any bigger?"

"She said she had to throw up, and I got her a bucket. Next time you go find one," he said, with derision.

Gently, he lifted Sienna off the floor and onto the nearby couch. Tears streamed down her face. Vaughn knelt beside the couch and positioned the container within easy reach. "The bucket is right here in case you need it, sweetheart. It's going to be okay," he turned to Sasha. "What else can I do? Should we take her to the hospital?"

"No. First thing we do is get her upstairs so she can lie down. The room needs to be dark. We need an ice pack. If she doesn't have one, a hand towel with ice wrapped in it will do."

His expression darkened. "You'd better know what you're doing."

Sasha's glare was instantaneous. "I've been taking care of her a lot longer than you have."

"Clearly, it's the quality, not the quantity."

He picked Sienna up and cradled her against his chest. His progression up the stairs was slow to keep from jostling her. Once he reached her bedroom, Vaughn laid her in the middle of the bed. Sasha was right behind him. "I've got her. You go get the ice pack."

He lingered a moment.

"You're wasting valuable time, Mr. Deveraux. Unless you enjoy seeing my sister suffer?"

"Be a bitch on your own time," he snapped, striding quickly from the room.

By the time Vaughn got back, the room was devoid of light except for a small candle sitting on a nearby table. He handed Sasha the ice pack and then hovered while she applied it to her sister's forehead. "I'll give her a therapeutic massage. That should relax her body and alleviate the stress. Hopefully that will put her to sleep. She should feel better when she wakes up."

"Shouldn't we get a professional?"

Sasha fixed him with a venomous stare. "I am a licensed massage therapist."

Vaughn looked skeptical. "Did you pick that up in beauty pageant school?"

"Be a bitch on your own time," she threw back at him. "There's a bag next to my suitcase in the trunk." She tossed him her keys. "I'll need it."

Vaughn retrieved her bag and then went downstairs so that Sasha could work on her sister in private.

At a loss for something to do, he made Sienna some tea. While the water was boiling, Vaughn wondered if giving her caffeine would be a good idea. Deciding to err on the side of caution, he turned the water off. A few minutes later, Vaughn alternated between pacing and checking his wrist watch. A loud ring pierced the silence. With a quick yank, he retrieved his phone from his front pocket. He saw the call was from Carlton. "Hello?"

"What happened? You stopped texting so suddenly. Has everyone gone to neutral corners?"

"At the moment, but only because Sienna is suffering from a migraine."

"A massage could help. Why didn't you call me? I would've come back over."

"No need. Sasha is a massage therapist, too. Besides, you're not seeing my girl partially dressed. No offense."

"None taken," Carlton assured him. "It appears this evening has been full of revelations."

"Tell me about it," Vaughn quipped.

"I'll let you go. You let me know if you need anything. I'm serious."

"I know. Thanks, Carl."

An hour later, Sasha descended the stairs. Vaughn was on his laptop reading message boards, scanning chat rooms and searching websites for anything he could find on migraine headaches. He glanced in her direction when she came into the room. He watched Sasha drop her bag on the rug next to a chair. She raised her arms over her head and then she stretched them one at a time across her chest.

Sliding the computer to the side he asked, "How is she?"

"She's doing much better." She reclined in the chair and stretched her legs out in front of her. "The massage helped. She was able to drift off to sleep. More than likely she'll be out for the rest of the night."

Vaughn nodded. "So, what brought this on?"

"She started getting them when we were in middle school. Usually there's a trigger. Sienna's is stress."

"Funny, she's never had them with me."

Sasha bristled. "Maybe you just haven't had a chance to thoroughly piss her off yet," her smile was overly bright. "Give it time."

With an insincere smile of his own, he continued questioning her. "So, what are Sienna's symptoms—besides you?"

"Blurry vision or bright flashes of light dancing before her eyes. Sometimes she mentions smelling green apples before a migraine hits," Sasha shrugged. "I guess we were so busy arguing she overlooked them."

"What about the nausea or vomiting," Vaughn added. "Did she throw up when you were upstairs?"

"No. Your precious bucket is still spotless."

Vaughn smirked at that. "Where did you pick up massage therapy?"

"I trained a few years ago. I worked at a spa for a while, but then changed career paths."

He placed his feet back up on the ottoman in front of the couch and folded his arms across his chest. He closed his eyes. "There are just so many issues with this evening I don't know where to begin."

Sasha studied him. A loud sigh escaped her lips. "I suppose we should start with my apologizing for what happened in the kitchen earlier. It . . . was uncalled for."

"If you're referring to not stopping me before I kissed you, then, hell yes, that was uncalled for."

Her gaze met his. "I'm sorry."

Vaughn inclined his head.

"I guess you heard everything Sienna and I talked about?"

"Not all of it. Still, it is surprising that with all the animosity the two of you share you still came to her rescue."

"Did you think I wouldn't?" she asked, incredulously. "She's my sister. Regardless of what we're going through, or how screwed up our relationship, I couldn't let her suffer."

"A headache," he said, pointedly.

She blanched at his insult. "I'm outta here." She jumped to her feet and slung her bag over her shoulder. "There's a great deal you don't know about, Mr. Deveraux."

"Enlighten me."

"Don't you find it strange you didn't know I existed? I'd wager you find Sienna's lack of honesty as bizarre as I do."

"Somewhat, but that's a conversation that I'll be having with my girlfriend—not her sister."

"Whatever." Sasha headed to the door. "I'll be at my parents' house. Call me if she needs anything."

Vaughn got up and followed her to the door. "Thank you, Sasha," he called after her.

She turned. "I didn't do it for you, Mr. Deveraux."

He watched out the door until she was in her car and backing down the driveway. He shut the door and turned off the porch light. Straightening up the downstairs and dousing all the candle lights went by quickly. He checked the doors to make sure they were locked before he headed to the second floor. Stealthily, he entered Sienna's bedroom. Going straight to the bed, Vaughn stared down at her. Her eyes were closed. *Good,* he told himself, *she needs the rest.* He caught himself before touching her. He wasn't sure if he would make matters worse, and there was no way he would risk causing her additional pain.

Though the bed was ample, Vaughn figured it would be better for him to sleep on the couch in her room. He didn't want to run the risk of rolling over in his sleep. Besides, he wanted to be near in case she needed him. He turned away.

"I thought you'd be gone," she said, weakly.

Astonished, Vaughn turned toward her. "Hey, what are you doing awake?"

"I heard you come in."

"Sorry about that. I was trying to be quiet," he sat softly on the side of the bed next to her. "You should try and go back to sleep."

"I'll be okay if you want to leave," she assured him.

"Sienna, I'm not going anywhere."

"I wouldn't blame you if you were angry with me . . . not after what happened earlier."

Vaughn took her hand in his. "I'm not angry, Doc. I won't lie, I am a bit disappointed, though," he kissed her fingers. "Regardless of what happened, I'm not about to leave you here alone, okay?"

Sienna nodded.

"Try and rest. If you need me I'm right over there on the couch."

"Vaughn, you don't have to sleep on the couch. That can't be comfortable. You can use the guestroom, or I'll move over and—"

"Sweetheart, I'll be fine. You just relax. I'll see you in the morning." He kissed her lightly on the lips. He went into the bathroom to grab his toothbrush and toothpaste. Quietly, he went down the hall to the guest bath so he wouldn't disturb her. He made quick work of brushing his teeth and showered. The hot water helped him unwind. *What a night,* he thought.

After he'd finished, Vaughn wrapped a towel around his waist and swept up his clothes from off the floor. He stopped at the linen closet and retrieved a pillow, sheet and blanket. Not wanting to turn the light on in her closet, Vaughn folded his clothes and placed them on the table.

The job of making up his makeshift bed complete, he walked over to the dresser and pulled a pair of pajama bottoms out of the drawer that

Sienna had assigned him. When he slid it open, he fondly recalled the night she had cleared her things out and ceremoniously announcing it was now his to use. The grin that plastered itself across his face prompted Sienna to comment, *"It's only a drawer."*

*"To you it may only be a drawer,"* he replied, taking her in his arms, *"but to me, it's my drawer."*

*"Then I'm glad you like it,"* she laughed.

He discarded the towel and replaced it with pajama bottoms. He lowered himself onto the sofa. With one arm stretched across his eyes and another over the top of the couch, Vaughn drifted in and out of a troubled sleep.

The next morning, Vaughn sat on the side of the sofa massaging his neck and the top of his shoulders. It may have started out heavenly, but the unforgiving couch quickly morphed into a chenille-covered torture device. Standing, Vaughn silently stretched. The room held the muted glow of the newly risen sun. He checked his watch. It was just after six in the morning. Luckily, it was light enough for him to retrieve a pair of boxer briefs, a T-shirt and jeans without turning on a lamp.

His gaze traveled to the bed. Sienna hadn't moved from the position he left her in last night. *She must have been out of it not to have tossed and turned like she normally does,* Vaughn told himself. His stomach growled, a reminder that they had skipped dinner the night before. He padded out of the room to go downstairs and fix breakfast.

He took a few minutes to research what foods fought headaches. He went with oatmeal. It was one of Sienna's favorite comfort foods, plus he had read it would be helpful after her episode.

The phone rang while he was in the kitchen. Vaughn answered on the first ring before it woke Sienna up. "Hello?"

"How's my baby girl?" Sienna's father asked, with concern. "Sasha told us what happened."

"Good morning, Colonel Lambert. Sienna may not have had the best night, but at least she slept through it."

"We can come. Do you need us to drop over and relieve you?"

"No, sir, things are fine here."

"All right. Call us if you need anything or when she wakes up, Deveraux. I mean it," he warned.

"Yes sir," Vaughn almost saluted the telephone. "Have a good day, Colonel."

"Cut the formalities son, and call me Gordon."

"Will do, Colonel—Gordon."

"That's better," he replied before hanging up.

Vaughn checked on Sienna often. Whenever he poked his head in the bedroom, she was asleep. He ate breakfast, and then took his laptop upstairs to work for a while. He always smiled when he went into Sienna's home office. It was almost a mirror image of the layout at her job and just as meticulous. "You are too efficient, baby," he chuckled before sliding the chair up to the desk. He had copy to write for a sporting goods client's new ad campaign. After about an hour, Vaughn tilted back in the chair and stared at the ceiling. He ran a hand over his stubble laden face. Silently, he pondered all that had transpired since arriving at Sienna's house fourteen hours earlier.

"Vaughn?"

His chair snapped forward. He got up and strode into Sienna's bedroom. She was sitting up slightly against the pillows.

"Hey," he replied, walking toward her.

"Hi," she said, in a voice deepened by sleep.

Disturbing the edge of her bed, Vaughn settled next to her. "How's my Sleeping Beauty?"

"Feeling like I've been asleep for a week," she yawned. She ran her tongue over her teeth. "Yuck. Do I look a mess, because I sure feel it?"

"Impossible. Your beauty will never fade. You did have me a little nervous, though." Vaughn admitted. "Are you hungry or thirsty? Is there anything I can get you?"

"No. I just need to take it easy for a while. I'll be my usual self in no time."

"By the way, your father called."

"Did he threaten to storm the place?"

"Nope. He called to see if I wanted him to relieve me of duty. I told him we were just fine."

Sienna's expression turned guarded. "I don't think that's entirely true."

Concern etched his features. "Do you want me to call your doctor or something?"

"No, I'm going to be fine soon. My headaches don't usually last that long, although, I may be nauseous until I regain my strength, but that's not what I meant."

An odd look crossed his face. "Sienna."

"I know I owe you an explanation."

Vaughn shook his head. "We aren't going to do this now."

"We have to talk about all this."

"And we will, just not right now."

"There must be a lot of questions running through your mind," she pressed.

A loud sigh escaped his lips. "You're right. I do have a lot of questions, and I had a lot of time to think about this whole scenario last night," he said, with irritation. "I've tried to think about this rationally, to come at this from different angles and to try and understand your circumstances, but I just can't. The only logical reason I could come up with for why you weren't open with me is that you don't trust me."

Sienna's eyes swept over his face. "Vaughn, that's not true. I trust you—completely."

Vaughn bounded off the bed. "How can you say that? You neglected to tell me you had a sister, Sienna. We're not talking about a shoe fetish, or you being a shopaholic. Sasha is a member of your family. Regardless of whether you two are on speaking terms, she is your twin sister. You also didn't think it pertinent to tell me you suffer from severe headaches?"

"You didn't tell me that you had another brother right away, either," Sienna argued.

Vaughn's eyes widened. "I don't have a blood feud going on with my brother, Sienna. This is hardly the same thing. I just didn't get around to telling you about Chase, but that wasn't because we aren't on speaking terms, or because of some master plan to deceive you."

"That wasn't what I was trying to do, Vaughn."

"Putting that aside for a minute, if it wasn't for your sister I wouldn't have known how to help you, Sienna. You can't see how upset that makes me feel? Did you think I enjoyed watching you in excruciating pain?"

"Of course not," she interjected.

"Then why did you keep something like that from me?" he demanded. "Those are two pretty big topics not to discuss with someone that's supposed to mean something to you, don't you think?"

"You mean a great deal to me, Vaughn. Please don't ever doubt that."

"That's just it, Doc. You've given me no reason not to disbelieve what you say. You say you trust me implicitly, and that I shouldn't doubt you. My question to you is why? I need a reason, Sienna."

When she remained silent, he shook his head and turned away.

"Vaughn, wait," she cried, jumping out of the bed and running toward him. She paused for a second and placed her hand on her head. Reaching him, she placed an arm on his shoulder. "Please . . . please don't leave. Not like this. I'm sorry. I should've said something and I didn't. I didn't tell you about the migraines because I don't get them that often. Just under extreme stress and—"

"And I still should've known. If you get them every damn week, once a month, or every five years, you still should have told me."

"I realize that now and I truly am sorry for upsetting you. As for my sister, she and I don't get along. Everyone assumes that twins are inseparable and share everything, but that's not the case for us. We're always rubbing each other the wrong way. We had that big blow up a long time ago and we've been barely civil to each other ever since."

"That's not telling me why you lied to me."

"I didn't lie Vaughn. It's not like I told you I had a sister and you found out I didn't."

"No," he shot back. "You didn't *say* anything. That's worse."

When he went to walk away she ran around and got in front of him. "What was I supposed to say? That I'm a psychologist that can't even sustain a healthy, meaningful relationship with her own sister, and a twin sister at that? How do you think that makes me feel? It's the one thing in my life that isn't orderly, that I can't control. I'm very good at what I do, Vaughn. I strive to be the archetype for my profession. I work with all types of people from every walk of life, yet I'm crazed when I'm around *her*. The only thing we see eye-to-eye on is that we can barely tolerate each other. Do you know how that makes me look?"

"Human?"

"This isn't a joke," she snapped. "Do you know that you are the longest lasting relationship I've ever had? Most of them implode before they even reach the two month mark, and somewhere in the back of my mind I'm always worrying that Sasha will show up and ruin everything just to get back at me. A psychologist that's paranoid." She ran her hand over eyes. "That's the most ridiculous thing I've ever heard."

"No, Sienna, it isn't. You can't control everything—or everybody. Life isn't perfect. It just *is*. You're going to have to deal with Sasha one way or another."

"I am dealing with it."

"No, you're avoiding it," he countered. Flicking a hand over the hair coiled at the nape of her neck, he studied her for a few seconds. He let out a long sigh. "At least I finally understand why you wear it. That bun and glasses are nothing more than camouflage. You say you and your sister aren't close, but I disagree. She's been in your head for years telling you that you weren't worthy of winning that crown. That it was only because of her that you achieved success, that you weren't beautiful in your own right. That you had nothing of your own to offer—and deep down you believed her, didn't you? You told her you won on your own merits, yet you discount them every time you hide behind props, Sienna. Every time you get crazed over having to deal with her. Every time a relationship comes along and you don't trust it," he said, with remorse.

Tears slid down Sienna's face of their own accord. "I'm sorry I kept this from you. You can't imagine how much I regret that decision. Please believe me; I do trust you, Vaughn."

He rubbed his thumb along her cheek. "I hope you're right, Doc, because without it we're dead in the water."

# Chapter Twenty-two

## Amends

Gordon and Cassandra sat at the dinner table chatting about the upcoming recital at her studio. He glanced across the table eyeing his silent daughters speculatively. "You two are supposed to be working on your relationship."

"Dad, we're sitting at the same table. We aren't arguing, nor are we fighting. I'd call that progress," Sasha reasoned.

Sienna stared at her food.

"Still bummed out over Vaughn?" Sasha inquired.

"What of it?" Sienna snapped.

"Don't bite my head off, I was only asking. It's been three days and you still haven't spoken to him or seen him?"

"And your point is?"

"My point," Sasha stressed, "is that I think you need to step up your quest to win him back."

"All of a sudden you're giving me dating advice?"

"She may have a point, sweetheart," her father chimed in. "Have you spoken to Vaughn since he went out of town on business?"

Sienna shoved her fork around on her plate. "No."

"Did you call him?"

"No, Dad I haven't called. He clearly doesn't want to talk to me."

"Coward," Sasha said, under her breath.

Sienna fixed her with a cold stare. "What do you know about it?"

"I know you messed up by not being truthful with him about me, I know I should be pissed at your for implying I don't exist. I know you have this hang up about relationships that looms over your head like a damn rain cloud. I know that ridiculous bun you're wearing would drive any man to drink, and I know that you are trying to pretend his desertion doesn't bother you, but you're scared as hell and crying on the inside."

She stared at Sasha several shocked seconds before bolting out of her chair. "Tell me something, Sasha. Whose fault is it that I have relationship problems? Did you ever bother to ask yourself that?" She looked at her sister in disgust. "No, I bet you didn't." Grabbing her purse, she said a curt good-bye to her parents and headed out the front door. Cassandra was fast on her heels.

Gordon turned a reproachful eye toward his daughter. "It's amazing. Neither one of you have to work at being hurtful. It just seems to come naturally, doesn't it? If your mother were still alive this animosity you two have would have broken her heart."

For the first time since Sasha arrived, her expression was one of genuine sadness.

At home later, Sienna dabbed furiously at her running nose and tear drenched eyes with a wad of tissues. She had been there less than an hour and had already gone through half a box of Kleenex. The accusations her sister hurled at her were painful, but true. She eyed the cordless phone on her ottoman. *Vaughn.* A pang of regret at how things ended between them made her stomach churn. *Had things really ended, or was this their first argument?* she wondered.

On the way back to her house she'd called Vivian to get another perspective. Her ears were still throbbing from the quadraphonic tongue lashing she'd received from her best friend. "It would appear everyone thinks I've lost my mind," she cried, aloud.

"Not everyone," a woman's voice sounded from across the room.

Sienna gasped loudly and jumped to her feet. Her hand went to her heart. "Don't ever scare me like that again. How did you even get in here?" she asked, breathlessly.

Sasha shook the house key that was in her hand.

Sienna watched her sister swing the chain from her finger. "How many times do I have to ask for that back?"

"Beats me," Sasha shrugged. Coming into the room, she sat across from the couch like she'd done with Vaughn.

"So, what brings you by?" Sienna inquired. "Here to twist the knife a little deeper?"

Sasha shook her head. "Not this time. I wanted to—apologize, for what I said earlier. I was wrong."

Sienna shrugged. "No, you weren't," she sniffed. "I handled things badly with Vaughn. It's my fault he hightailed it out of town."

"It was work related," Sasha said, optimistically.

He's been on location before and he's called me every night, but not this time. I think I've lost him. Rule number twenty: quit kicking a dead camel."

"I think that's horse," Sasha remarked.

She blew her nose loudly. "These are my rules. I'll make up whatever I want."

Sasha took a breath. "Sienna, I—I owe you an apology. About what happened with Vaughn, about what I said earlier," she looked at her sister. "Most importantly, about what happened at the Beauty Pageant." Sasha looked remorseful. "I've done many things in my life that I am not proud of, Sienna, most of them to you. I want you to know that it's haunted me—my not being there when you needed me. Not taking up for you with that poor excuse for a human being. It was my darkest hour, Sienna. I'm ashamed of myself and not a day goes by that I don't wish I could take it back, that I could have made him pay for what he did to you," she brushed tears from her eyes, "to us. I am not asking you to ever forget what happened. I just hope that you are able to forgive me. I miss being your sister, Sienna, and I'd give anything to have that back." Sasha's voice shook with emotion. She took one final look at her sister and then got up to leave.

"Wait."

Sasha turned around.

"I'm sorry for what I said earlier, too."

"No, you had every right."

"You aren't to blame for me having relationship problems. He was. I'm trying not to let him continue to have that power over me. I realize that if there's ever going to be a change it has to start with me."

Sienna got up and walked toward her sister. "Thanks again for last night."

Sasha met her in the middle. "You're welcome."

Awkwardly, they hugged. After a few tears and more hugs Sasha pulled back. "Okay, enough with the pity party. Get off your butt; get showered, dressed, and go find your man."

She pushed Sienna toward the steps.

"I can't. I don't know where he is." Sienna protested.

"Think, Dr. Lambert. You interview people for a living, don't you? Yes, you do," Sasha answered for her. "Then go interview people until your find your boyfriend."

By the time Sienna had returned from her shower, Sasha had rifled through her closet and dresser drawers as well as located an overnight bag. Thanks to her sister, Sienna was completely packed and ready to go.

"I don't—"

"Sienna, don't even think about starting that sentence with something negative. Get dressed and start making calls. I'm sure you know some-one who can tell you Vaughn's whereabouts."

Realizing her sister was right, Sienna sat on the edge of the bed and started calling. Ten min-utes later, after hanging up the phone Sienna exclaimed, "Success. Carlton was in the shower, but Angella told me Vaughn's flying in tonight from a business meeting. His plane gets in around nine thirty."

Flipping her wrist, Sasha took a peek at her watch. "Okay, that doesn't give us much time."

Sienna glanced up. "Us?"

"Yes, us." Sasha informed her. "We may still have a lot of issues, but there's no way you can pull this off by yourself. You'd go over there with that damned jacked up hairdo and it would be over before it began."

Sienna eyed her sister suspiciously. "Have you been talking to Vivian?"

Sasha had the temerity to chuckle. "Actually, she did call while you were in the shower. We've planned the perfect seduction. It's guaranteed to work."

"I don't need a seduction; I need a sure-fire way to get him to forgive me and—ow." Sienna yelled when Sasha yanked her hair out of a pony tail and dragged her to the bathroom.

"That was from Vivian," Sasha informed her. "Look maid Marion, this isn't Sherwood forest. Don't go over Vaughn's house and talk him to death. You want to flash the panties and get him to forgive you for being stupid."

Sienna stared at their reflection in the mirror. "Why are you helping me?"

Sasha shrugged. "It's about time one of us is happy and in a relationship, and . . . I owe you."

"You and I will take some work. Things between us aren't going to change overnight. No matter what Mom and Dad want, I'm still mad at you," Sienna clarified.

Her sister met her gaze head on. "I know, but this is worth a momentary cease fire, wouldn't you agree? Don't get me wrong, I'm still mad at you, too. We'll deal with our issues after you make up with Mr. Fantastic."

Sienna's eyes widened. "Good grief, you *have* been talking to Vivian."


Vaughn was driving home when his cell phone rang. He looked at the display and then at the time. He answered it without a prelude. "Isn't it a bit late for you to be calling me? Aren't you supposed to be otherwise engaged by now?"

"No can do," Pierce replied. "I'm flying out in the morning to tape a show for the shopping network. I've got to be at the top of my game tomorrow."

"So, no honeys before the money?"

"Hey, that's a good one. Do you mind if I use it?"

"Not at all, little brother." Vaughn tried to stifle a yawn.

"Tough week?"

"Yes. Murphy's law in effect at the photo shoot. Two sick models, on average five hours of sleep a night, six botched props, and one irate client."

"Sounds like my kind of fun," Pierce joked. "Seriously though, have you talked to Sienna since you've been gone?"

His expression darkened. "No."

"Granted monogamy isn't my bag, but you've got to fix this. You and Sienna are good together."

Vaughn sighed. "I know. I'm home, now. Have fun and call me after the show."

"Will do. Later man, and remember what I said."

Vaughn watched the line disconnect. He checked for messages. There were none. *What did you expect? She hasn't called you all week. Why would she now?* his inner voice reasoned. Vaughn threw his cell phone on the passenger seat. The past week had been pure hell for him.

Work had sucked, and it was the longest he'd gone without speaking to Sienna since they'd gotten together. He wondered at their status now. They hadn't exactly parted on the best terms. *This is insane.* Granted, he was still a bit annoyed at the whole situation, but enough was enough. If she didn't call him by tomorrow, he'd call her.

Vaughn felt better now that he had settled on a course of action. He drove his car down the long driveway to his house. As he got closer, he noticed a car parked in front of his garage. He pulled in behind it and parked. He pressed the garage door opener before he turned off the motor and got out.

"Sienna," he replied with surprise.

Flooded in light, she walked slowly toward him. Even in the dark the first thing he noticed was that her hair was down and curled to riotously frame her face. The second was that she was wearing a short, form-fitting dress and high heels.

"Hello Vaughn," she replied.

Suitcase forgotten, he stared down at her. His eyes traveled across every square inch of her. "What are you doing here?"

"I had to see you. Do you mind if I come in?"

"Sure," he walked toward the garage.

She followed him into the house. He bypassed the kitchen and went to the family room instead. Striding over to the table, Vaughn flipped on a lamp. When he got a good look at Sienna, he almost dropped into the chair behind him. Her dress was not only short; it was red leather and it fit her body like *Cling Wrap*. His mouth went dry.

"I guess you're wondering why I'm here."

*It doesn't matter when you're in a dress like that*, his inner voice fairly shouted.

"I'd have to say to talk?"

She nodded. "There's something we need to discuss. Actually I need to discuss, you need to listen."

Vaughn lowered himself into the chair while Sienna went over to sit on the couch on the other side of the room. She placed her hands in her lap and began.

"You told me I didn't trust you. That wasn't entirely true. It's me I didn't trust. You know about the pageant and that I traded places with Sasha because she injured herself, but did you hear all of our argument that night?"

"No. I was texting Carlton on the phone right before you collapsed," Vaughn admitted.

She nodded. "Well, what you don't know is that something else happened that night; something a lot more detrimental than Sasha being angry with me for taking her crown." Distraught, she looked up at him.

Their eyes met across the room. When he got up to close the distance between them she stopped him.

"No . . . I won't finish if you . . . I need you to stay where you are."

"Okay," he said quickly.

She clasped her hands in her lap.

"Hey," Vaughn said softly. "You can tell me anything, Doc." he assured her.

She looked over at him and began. "Sasha had a boyfriend. They had been going out for over a year. He was at the pageant as well. He never missed one. He loved boasting about his girlfriend, the beauty queen. When it was over, he told me that we were going to celebrate. Sasha and I switched places all the time. We never told anyone when we did it. This time was no different. I wanted to go home and told him as much, but he wouldn't take no for an answer. I thought we'd just go out to eat or something and be done with it. I couldn't have been more wrong. He'd been drinking and the type of party he had in mind was a lot different."

A frown immediately creased Vaughn's forehead. "Sienna—"

She held her hand up. "I need to finish. He pulled me into a vacant room. I tried to tell him who I was, that I wasn't Sasha, but he didn't believe me. I tried to reason with him but it didn't help. He was fixated. He kept repeating how he was going to love making it with his Beauty Queen, his own personal Beauty Queen. He tried to rape me, Vaughn. He would have if someone hadn't come in and discovered us. I ran and didn't look back. When I got home I told Sasha what happened—everything"

"She didn't believe you, did she?" he surmised.

Sienna shook her head. "No, she didn't. She and I got into a huge fight. She accused me of being jealous of her, of trying to take away the two things that mattered to her most. She—was so hurtful in the things she said to me, but what hurt the most was that she took his side. He told her that he thought it was her—and she believed him. He turned it around and made Sasha feel bad for us switching places. He lied. He knew it was me. I told him it was me, Vaughn." She wiped the tears from her eyes. "Why would I make up something like that? The bastard knew it was me," she cried.

Vaughn went to her. He knelt down in front of her. He gathered her trembling hands in his. "Sienna, listen to me. You aren't to blame for what the jackass did to you. Do you hear me? What he did to you was despicable, but it wasn't your fault. You switching places with Sasha made no difference. Nothing warranted him trying to force himself on you. You understand, don't you?"

Tears resumed sliding down her face. "I figured if I could make myself stand out less and blend in more . . . I'm sorry I didn't tell you sooner."

"Sienna, it's okay. I'm so sorry you had to go through that. That you felt there was nowhere you could turn. Do your parents know?"

"No," she sobbed. "I couldn't—I couldn't say anything to them. My father would've—I just couldn't do it. Sasha would've denied it ever happened anyway. My father would've gone after him." She shook her head. "Our family couldn't have survived it, Vaughn."

"He thinks all the bad blood between you and your sister is about a beauty pageant?" Vaughn said, incredulously.

"More or less. He knows there's more to it than that, but he doesn't have a clue it's this serious. This would hurt him, Vaughn, badly. I couldn't do that to him. Regardless of our animosity, I know Sasha wouldn't either. We've seen him destroyed once, when our mother died. He can't go through that again."

"So you're going to carry this burden all by yourself?"

Sienna looked at Vaughn with determination. "If that's what it takes."

Vaughn guided her hand to his lips and kissed it. "I wish I knew you back then. I swear to you I would have broken his jaw—or worse. He'd have ended up in the hospital or the morgue."

She touched his cheek with her other hand. "I know."

Vaughn pulled her up to her feet and embraced her. He lost track of how long he stood there just holding her. "I'm here for you in any way I can be, Sienna. I swear to you that nobody will ever hurt you like that again."

"I'm not afraid anymore, Vaughn. I just wanted you to know. I didn't want there to be any secrets between us. I wanted you to know that I trust you, and I'm sorry about not being open with you about Sasha."

"I know." He lightly kissed the bridge of her nose. "We're okay, sweetheart. Look, if you want to talk about it some more —"

She looked up at him. "Actually, I don't. It was in my past. I'm tired of living in it. I'd rather be here in the present—with you." Sienna leaned up and kissed him on the lips.

When he went to end their embrace Sienna tightened it. Eventually, she released him. When Vaughn gazed down at her, he noticed she was wearing the necklace he'd given her. It hung low nestled in her open cleavage. Her plunging neckline made his fingers want to follow the path of that charm. His hands flexed at his sides. As if she had read his mind, Sienna guided his hand up to her chest and traced a path over her charm.

"It's where all the magic began." She leaned in to kiss his neck.

Sienna walked an unhurried circle around him like she was an orbiting planet. She stopped behind him. His jaw ticked. Her fingers slid up the back of his shirt to his neck, and then ran slowly down his back. She stopped at his belt buckle. With deliberate movements, Sienna went lower until her hand cupped his rear end. Her fingers trailed lightly across his side and around to the front of his chest.

Sienna unbuttoned his shirt with precise, deliberate movements.

Vaughn stilled her fingers. "Sweetheart, we don't—if you're not—"

She walked around until she was back in front of him. "Shhh." She whispered. "No words—not yet."

With a slight nod, Vaughn remained silent.

After the task of unbuttoning his shirt was complete, she eased her right hand inside and caressed his chiseled pectoral. She gave the left side of his chest equal attention. Moments later, she slid his shirt down until it landed in a noiseless heap on the floor.

Her fingers played with the buckle on his belt. Eventually, she flicked the strap from the belt loops on his pants. She continued to apply tension until the belt was released. Sienna's eyes locked with Vaughn's as she unbuttoned his pants and unzipped them. The noise was a stark contrast against the silence. She moved back while Vaughn stepped out of his trousers. He watched with fascination as Sienna turned her back to him.

"Your turn."

Vaughn ran a hand down the back of her dress. Ignoring the zipper for a moment, his hand trailed from the nape of her neck to the small of her back. It was his turn to outline her rear end with his hand. Just as she'd done, his fingers slid up her waist as he walked around to the front of her. His fingers teased her breasts through the soft leather. Sienna swayed against him. He moved until he was behind her again. His thumb and index finger slid the zipper of her dress down.

Both hands went inside the dress to cup her shoulders. He eased her against his front and then lowered the dress inches at a time until it too littered the carpeted floor. Vaughn's arms encircled her waist while he buried his lips against her neck. He kissed her shoulder blade before retracing the path with his tongue.

He turned her around. His thumb traced a slow path across her lower lip. His eyes searched her face. "Sweetheart—"

"Yes, I'm sure." She finished. "I want to make amends—for everything."

"Baby, you were forgiven the moment I pulled into my driveway and saw you," he confessed, and then sobered. "I'm sorry I haven't called you. It was childish of me, Sienna."

She silenced him when her hand followed a deliberate path down his abdomen.

When she traveled lower Vaughn moved her hand and crushed her body to his. He kissed her with a force that made her grab onto him for support. In one swift movement, Vaughn picked her up. Her legs locked around his middle. He leaned her against the nearest wall for support. His lips found hers again.

"Are we all kissed and made up?" he grinned, lasciviously.

"Not yet. There's one more thing you need to do."

"Name it."

"Make love to me. I'm not leaving this house until you do," she whispered in his ear.

"News flash," he whispered back. "You aren't leaving the entire weekend. We're making love in every room in this house."

She mentally calculated the square footage. Her heart skipped a beat. "Say that again," she said, eagerly.

Vaughn let her down long enough to swing her up into his arms. He headed for the wide staircase. "I think I'd rather show you."

# Chapter Twenty-three

## The Light of Day

Sienna was awakened by Vaughn trailing kisses along her back. She waited until he'd traveled the entire length before she murmured, "You missed a spot."

"Is that so? Well, never let it be said that I didn't take care of my woman—thoroughly," he said in a seductive voice. This time he slowed his progress, taking special care to give every inch of her warm skin his complete attention.

Unable to keep still, she turned over until she was facing him. "Good morning," she beamed.

He kissed the bridge of her nose. "It's a spectacular morning, darling. How is my beautiful, sexy, intensely desirable girlfriend?"

She stretched languidly. "Pleasantly tired, yet incredibly happy to be waking up next to my virile, ultra handsome, hunk of an amazing boyfriend."

"Ugh." Vaughn made a face. "Somewhere there's a greeting card author that just ran for a pen and pad."

Sienna giggled. "You think? I hope we inspire couples the whole world over to wake up just as happy and satiated as we are. You know it's odd. We've known each other for months and this is the first time I've ever been on the second floor."

"That's probably because we both knew that if you'd gotten anywhere near this bed I wouldn't have been responsible for what transpired on it." He trailed kisses down her face."

"Whatever it was would have been fine with me."

He burrowed his face into her neck. "Is that so?" he responded in a muffled voice. "Now she tells me."

His five o'clock shadow tickled her neck. "Stop," she laughed. "That tickles."

"What? Did you say tickle you?" he slid his hands to her waist.

"No, don't you dare," she screamed writhing underneath him. "Vaughn, I mean it. Stop it right now." She wrapped her legs around his middle.

The contact made them sober instantly. Their playful teasing quickly turned to burgeoning desire. Vaughn lowered his head and claimed her lips possessively before trailing down the nape of her neck. He moved lower still.

"Vaughn," her voice took on a pleading tone.

When he traveled back up, Sienna grabbed his head in her hands and kissed him. Their contact was explosive. A few moments later, Vaughn lifted his head. "Come on," he said, disentangling himself.

Surprise crossed her face when he rose off the bed and held his hand out for hers. She let her fingers settle into his grasp. He sauntered toward the bathroom with Sienna in tow.

When they reached it Sienna's eyes grew wide. "Vaughn, you could land a plane in here."

He turned the shower faucets on. When the water was the correct temperature he slid under the hot spray. He helped her in next. "Not a plane, Doc. Maybe a Mini Cooper, though."

Sienna turned in a complete circle in the seven foot walk-in shower. There was an oversized head cascading water over them like a rain shower. Her mouth was still hanging open. "This is awesome."

He got in front of her and didn't stop walking until she was up against the wall. His fingers followed the trails of water running down her chest. "I think you might want to delay that sentiment—until later."

Sienna's eyes fluttered closed as Vaughn caressed her wet skin with consummate detail. He tuned in to the changes in her breathing pattern. That acuity allowed him to concentrate on the places that gave her the most pleasure. When he picked her up, he wrapped her legs around his waist.

"Now you're killing me," Sienna confessed in a shaky voice.

"Not yet, baby," he whispered against her wet ear. He pulled back to look into her passion soaked eyes. "Soon."

Vaughn took his time making love to Sienna. When they finally came together, Sienna's face mirrored the intense emotions consuming her from the inside out. She held onto him as if her life depended on their bodies remaining connected. Each thrust he delivered ignited a spark within her.

Sienna could feel each speck of desire mounting to form one massive explosion. *Never in her life had she felt this way.* When she opened her eyes, their gazes locked. In that moment she knew. Vaughn was the difference. It would be this way with him, and only him. "Pleasurable torture," she whispered. After that, she lost herself in the escalating currents that short circuited her senses. Last night she was in control, but this time Vaughn took the lead. He brought Sienna to heights she'd never encountered. Slow and deliberate was how he loved her. When the world faded and nothing remained but Vaughn, Sienna embraced the maelstrom washing over her. Sure and steady. Like the unyielding waves of the evening tide hitting the shore. He consumed her.

This time when Sienna awoke hours later, Vaughn wasn't by her side. Closing her eyes, she stretched languidly. He may not be there, but she could still smell his scent. Smiling she wrapped herself tighter in the bed covers. The last two days replayed in her head. Her body tingled just thinking about him—and the things he did to her. "He really is going to be the death of me," she moaned, aloud. Sitting up, her eyes focused on the nightstand clock. It was almost dinner time. *I can't believe I slept this long.* She said to herself. Realizing that her suitcase was still in her car, Sienna got up and practically floated to Vaughn's dresser. She found a pair of cotton pajamas. Eagerly she put them on tying the drawstring at the waist as tight as it would go. Next Sienna slipped on the shirt. She buttoned it up and rolled the sleeves to her elbows. *Perfect.*

She went to the bathroom to check her appearance. Thankfully, her hair wasn't a complete disaster. It was slightly damp from their assignation in the shower, but it would air dry. A blush suffused her face. Consummating their relationship had exceeded her expectations. Thus far, everything about their relationship did.

When she arrived in the kitchen, she found Vaughn cooking hamburgers on his indoor grill. He looked up when she entered. Their eyes connected across the room. Vaughn's smile was blinding. So was Sienna's blush.

He studied her, an appreciative glint in his eyes. "You look sexy in my pajamas."

"Thanks," she said noting the pajama bottoms he wore were similar to hers. "You don't look to shabby, either,"

"Are you hungry?" he inquired.

"Like a bear in the springtime."

"Good. I made burgers."

She walked further into the room. When she came to his side, he grabbed her and sat her on the granite countertop next to him. "Feeling okay?"

Her teeth clamped down on her lower lip before she broke out into an ear splitting grin. "You mean now that I have feeling back in my legs and can speak coherently?"

Vaughn didn't try hiding his satisfied smile. "Me, too." He kissed her soundly before turning his attention back to their dinner.

"What can I do to help?" she asked him.

"That depends. Which room would you like to eat in?"

"I guess the kitchen is good. So what would you like me to do?"

"You can gather the rest of the condiments. They're in the fridge."

After washing her hands, Sienna got to work. She sliced tomatoes and onions, tore a few leaves of Romaine lettuce and arranged the ketchup, mustard, relish, and kosher pickles on the counter. She perused the pantry and located a bag of tortilla chips. When the burgers were ready, Vaughn brought them over to the island. They each built a burger and laughed at how similar they were.

Sienna eyed the loaded hamburgers. "It would appear that we like the same fixings."

"Hey, we can't fight it. We've got good taste," he bragged.

They laughed and talked while they ate. When dinner was over, Sienna helped Vaughn clean up the kitchen. Their task complete, they went downstairs to the basement. He convinced Sienna to play him in a game of pool after which she promptly lost her shirt.

"Good thing it wasn't literally," she mused after they'd finished.

"Strip pool," he slapped his forehead in mock chagrin. "Now why didn't I think of that?"

Agreeing to watch a movie, Sienna made popcorn while Vaughn picked a DVD from his library. They met up on the couch.

"Having a kitchen down here definitely has its advantages," she observed between mouthfuls of food.

"I thought so. What would you like to do tomorrow? It's supposed to be a wonderful day. How about a picnic after the game? We could go to the lake?"

"Hmm . . . Sounds like fun."

"That'll work."

They decided to go to Falls Lake, and then go visit her parents. With their day planned, they returned to the movie. When it was over, Vaughn turned off the projection screen and DVD player. He encircled her shoulder and pulled her into his lap.

"So, do you want to go to bed now or are you open to other—suggestions?"

"I don't know, Mr. Deveraux," she smiled, innocently. "What other things did you have in mind?"

He lay down on the couch so that she straddled him. "There was that one idea I had earlier about christening every room in the house. So far we've only broke in two. We're behind schedule," he said, lasciviously. "Batter up."

Sienna's hand caressed his chest. "I think we'd better rectify that situation immediately, don't you?"

His eyes glowed like smoldering embers. He rose up to meet her for a searing kiss filled with promise. "Absolutely," he breathed against her lips. "Absolutely."

# Chapter Twenty-four

## Family Night

They got up early to get everything ready. Vaughn headed for the garage while Sienna organized the food for their picnic.

"I don't suppose you have a picnic basket do you?" she called after him.

"Actually I do," he boasted, coming back into the room. He sauntered to a nearby cabinet and retrieved it from the bottom shelf. He walked over and ceremoniously placed the basket on the counter in front of her.

Sienna opened it, and then laughed. "Vaughn, it still has the tags on it. How long have you had it?"

"It was a gift from my mother," he replied. "Hey, I said I had one, not that I'd ever used it."

Vaughn went out to pack up the truck. Sienna sat down at the kitchen table and made a list of items they'd need to take with them to the lake.

Her task done, she went through Vaughn's house like she was on a scavenger hunt.

By the time he returned, Sienna had a mound of things sprawled out on the table in organized piles.

He came over and kissed her, "I brought your suitcase in from the car."

"Great. I'm just about done here, so I'll go shower and change."

He perused the items she'd found. "You've been busy."

"Yep. I've always had an innate ability to scrounge around and find whatever I need. It's a gift," she bragged.

Gathering her in his arms, he nuzzled her neck. "Thank God that ability extends to your private life," he said meaningfully.

Sienna's eyes brightened. "I'm glad it does, too."

Vaughn took the picnic basket outside while Sienna showered and changed clothes. She made up the bed and tidied up the room before coming back downstairs.

Before leaving the house, Sienna phoned her parents. She filled her dad in on their plans for the day and asked about coming over for dinner.

"Sweetheart, you never need an invitation to join us for dinner."

"I know Dad, but I'm bringing Vaughn. I didn't want to assume you had enough food for all of us."

"We've got plenty, so come on over when you're done at Falls Lake."

"Will Sasha be there?"

"I'm not sure of your sister's plans, but I think so. Will that be a problem?" her father asked, warily.

She thought back to her sister helping her the day before. "Not really, Dad."

"Hallelujah," he yelled into the phone. "Progress."

"Ha-ha," she said, sardonically before saying good-bye.


Surprisingly, it wasn't too congested. Vaughn parked at the boat launch area off of Route 50. "There's an embankment over there," he pointed as they were getting out of the truck. "It's a primo spot for a picnic." Sienna retrieved items from the back seat while Vaughn pulled a cooler and canopy from out of the tail gate.

By the time he reached their spot Sienna had already spread their blanket out and had begun organizing the bug repellant and sun block.

"Has anyone ever told you you're an over-achiever?" Vaughn asked as he began setting up the canopy.

"Not today," she said, serenely.

The two of them worked together to set up the area. When they were done, Vaughn tossed the container of sunblock to her. "I'll get your back when you've finished."

Sienna stripped down to her bathing suit before lathering up with sunscreen. Vaughn followed suit. After she'd folded their clothes and placed them back in a duffle bag, they strode down the embankment to the water's edge.

Sienna slipped her sandal off and dipped her foot into the water. "Wow, it's like stepping into a lukewarm bath."

"In an aquarium," he teased.

They frolicked around in the lake for over an hour before Sienna announced that she was starving. They went back and toweled off before sitting down on the blanket.

"This is a great spot," she announced as she spread out the food.

Vaughn retrieved two bottled waters from the cooler and handed her one. "Glad you like it. I come here a lot to go jet skiing. We should do that next time. You'd love it."

"What else do you have tucked away in that garage of yours, you adrenaline junkie?" she giggled.

"You'll find out soon enough," he joked.

Later, Vaughn drove them back to his house to drop off their stuff and change. He put away their gear while Sienna disposed of the leftovers. When she was finished, she headed upstairs to shower. By the time Vaughn entered his bedroom she was done and blow drying her hair.

"Are we going casual?" he asked as he stepped into the shower to turn the water on.

"Yep. Just some shorts and a shirt will suffice."

He looked at her bright sundress. "Uh-huh." He headed to his closet and came back out with a pair of khakis and a button up short-sleeve shirt.

She shook her head. "You're really over doing it."

"If that's the case, you'd been in shorts and a tank top," he observed.

Sienna sat on the bed with her laptop while Vaughn showered.

When he was done he headed out in a towel. "What are you working on?"

A glance in his direction made her mouth go dry. His skin glistened with leftover water. She watched in fascination as a line of it traveled down his chest and disappeared beneath his towel. She swallowed hard. He was altogether sexy and her desire was mounting by the minute.

Her hand went to her chest to quell her rapid heartbeat.

"Well?"

She looked baffled. "Hmm?"

Vaughn pointed to the laptop. "I asked what you were working on."

"Oh," she cleared her throat. "I've got a focus group next week and I'm just going over some details," she replied, trying hard not to stare the towel out of his hands. She figured her drooling would be less obvious if she returned to her work.

"I'll be in Vegas next weekend. Wanna meet me there?"

"I'd love to, but I can't. Vivian and I have already planned a girl's weekend out."

"So whatever you two are up to couldn't fit into just an evening out?"

"Something like that."

"Don't get into too much trouble," he teased. "Are you inviting your sister?"

Sienna stopped typing and looked up. Setting her computer aside, she pondered his question. "I hadn't planned on it. Sasha doesn't breeze into town that often so I didn't even think to ask her." Her face wrinkled in contemplation. "Do you think I should?"

"That's up to you, Doc," he said, sliding up a pair of boxer briefs. He sat on the edge of the bed to put lotion on. "It would be a nice gesture considering you two are on shaky ground right now. Maybe this would help get you guys back on track."

*Do I even want to get back on track?* She asked herself. Her thoughts turned to her parents and the strain she and Sasha were putting them through. "I honestly don't know. The two of us mix like water and oil, Vaughn. That's not exactly my idea of a rollicking night out," she confessed.

Vaughn smiled. "Rollicking?"

"Shut up. Plenty of people use that word."

"Are they under eighty?"

Vaughn took Sienna in his arms and leaned back on the bed. He kissed the sensitive area between her neck and collar bone. When his eyes found hers, his expression was smug. "Don't think I didn't notice you checking me out."

"What? I—I wasn't checking you out. I see drop-dead-sexy men all the time," she said, dismissively.

"Is that so? Sounds like a challenge for me. I may have to step up my game in order to compete with all those men catching your eye, especially when you're out of town doing focus groups."

"I have a rule never to involve myself with respondents," she informed him.

"A rule?"

She nodded.

His hand slid inside her bodice. "I'm curious, Dr. Lambert, what other rules do you have?"

Holding a thought in her head was becoming difficult. Heat suffused her skin flushing it red. The devilish grin he wore made her heart leap in anticipation. "I'd rather show you," she countered, reciting his words back to him.

An hour later, they were pulling into her parent's driveway. Vaughn eased out of his convertible and walked around to open Sienna's door. She reached into the backseat to retrieve the bag she'd brought with them. She entwined her fingers with Vaughn's and led him toward the front door.

True to form, her father opened it before they reached it.

"Hey, kiddo, Vaughn," Gordon said, enthusiastically. "Come on in."

Vaughn shook Gordon's hand and followed Sienna inside.

"Welcome, Vaughn," Cassandra appeared out of nowhere. She gave him a big hug and guided him toward the family room.

"Thank you, Cassie," he replied.

Vaughn looked around as he followed behind her. The large white house with the wraparound porch and bright, open floor plan emitted warmth and well being. He felt the same ease he did at Sienna's house. Sienna joined him on the couch while her parents went to check on dinner.

"Can we help you with anything?" Sienna called after them.

"No dear, we're fine," Cassandra replied over her shoulder. "You two just relax."

Sienna leaned back on the couch. She closed her eyes and sighed.

"What are you doing?" Vaughn inquired.

"Relaxing."

He leaned closer. "You sure you aren't remembering our tryst on that big bed of mine earlier?"

Her eyes flew open, but before she could respond Sasha entered.

"Hey."

Vaughn spoke first. "Hello, Sasha."

"How are you?" Sienna asked sitting up on the couch.

"Great. How about you? You seem—well," Sasha smiled, knowingly.

Sienna immediately blushed. "I am, thanks for asking."

Before more could be said, Gordon asked Sienna to come open a bottle of wine.

"Oh, wine. That's right," she leaped off the couch and picked up the bag she'd placed on the table. "We brought wine. I'll be back," she said, practically running from the room.

Sasha sat on a nearby chair. She regarded Vaughn with amusement.

He returned her frank stare. "So, do you always take pleasure in ribbing your sister about her boyfriends?"

She shrugged. "Every chance I get, which believe me hasn't been too often."

"So, from that none-too-subtle comment earlier, I gather you had a hand in Friday's little red dress?"

"Maybe."

Vaughn couldn't contain the grin at the recollection. "Well, if you did, my undying thanks."

Sasha smiled as well. "So tell me, how did you and Sienna meet?"

"A client outing. We were playing baseball."

Sasha looked shocked. "Sienna? Playing baseball? That doesn't sound like my sister."

"She did quite well considering it was her first time," he said, proudly. "Unfortunately, she was in front of the base when I was trying to slide in."

"An obstruction," Sasha retorted.

Surprise registered on his face.

"Now that does sound like Sienna. So you swept her off her feet?"

"Literally," Vaughn chuckled at the memory.

"It sounds like everything worked out in the end, though."

"We've had our ups and downs."

"From the looks of things, you two are back on track. I'm glad for her."

"Are you?"

"Of course. Contrary to popular belief, I want my sister to be happy, Mr. Deveraux."

"Sasha, I think you can call me Vaughn now, don't you?"

She studied him. "If you say so."

"So, what do you do in London?"

"I'm a flight attendant for British Airways."

"That must be interesting. I take it you've traveled a lot?"

"I've been all over the world. My boyfriend's job is very demanding and takes him to many countries. I go with him when I can."

"Really? What's he do?"

"He owns a soccer team."

"Which one?"

"The Meteros."

Vaughn sat forward. "Milo Georgopoulos is your boyfriend?"

Sasha glanced up.. "You know him? How?"

"My company did an ad campaign to promote his team."

"Small world," she noted.

Just then, Sienna entered holding a tray with three wineglasses and a plate of assorted snacks. She handed them both a glass before taking hers. She sat down next to Vaughn. "Mom's elated we're all here. You'd think it was Christmas," Sienna remarked.

He placed a hand on her leg. "For your parents maybe it is. Getting the two of you together often must be just short of a miracle."

"So what were you two chatting about when I came in?"

"Just work stuff," Sasha answered, quickly.

Vaughn's eyebrow rose, but he remained silent.

"Chow time," her father's voice boomed from down the hall.


Dinner was a lighthearted affair. Everyone chatted amicably while Gordon recounted stories about his two girls' antics growing up. When it was over, Sasha and Sienna handled the dishes while Gordon, Cassandra and Vaughn went into the family room to chat.

"Do you have any other family in the area, Vaughn?"

"No sir, my father's family is on the West Coast. My parents live in Michigan near my mother's family."

"And what are your intentions toward my daughter?" Gordon asked cutting to the chase.

"Colonel Lambert," Vaughn began.

Gordon shot him a stern glance.

"Sorry, Gordon," he corrected.

The older man nodded his approval.

"I care about your daughter very much, sir."

"I can see that. Tell me, have you ever been married?"

"No, I haven't."

"Any children?"

"None."

"That you're aware of, or not at all?"

Vaughn didn't take offense. "Not at all, sir."

When her husband showed no signs of letting up on the interrogation, Cassandra excused herself and went into the kitchen.

"Hey Mom, what's Dad up to?" Sienna inquired.

"Nothing much, just interrogating your boyfriend."

"What? Mom," Sienna dropped the dish towel she was using. *Rule number twenty-one: Never let your parents' one-on-one time with your boyfriend exceed ten minutes.* "Why didn't you warn me?" she accused, dashing out of the room.

"I just did," Cassandra called after her.

By the time Sienna made it to the family room they were gone. She ran downstairs, but they weren't in the basement either. She checked the garage, and then the office.

Poking her head in, Sienna was about to leave when the telephone rang. "I'll get it," she called out. Walking quickly to the desk, Sienna picked up the receiver. "Hello?"

"Have they pulled out the baby pictures, yet?"

Sienna plopped down into the chair. "Please don't give them any ideas. Don't get me wrong, I'm happy to hear from you, but how did you find me?"

"Sienna, it wasn't that hard. The places you like to frequent can still be counted on one hand," Vivian informed her.

"Dad's somewhere around the house grilling Vaughn, I can feel it. I'm trying to find them to run interference."

"Don't go getting all nervous," her friend soothed. "I'm sure it isn't as bad as you're thinking."

"I don't know. My imagination is pretty extensive."

A loud ding sounded from the laptop on the desk in front of Sienna. She immediately moved the mouse. The dark screen disappeared allowing Sienna to see what was on the screen. As her eyes scanned across the page her expression turned from curiosity to shock and then anger. "That little bitch," she said, venomously.

"What? Who?"

"My poor excuse for a sister. I knew it," she said, in a raised voice. "Viv, I've got to go," she informed her before disconnecting the line. She unplugged the laptop from the wall outlet. Picking it up, she stormed from the room.

# Chapter Twenty-five

## Hidden Agenda

Going into the kitchen, Sienna spotted her sister. "This whole thing was a ruse, wasn't it?" she accused.

Sasha turned around to face her sister. When she saw her laptop being waved through the air her expression darkened. "Why do you have my laptop?"

"You didn't answer my question. Suppose you tell us what's really going on?"

Cassandra looked from one sister to the other. "What's this about?"

"She's been lying to us this whole time," she told their mother. She reeled around again. "You weren't here to relax and commune with your family. That was just how you got your sorry foot in the door. What you were really doing was spying on me for some book you're writing about twins and how we don't get along. Admit it."

Cassandra placed a hand over her mouth. "Sasha, is this true?"

Sasha looked at her sister, her expression venomous. "Not exactly, mom."

"Don't you dare try to spin this around. I saw it myself," Sienna told her family.

Sasha glared at her sister. "You had no right snooping on my computer and reading mail that wasn't addressed to you."

"And you had no right being here under false pretenses," Sienna's voice shook with indignation.

"I'm not here to gather information on you for my book. I merely wanted to visit. No more, no less."

"I don't believe you," Sienna shoved the laptop at her. "Besides, it's not the first time you've done something under false pretenses."

Sasha sat the computer on the kitchen table and regarded Sienna with annoyance. "Oh, for once would you stop acting like a victim? If you would've just asked me I would've told you, but no. That's not how Miss Holier-Than-Thou operates. You have to lecture people to death until you get your way."

"All right stop it—both of you," Cassandra's voice carried over their bickering. "I will not tolerate you two going twenty rounds in my kitchen.

Let's all sit down and discuss this rationally."

"You do know you're talking about Sienna, don't you Mom?" Sasha said, dryly. "I don't think rational is in her psychic bag of tricks."

"Really? Well, it's pretty obvious family loyalty isn't in yours," Sienna shot back. "I'm leaving. Mom, I'm sorry but I have to go."

"Neither of you is going anywhere until I know what's going on," Gordon's authoritative voice sounded from the door.

The three women turned to see Gordon and Vaughn standing just inside the entryway. Vaughn walked over and stood protectively beside Sienna.

Eventually everyone moved into the family room. Sienna and Vaughn shared a couch while Sasha, Gordon and Cassandra seated themselves in nearby chairs. Sienna relayed the details to her father and Vaughn.

"Her agent, Jewel Lieberman, sent her an e-mail asking if she'd gotten more examples of our dysfunctional relationship for the book."

Gordon shook his head in disbelief. "Sasha—is this—tell me it's not true."

"Daddy I swear I didn't come here to spy on my family."

"The hell you didn't," Sienna raged.

Sasha sighed. "I am writing a book, it's true," she looked toward her sister, "but I wouldn't put anything damaging in it about any of you."

"Really? Sienna said, skeptically. "Then I suggest you clue what's-her-name in because that's what she thinks you're here to do."

Silence descended on the large room. Finally Cassandra spoke up. "With all the commotion, I never got to ask about the book you're writing."

"It's a work of fiction—more or less."

"You must be thrilled to be writing a book," her mother exclaimed.

"I am, Mom. I've just started. I'm still working on the research and character development."

"Sasha, may I speak with you in private?" Sienna asked.

"Sure," she said, reluctantly.

The sisters went to the office. Sasha closed the door. "What do you want, Sienna?"

"You may have our parents fooled, but I'm not so gullible."

"I don't know what you mean. As usual, you're jumping to conclusions."

"Don't even think about trying to turn this around on me. I'm not jumping to anything. It was all there in black and white, Sasha. Or are you now going to call your agent a liar, too?"

"You had no right to invade my privacy."

"And you have no right to be here under false pretenses."

"I'm not." Sasha threw her hands up. "This is ridiculous! Why do we rub each other the wrong way all the time? Don't you get tired of us bickering? Can't you for once be happy for me? I'm writing a book that will be a best seller. I will be recognized for what I say. People come to you every day for your advice, now I'll have people wanting to know what I think."

"Just remember, your actions have consequences. Sometimes people get hurt because of them."

"This isn't one of those times."

Sienna eyed her sister with contempt. "We'll see. I'm sure if given enough opportunities you'll reveal yourself. For your sake, you'd better not be here with a hidden agenda. Whatever book you're writing better not have me in it or I promise you'll regret it."

Sasha arched an eyebrow. "Is that a threat?"

"You better believe it."

They regarded each other a few seconds longer before Sienna turned around and left the room slamming the door behind her.

"You know, Dr. Lambert, I think this little run-in would make a great scene for my book." Sasha retrieved her cell phone from her jean pocket, dialed a number and waited. "Hey, it's me. Yes, I got your e-mail. My sister stumbled across your message. Don't worry about it; it's not your fault. Just to be safe though, call my cell phone if you need to reach me. No, I'll send you the outline as soon as I've finished up. It will definitely be worth the wait."

While driving back to Vaughn's house, they discussed the happenings of the night.

"Well, that went well," Sienna sighed heavily. "I'm sorry about that. I'm sure you got more than you bargained for with my family; my father's interrogation, and my sister with her sordid book on our tumultuous relationship."

Vaughn reached over and eased her hand into his. He kissed it. "Sweetheart, it wasn't as bad as that. Your dad wants what's best for you, and wanted to be sure I did, too."

"Of course you do," Sienna sniffed. "It's just my evil twin sister that wants to cause me harm."

"Do you really think that's what she's doing?"

Sienna glanced out the window. "Honestly, I don't know. I don't trust that she's being completely honest about her intentions. I know what I saw. The last thing I need is her to be painting me as some psychologist that can't even have a healthy relationship with her own flesh and blood. I can tell companies all day long what's on consumer's minds, but when it comes to my own sister, I'm clueless."

"You'll get to the bottom of things. Of that I have no doubt," Vaughn assured her.

"I hope so. I'm going to be watching her every move. If she thinks I'm going to stand by and let her use me for target practice, she can think again."

It was silent for some time before Vaughn spoke up. "How about we invite Carlton and Angella out for breakfast tomorrow?" he asked, changing the subject.

"That sounds great."

He waited until he got to a red light before he took his hand and tilted her face toward his. He regarded her. "Are you sure, Doc?"

"Vaughn, I'm fine with it," she said, smiling. "It's just what I need to get my mind off of my sister. So, what time?"

"Good question."

Vaughn dialed Carlton's number and put him on speaker. When he answered, Vaughn invited the two of them to breakfast.

"I think we can make it. Where are you going?"

"I think we should let Angella choose." Sienna concluded.

"Angella, pick up the phone," her father said, loudly.

Seconds later she was on the telephone. Her dad filled her in on their impromptu breakfast plans.

"It's your choice honey," Carlton informed her. "Where would you like to eat?"

"Dad, I can't believe you even have to ask," Angella said, with excitement. "IHOP."

"IHOP it is," Vaughn agreed. "Do you want us to meet you both there Carl, or stop by your house first?"

They decided to meet up at the restaurant since Carlton and Angella would be going shopping after breakfast. With their plans made, Vaughn ended the call.

"How about we invite Pierce?" Sienna asked.

"That's way too early for my brother to be out and about. Especially on a Sunday," Vaughn snickered. "Besides, he may not have seen off his latest date by then."

"He's a ladies' man extraordinaire. Honestly, I wonder how he finds time to market his new scents and endorsements with his busy schedule."

"Where there's a libido, there's a way," Vaughn chuckled.

"Speaking from experience are you?"

He took his right hand off the wheel, and rested it on her thigh. "Absolutely not. I was too busy with work to even think about having an entourage. Not my style, anyway," his gaze swept over her. "What about you?"

"I already told you my longest dating experience lasted two months. I wasn't being facetious, you know."

Vaughn recalled her sister's words to that effect. There was a lull in the conversation for a while. As if she'd just remembered something, Sienna turned sharply toward Vaughn. "My dad," she exclaimed.

Vaughn looked confused. "What about him?"

"Will you tell me what happened? Was it the Spanish Inquisition two thousand and nine, or did he decide to take it easy on the civilian?"

He laughed heartily. His voice carried throughout the small space. Seconds later she joined in.

"It wasn't as bad as that, Doc. Your father was just trying to see where I'm coming from."

"You don't have to try and spare me, Vaughn. I know my father is overzealous when it comes to protecting his family. Did he say you were one-of-a-kind?" she prodded.

"I don't know, why?"

"That's code for he's going to be delving into your background. He doesn't think Sasha and I know, but we overheard him talking on the phone to one of the guys from his troop. That means he's going to have you investigated. I'm going to check with Mom and—"

"Hey," he said, quietly. So quiet that she stopped rambling and turned a worried face toward him.

"Yes?"

"I wasn't kidding, Sienna. Your father and I had a very good chat. He knows I'd never do anything to hurt you. I'm crazy happy that you're in my life to begin with. Considering our rough start I don't plan on doing anything to jeopardize that."

She stared at him dumfounded. "Oh," was all she could manage to say.

"At first he was a little concerned about an issue in my past, but once I showed him the paternity test results he relaxed."

"What!?" she screeched.

Vaughn couldn't continue the joke. He dissolved into non-stop laughter. Annoyed at his not-so-funny hoax, Sienna took great pleasure in punching him in the leg.

"Very funny," she said, wryly. "Don't quit your day job, you're not that good."

His hand come over and rested on her leg. He gave it an affectionate squeeze. "Come on, we both know my humor is one of the many things you love about me."

Her facial expression grew serious. Her response wasn't immediate and when she did speak up her voice sounded oddly uneven to her. "Yeah," she answered quietly, "one of the many things."

When they got back to his house, Vaughn parked the car and escorted Sienna in. Before she could ask what they were going to do, he said, "I'd like to show you something."

"Okay."

Taking her hand Vaughn guided her to a part of the house she'd never seen. He went up a staircase at the back of the house. At the top was a wide glass door. "I call this the observatory," he said, opening the door and stepping outside.

The space was big enough to hold what Sienna thought looked like a large bed or extra wide futon-type structure that sat in the middle of the wooden floor. There was a canopy around it with netting cascading down like drapes secured with tie backs. Multiple pillows and a thick mattress beckoned her to try it out. The decking extended out past the house to take full advantage of the unencumbered view of the sky. Guard rails went around the perimeter, but other than that the outdoor space gave you a sense of being one with nature.

"Vaughn," she breathed, turning toward him. "This is amazing."

"Not yet," he told her. He took a lighter off a nearby shelf and lit the candles that were strategically placed around the area.

Sienna stood there watching him. With his task completed, Vaughn came over and crouched down in front of her. He removed her sandals and ran his hands gently up her legs. They didn't stop until they were encircling her waist. "I've wanted to get my hands on you all evening," he admitted.

Her arms snaked around his neck. "Me too. You always know what I need."

When they kissed, it was unhurried and full of promise.

"You look beautiful, Doc," he kissed her neck. "Though I hope we've seen the last of that bun," he mocked. His fingers looped around the straps of her sundress and eased them down her shoulders.

Sienna was finding it difficult to form coherent thoughts. "With you—or at all?"

His hands continued to coerce the dress down her body. "I would be thrilled to never see it again," his voice caressed her like warm butter sliding down a hot piece of bread.

"Consider it gone," she said, huskily.

He stopped. "Sienna, are you sure? I know you—"

She silenced him with her finger across his lips. "I'm sure. It's gone."

Vaughn knew how significant that gesture was for her. "Kind of like this dress," his voice was thick with emotion. He waved it in front of her before laying it on a nearby bench. His eyes scanned appreciatively over her candlelit body. He watched in fascination as the muted shadows danced across her body. Vaughn's hand stroked her skin over and around her satin bra and matching panties.

Unable to remain a spectator, Sienna unbuttoned his shirt and helped him out of it. Next, she went to work removing his pants.

They faced each other in their underwear.

Vaughn caressed her cheek. "Are you cold?"

"Are you kidding? Right now, I feel like you could melt candle wax on me."

She saw a gleam in his eyes. "Theoretically," she clarified.

He picked her up. "Tease."

Vaughn lowered her onto the bed. When he lay down beside her he gathered her in his arms.

Her head rested on his chest. Silently, they observed the stars above them. They took turns pointing out constellations to each other. "Doc?" Vaughn said, softly.

She didn't look up when she spoke, "Yes?"

"Now, this is amazing."

# Chapter Twenty-six

## Girls Night Out

Vaughn and Sienna were sitting inside the restaurant when Carlton and Angella arrived. When she spotted Vaughn, she ran toward him. He was waiting for her with outstretched arms. "How's my Angel?"

"Uncle Vaughn," she said, gleefully. "It's been forever since I've seen you."

"Forever has lasted a week," he teased. "How's my favorite short stop?"

"Great," Angella enthused. She turned her attention toward Sienna. "Hi, Ms. Sienna."

Extending her hand, Sienna squeezed Angella's. "It's a pleasure to finally be able to meet you. The last time doesn't count since we were in the middle of some drama."

"Total drama," Angella agreed.

Carlton stepped over to his daughter's side. He leaned in to hug Sienna. "Nice to see you again," he smiled.

"I'm glad it's under better circumstances this time," Sienna countered.

"I hope you brought an appetite, Angel."

"Uncle Vaughn, this is IHOP. Since when haven't I been in the mood for their pancakes?"


They enjoyed each other's company throughout breakfast. Angella discussed her last soccer game with Vaughn while Carlton discussed migraines and ways to alleviate the effects with Sienna. After Vaughn paid the bill, they all walked to the parking lot. Angella and Sienna were animatedly discussing Cassandra's dance studio.

Carlton pulled his friend aside. "She's a great woman, Vaughn. Seriously, I'm glad everything is working out for you."

"Thanks, man. At least now we know she has a sister," he said, dryly.

"True, though she's not exactly my type," Carlton said, heaving a sigh of relief. "And honestly, it would be too weird for you and I to be dating twins."

"From what Sasha said, she's already taken anyway."

"Back to the drawing board then," his friend joked.

Vaughn gave Carlton a quick pat on the back. "It looks that way."

*Six days later . . .*

Vivian rolled a small suitcase into Sienna's office. She took a quick peek at her watch. "Girl, will you please hurry up so we can get going? Fooling around with you we're going to be late."

"Almost finished," Sienna said, calmly. "Viv, I've got some news."

Vivian arched an eyebrow. "Uh-oh. What's going on? Every time you use that tone something happens that I don't like."

"Sasha is coming along."

Vivian's eyes grew huge. "What? How the hell did that happen? After what you told me I thought you all were on the outs. More so than usual, that is."

"Cassie happened. She let it slip in front of my dad that you and I were going away for our girl's weekend. Before she could stop him, he'd invited Sasha along."

"Well, he can just uninvite her. Besides, she said no, right?"

Sienna shook her head. "We're not that lucky. She agreed to go. I'm sure it was to placate my dad."

"Oh, this is just great," Vivian moaned flopping into a nearby chair. "Talk about buzz kill. We're going to be stuck an entire weekend with your twin from a parallel universe. Splendid."

Sienna tried to put a good spin on it. "Look at it this way, if she's with us, she can't be here trying to probe my parents for stuff to write in her book. This way we can keep our eye on her."

"I thought she told you she wasn't using you for it?"

Sienna looked skeptical. "That's what she said, but I don't trust her, Viv."

"Fine," Vivian acquiesced. "Is she coming here or meeting us at the airport?"

"At the airport."

Suddenly Sienna looked up. "I wish you'd tell me where we are going."

"Not a chance. After that big bombshell you just dropped I need to have some fun. You'll have to wait until we get to the airport. You picked the place last year and we agreed remember? No telling where we're going until we're practically on the plane."

"You do realize that makes it hard to pack don't you?"

Vivian pondered that predicament. "You're right. Okay, if the destination will be a climate change for us then we can give hints."

"So you're saying I packed satisfactorily for where we're going?"

"Yes, Crazy, now let's go."

Despite finding out last minute that Sasha was tagging along, by the time they made it through into RDU, Sienna was getting excited. Work had kept her busy up until the moment they walked out the door and Vaughn had been on deadlines and travel so they hadn't seen each other but once that whole week. They'd conversed on the phone, but it wasn't enough for either of them. Just remembering that night they had spent together caused her to sigh in delight at the memory. Her stomach flip-flopped just thinking about their passionate encounter in Vaughn's Observatory.

"Okay, new rule," Vivian announced. "What number are you on? Anyway, no thinking about your man to the point that you're eyes glaze over, and you're sweating in front of me. Unless I have a man, and then it's okay. Since I don't right now—cut that crap out."

Sienna ignored Vivian's protests. She opened her cell phone and dialed Vaughn's number. When she got his voicemail she left a message. "I'm missing you like crazy. This week has been intolerable. I can't begin to tell you how lonely it's been without you—especially at night," she whispered.

Vivian rolled her eyes so Sienna turned and faced the other direction. "I still don't know where we're going. We've had a hiccup in the program, too. Sasha's coming along. Don't ask, I'll call you later tonight with those sordid details," she promised. "I hope you're having fun being in Las Vegas without me. We will have to plan these excursions better in the future. Anyway, have a safe trip and I'll talk to you soon."After she hung up she turned back around. Vivian was shaking her head at her. "I don't know why you didn't tell the man you loved him."

Sienna blushed profusely. "Who says I love him?"

"Anybody that has a brain in their head or eyeballs or—"

"I get it," she interrupted. Thoughts of Vaughn and how she felt about him rocketed to the forefront. Sienna knew Vivian wasn't telling her anything that she hadn't asked herself already. *Are you in love with Vaughn Deveraux?* she pondered. Her hand went to the necklace he'd given her. She wore it more times than not. His sentiments when he'd presented it to her made her almost blurt out how she felt about him right then and there.

"Earth to Sienna?" Vivian waved a hand in front of her face. "You're sister's coming."

Sienna pushed her thoughts aside and watched Sasha come into view.

When she reached them, Sasha smiled. "Hello, ladies."

"Sasha, what an—unexpected surprise." Vivian smiled overly bright.

"I hope you won't mind me tagging along. Dad sort of insisted, and you know how he gets when you try to disagree with him. He went straight to 'Colonel Mode.'"

"Don't I know it," Sienna chimed in despite herself.

A few seconds of awkward silence passed. Eventually, Sienna spoke up. "Enough of the mystery, Vivian. Where are we going?"

"Okay, okay, I'll tell you," she replied, ceremoniously putting her hand into her bag and pulling out their tickets. "We're going to New York."

"New York?" Sasha repeated with minute enthusiasm.

"Don't give me that bored look. We are having the time of our lives this weekend. If you'd rather not participate—"

"I'm here, aren't I?"

Vivian turned to Sienna. "I've got all sorts of excitement planned so get your game face on and let's get to partying."

The plane ride was uneventful. On the taxi ride to the hotel, Vivian finally gave them a few details.

"We're staying at the Plaza, ladies."

"Vivian, are you insane? The Plaza?" Sienna's eyes bugged out of her head. "Do you know how much a night there costs? And you've booked us for two?"

"Yes, I do and yes, I have," Vivian informed her in her not-too-be-messed-with voice. "Sienna, relax. We've earned this. It's been a fantastic year thus far and we have a girl's weekend every year. We spent more than this last year on a cruise."

"Yeah, but that was a cruise—for five days—to the Caribbean."

"I was there, remember?"

"Vivian, this will cost a fortune," Sienna groused.

"Only half a fortune and sometimes you just have to go with the flow. Besides, if you meet with at least one client, we can write the hotel room off."

Sienna looked thoughtful.

"I'm kidding. You will do nothing of the sort. This weekend is about having a good time. We've got reservations tomorrow night for dinner at Le Cirque, and after breakfast we've got spa appointments. Not once this entire weekend do I want to hear or see you worrying about money.

It's all about those hour long massages, which I hope will be given by some incredibly gorgeous, virile men—accents optional."

Before Sienna could say anything, Sasha spoke up, "Now this trip sounds like fun. Don't worry sis, neither one of us will tell Vaughn about Sven."

Sienna glared at her sister. "First of all, I am not so frugal that I can't have a good time and enjoy myself. Secondly, Sven? There will be no Sven."

"Maybe his name will be Derrick," Vivian gushed. "What if he looks like Shemar Moore from *Criminal Minds?*" she threw her hand over her eyes for effect. "I'm telling you right now, if my masseuse has an island accent I'll have to catch up with you all later."

Shock registered on Sienna's face. "You wouldn't."

"Watch me. I'll be quoting nine famous words."

Sasha looked over curiously. "What?"

"Exactly," Vivian said. "What happens in New York stays in New York."

"Oh, please," Sasha scoffed. "You aren't having a one-night stand."

"You're right, because I sure won't be standing."

They all roared with laughter.

By the time the cab arrived at their hotel even the cab driver was caught up in their excitement. They ogled the hotel while they checked in.

"It's beautiful," Sienna commented as she looked around. "Sasha, isn't it incredible?"

"You've forgotten I've traveled all over the world. This kind of luxury is commonplace for me."

Vivian rolled her eyes. "Snob."

After they checked in, they headed upstairs. Vivian had booked two adjoining rooms. Sasha and Sienna shared one while Vivian took the other. "There's no way I'm sleeping in the same room with her," Vivian had whispered while they were waiting for their room keys. "I'm telling you right now if I do, both of us are going to sleep, but only one of us is waking up."

"Viv," Sienna hissed.

"Don't you Viv, me. She's your crazy relative, you deal with her."

When she was done putting her clothes away, Vivian knocked on their shared door and came in. "Is this awesome or what? Did you see the bathroom; marble floors, gold fixtures? I don't think I'll get any sleep. I'll be too busy gawking at the room."

"Kudos, Vivi. You did a fantastic job of setting this whole thing up. You're right, it was worth it," Sienna concluded.

"I know. Here we are living it up in the Big Apple. Hey, I've got an idea. How about we have a slumber party and order room service instead of going down to the restaurant?"

Sienna and Sasha glanced at each other. When Sasha remained silent Sienna shook her head. "Look, you insisted on coming, the least you can do is make the best of it."

"Sure, sounds like a plan," Sasha retorted.

"Fantastic. I'm going to shower and change. See you two shortly," Vivian replied heading back to her room.

The sisters attempted to chat amiably while putting their clothes away.

"You want to hit the bathroom first, Sasha? I want to call Vaughn."

"Sure. Tell him I said, hi."

A surprised expression crossed Sienna's face. "What?"

"Nothing, I didn't think you liked Vaughn that much is all."

"Come on, if you can't rake your sister's boyfriend over the coals every once in a while, what's the point? Besides, he's no wilting flower," Sasha noted. "He gives as good as he gets. I like that."

Sienna stared at her sister in disbelief before she shook her head. "You're as twisted as I remember."

Sasha's hand went to her heart. False tears glistened in her eyes. "Oh sis, that was the nicest thing you've ever said to me. Wow, you really are lightening up. Not too long ago my declaration would have left you all indignant with your Best Kept Secrets in a bunch," she said, dryly.

A gasp left Sienna's mouth. "How'd you find out about that?"

"Mom filled me in on your underwear experiment," Sasha admitted. "You know, you're not as boring as I remember."

"Funny, you're still as bitchy as I remember," Sienna shot back.

"Okay, where's the most public place you've ever made love?" Vivian asked.

Silence permeated the suite as everyone pondered the question.

"Come on, times up. We're not suppose to think too much about the answers remember? You just blurt them out before you have a chance to lie," Vivian added for good measure.

"A park bench in Prague."

"What?" Sienna sputtered.

"It was at night," Sasha added.

"Come on, Sienna," her friend prodded.

"Outside my old high school."

"Were you in a car?" Vivian asked.

"No. Enough about me, it's your turn, Vivi."

"A parking garage elevator."

"No way!" Sienna shrieked. "How did you manage that?"

"Uh, hello? The elevator has a stop button."

Sienna took a bite of her brownie. "Yeah, but doesn't that sound an alarm or something?"

"Yeah, it does. That's what made it fun," Vivian sighed, languidly.

"Okay, moving on," Sasha announced. "How many O's have you had in a single session?"

"Four."

"Three."

"Seven."

"What?" Vivian and Sasha both stared incredulously at Sienna.

"Seven?" They both repeated.

"Yes," Sienna replied before taking a sip of her wine.

Vivian peeled with laughter. "Were there battery operated accessories involved?"

"No," Sienna blushed.

"You freak," Sasha laughed so hard she started to hiccup. "I can't believe Dr. Bookworm here is a closet Kama Sutra expert."

"Well, it is a book," Vivian reasoned.

"I did not read the Kama Sutra," Sienna clarified.

"We'll you're going to have to give up some details about this encounter with Vaughn, freak girl," Vivian giggled. "Because I know it wasn't with any of your old tired, raggedy two-week boyfriends."

A few minutes later, Sienna's cell phone rang. Three pairs of eyes glanced across the room. Determination crossed Vivian's face.

Sienna gasped. "You wouldn't?"

"Watch me," Vivian cried out, as she jumped off the bed and went running for Sienna's phone.

"No," Sienna practically screamed giving chase. "You'd better not."

"Sasha, I need back up," Vivian called over her shoulder.

Sienna made it across the room before Sasha had even looked up.

"Dr. Lambert's telephone," Vivian answered, with a hint of amusement.

"Hi Vivian, may I speak with the good Doctor, please?"

"Oh, hello Vaughn," Vivian said, turning so Sienna wouldn't pull the phone out of her hand. She ducked and weaved as her friend attempted to retrieve her cell phone. "Sure. You know we've been having such a good time this evening. Do you know it only took us seven minutes to get checked in at the hotel? And between the three of us we've only had seven drinks?"

"You don't say?" Vaughn chuckled with amusement.

"Vivian, if you don't hand me that phone, so help me," Sienna threatened.

"Fine," her friend giggled, relinquishing her iron grip. Calmly, she gave it over to Sienna. "He's all yours."

Sienna snatched the phone away. "Hello?"

"Hi, sweetheart."

Sienna's heart thudded. "Hi."

"Do I even want to know what that was about?"

"Um, not really," Sienna laughed scurrying into the bathroom. Once inside, she shut and locked the door. She lowered the lid on the toilet seat and sat down. "How's Las Vegas?"

"Lonely as hell without you. I'm about to go back into a meeting shortly. I just wanted to hear your voice."

She beamed at the compliment. "Vaughn, isn't it kind of late for a meeting?"

"Not for my client. You and Vivian having a good time?"

"It's getting there. Sasha's with us."

"Really? How'd that come about?"

"The parents' machinations. They're hoping we'll learn to be more civil to each other."

"I'm sure it would make things a lot easier for them, sweetheart."

Sienna sighed into the phone. "I know, Vaughn. I'm trying, but I swear she rubs me the wrong way almost every time she opens her mouth."

"Hey," he soothed. "You'll be fine. So, what do you have on?"

Sienna crossed her legs and leaned back. "Nothing glamorous, I assure you. Just some of my usual cotton pajamas."

"Mine?"

She glanced at the phone in astonishment. "How'd you know?"

"Lucky guess," he bragged.

"They make me feel closer to you," she admitted. "I miss you."

"I miss you too, Doc. Though I have to admit, you won't find me wearing your pajamas."

"Not even a bra?"

"Especially not a bra," he snorted. "Though I might bring one with me the next time, or some other intimate article of clothing," his voice lowered.

Sienna heard background noise. "Vaughn, where are you?"

"In a conference room. The meeting just started back up."

Sienna's cheeks reddened. "Will you stop talking about my underwear in front of people?"

"Would you rather I talked about you out of them in front of people?"

"Crazy seems to be contagious tonight."

"You and I have a date when we return home."

She beamed. "I can't wait."

"I think it fair to warn you that neither of us will be wearing any clothes."

"My kind of date," she said seductively.

Vaughn expelled a ragged breath. "You do that thing you just did with your voice again, and I'm hopping on a plane."

Sienna closed her eyes. His face materialized before her. "Will you call me tomorrow?"

"Try and stop me."

"Good night, Vaughn."

"Good night, Doc."

After Sienna hung up, she sat a long time just staring at the phone. She ran her thumb over the darkened screen. Her heart ached when she was away from him. She fingered her necklace. In the span of a few months, her world had been turned upside down. It was hard to imagine what she did to occupy herself prior to meeting Vaughn.

*Who are you kidding?* She chided. It was all about work. Though work was essential, she was also anticipating the time she spent in his company. Vaughn had introduced her to a world of fun that she'd only read about. She wasn't as much of an adrenaline junkie as he was by any means, and no matter what he said, rock climbing and sky diving were out, but so far she liked everything else he'd taught her. It made her feel alive.

*He makes you feel alive.* She corrected herself. "Oh Vaughn, it looks like Vivian was right," she whispered. "I have gone and fallen in love with you."

# Chapter Twenty-seven

## In Plain Sight

"What are you wearing tonight?" Sasha asked.

"Hmm . . . I think I'll wear my short black dress. It's off the shoulders and makes me look amazing. Wait till you see the new strappy heels I found to go with them. I'm going to be all sorts of sexy," Sienna exclaimed.

"And you call me the narcissist," Sasha quipped.

Before Sienna could retort Vivian made a grand entrance into their room. She'd chosen a red halter dress with matching stiletto heels. Sasha's dress was deep purple.

"I can't believe dinner is so late. Do you know I had to eat a pre-dinner snack earlier just to keep from getting gas pains?" Sienna groused.

"First off, that was seriously too much information. Secondly, quit complaining. The later the reservation, the more likely we'll see a few celebrities," Vivian concluded pushing Sienna toward the door.

Before they left the hotel, they asked an employee to take two pictures of them.

"We really appreciate it, Vivian told the man. "This way when we tell people how hot we looked and they don't believe us, we'll have another picture to show them as backup."

"You're ridiculous," Sasha observed. "Sienna, how in the world have you tolerated her all these years?"

"Partially because I'm the only one that will put up with her for prolonged periods of time," Sienna said jokingly.

"Kind of like you." Vivian eyed Sasha.

Without a word, Sasha swept past them and out the door.


Dinner reservations at Le Cirque were for eight o'clock. Sienna had difficulty not staring at her surroundings. The place was packed and there were lots of beautiful people enjoying the ambiance.

Vivian made sure she was positioned so she'd have a bird's eye view of the door. They ordered appetizers and a bottle of wine. While their server was filling their glasses, Sienna glanced around. "Sasha, there's a guy to your left staring at you," she said quietly while staring at her menu.

"Not interested," she replied. "Besides, we're twins. How do you know he's not staring at you?"

Vivian followed Sienna's gaze. "She's got a point. You don't want to at least look over at him? The man is fine. Somewhere in this city is a magazine cover missing its model."

"Hardly. I've got a boyfriend already, and trust me none of these men can match what perks I get being with him."

Sienna and Vivian both glanced up over their menus. "Perks? What kind of perks?"

"The usual; house, trips, jets, boats, top shelf vacations."

Sienna's eyes widened. "What a minute, why are we just now hearing about a boyfriend?"

"Maybe because it just came up," Sasha reasoned.

"So, who is this man of means?"

"Milo Georgopoulos."

"He's Greek?"

Sasha nodded.

Vivian took a sip of her wine. "How long have you been dating?"

"Four years."

"Good grief girl, I'm sure the man has traded in a car or two in that time frame. Do you plan on getting married any time soon?"

"No."

Unable to help herself, Sienna eyed her sister curiously. "Why not?"

"Because he's already married."

Vivian choked on her wine. "Are you serious? Interesting. I wouldn't have pegged you for the other woman type."

"Sasha, why are you involved with a married man? You can't be thinking he'll leave his wife for you no matter what he promises."

"They aren't together, Sienna. His father-in-law is a high-powered banker with global connections. His wife is worth billions. It's a marriage of convenience for him—nothing more. They will get divorced, it's just taking longer. It's complicated"

"Do they have any children?" Sienna asked.

Sasha fingered her wine glass. "Three."

"I'd say that was more than just convenience," Vivian said, dryly.

"Viv," Sienna admonished.

"What? You aren't saying it, but you're thinking that it's all kinds of crazy, too. Sasha, you are a beautiful, intelligent woman. Granted, you get on my nerves, but I'm sure you could get any man you set your sights on. Why waste it on someone that can never be completely yours?"

"He will be soon!" Sasha replied.

Sienna scrutinized her sister. "Do you love him?"

"Like a woman possessed," she laughed, but there was no humor in it. She took a sip of wine, and then cleared her throat. "Now, can we please talk about something else?"

Everyone pretended to study the menu, but each was lost in their own thoughts.

"We are sitting in one of the most popular dining establishments in this city. I've personally seen three famous people, and I'm trying my damndest not to stare them down like they owe me money. We're supposed to be having a great time not sitting here all morose," Vivian reached over and grabbed their wine bottle topping off everyone's drink. "A toast ladies. No men problems or cat fights. This weekend, it's all about us."

Sienna and Sasha both raised their glasses and clinked Vivian's. Taking a sip, she set her glass on the table. "So, what are we eating?"

"Sorry you didn't get your island man with the killer accent," Sasha told her later. "Todd wasn't so bad, though."

"Wasn't bad? He was all kinds of hot. I don't know how I relaxed enough to even enjoy it. Every time he laid his hands on me all sorts of sexy images would pop into my head. Yum. Talk about torture," Vivian leaned her head back and sighed.

"Well, I enjoyed the woman who did my massage. She was great."

"Sienna, you're a coward. I can't believe you picked a woman. You could do that any time."

"I don't think Vaughn would appreciate my being rubbed all over by another man."

"Girl please, he tripped your light fantastic seven times in a row," Vivian cracked up laughing.

Sasha glanced curiously at her sister. "What does dancing have to do with anything?"

"Not a thing. That's Sienna's code name for seriously intense, butt naked sex. Trust me, right about now Vaughn Deveraux is hardly worried about Sven, one hour, and a tiny bottle of massage oil."


"I must tell you, I'm thrilled to finally get to meet you and, trust me, I don't say that very often. I heard you're the best, and that's exactly what my new lines need. I've done my homework, Mr. Deveraux. You come very highly recommended and that was enough to get my attention."

"Thank you, Ms. Simone, for giving Chase & Burroughs this opportunity."

"It was my pleasure. I appreciate you being able to accommodate me last minute. I met your brother while at the Shopping Network, you know. When Pierce told me about your company and some of your work, I knew we'd be a great fit. The Best Kept Secrets campaign was brilliant."

"I appreciate the praise, Ms. Simone. I wrote down some ideas on the plane ride here that I think would fit your new line. You indicated your target audience is women from every background, ethnicity, and age group and that you wanted a truly universal appeal."

"That's right, Mr. Deveraux."

"Call me Vaughn."

"Then I'm Natalia, darling. Ms. Simone is my mother." She flashed a cosmetically flawless smile.

"Fair enough."

"You see Vaughn; I wanted to create that special scent that sets the wearer apart. We created a remarkable line of cosmetics as well that makes a woman feel truly desirable, and not just to a potential love interest, but to themselves. It's bold, timeless, and hard to resist—like me."

Vaughn hid a smile. "So you want it to boost their confidence. To give them that edge which ultimately carries over into every nuance of their lives, correct? That meeting with the new boss, the marathon they just ran, the first day of kicking a habit, helping a friend or loved one through a crisis, or dealing with one of their own. Inner Beauty accentuates the inner strength women have to go above and beyond in their day-to-day lives."

"I knew you'd get it," she said, excitedly. "My instincts are never wrong when it pertains to money, fashion, and people."

"My team will get to work on it immediately."

"You'll be working on this personally, right? I won't be pawned off on some junior team. That doesn't suit me at all, darling."

"Of course not. I'm the lead on this from start to finish."

"Good, because I'm not investing millions on a campaign being led by an amateur; I demand the best at all times, and there's nothing I won't do to get it."

"That is absolutely what you'll have. I give you my word."

She put her arm on his shoulder and squeezed. "I certainly hope so, Vaughn. I will admit many find me difficult to work for. That's their problem. I make no apologies for my aggressive nature.

In my industry, you have to be powerful or you get eaten by the wolves. I don't plan on being eaten, darling—at least not by wolves," she said, brazenly.

At that moment, Pierce returned to the table. "Sorry about that. One of my fans wanted to get a photo and an autograph."

"No need to apologize, your brother and I were going over our respective visions for Inner Beauty. I must say he's got it all—you both do. Talent, looks, and a keen intellect, I'm telling you, it's an explosive combination," her smile encompassed both men. "I'm sure I'm the envy of every woman in here."

"Maybe not every woman," Pierce chuckled.

"Come now, you know exactly what affect you have on the opposite sex," Natasha replied. "I find that utterly fascinating in a man."

Their waiter returned. "Are you ready to order, or do you need more time?"

Natasha observed Vaughn as he perused the menu. "Oh, I don't need any more time. I definitely know what I want."

"Anyone want dessert?"

"You two have at it. I'm going to the bathroom," Sasha announced.

When she'd gone, Vivian leaned toward Sienna. "Can you believe she's having an affair with a married man? You didn't know anything about it?"

"No, I didn't. You know this is the most we've talked or been civil to each other in I don't know how long."

"You're her sister, give her all that analytical advice you're always boring me to death with."

"Very funny," Sienna said, sarcastically. "When it comes to Sasha, I find my analytical skills are—ineffective. Besides, what am I supposed to say that she doesn't already know?"

They stopped talking when they saw Sasha approaching. Her facial expression was strained. When she sat down, she placed her hands in her lap. Sienna touched her sister's arm.

"Sasha? What's wrong?"

"I'm uh, I'm not feeling that well. Do you mind if we leave?"

Vivian and Sienna exchanged glances. "Sure. We'll signal the waiter and pay the bill."

"I've got to get some air," Sasha announced standing up. "Sienna—um, could you walk me out while Vivian takes care of it?"

"Sure." Sienna stood up and put her hand at her sister's elbow. "Viv, you got it?"

"Yeah, go ahead I'll be out in a minute."

Sasha was walking quickly, but their progress was hindered by a large party trying to get by. "They'll be all day," Sasha complained.

"Don't worry," Sienna soothed. "We can go this way." She guided Sasha around the throng of people. There was a loud high-pitched laugh a few tables away. Sienna's head turned in that direction. When she saw the occupants, she stopped dead in her tracks. The color drained from her face.

Sasha tugged on her sister's arm. "Come on, Sienna. Let's go."

Sienna stood transfixed. Her breathing stilted. Her hand covered her heart as if to protect it. "Vaughn."

Vaughn was casually seated at a table near them with a well-dressed woman who was literally draped over him like a coat, laughing up at him.

Vivian came up on Sienna's left side. "Honey, maybe one of us should go over and —"

"No," Sienna's tortured reply was barely heard over the activity around them.

Time slowed and the noise around her receded. All Sienna could focus on was Vaughn with a gorgeous, well-endowed redhead gazing at him like he was an after dinner mint. She watched him lean in to tell her something. Her smile was feline. *Was he asking her back to his room?* she asked herself. Sienna started shaking. Her body felt hot and cold simultaneously. The fight or flight instinct kicked in. She wrenched free of her sister's grasp. Her feet were moving before her brain caught up.

"No, wait," Vivian cautioned, loudly.

In her haste to leave, Sienna collided with a waiter. They both went tumbling to the floor. The plates of food he was carrying shattered on impact. All eyes turned toward the deafening sound.

"Miss, I'm so sorry, I didn't see you," the man apologized, helping her up off the ground, and then wiping the food off her dress. "Are you all right?"

"Fine," she said, batting his hand away. Once she'd gotten back on her feet she didn't waste a second. She bolted for the door.

"Sienna?" Vaughn's voice boomed over the chaos.

*Don't stop. Don't look back.* Her inner voice prodded her forward. She ran as fast as her heels would allow.

He caught her before she reached the door. He wheeled her around to face him, his hands on her shoulders. "What are you doing here? Baby, are you okay? Did you hurt yourself?"

"No," she said, softly and then louder. "No, I'm not okay. Get your hands off me."

"First, tell me why you're leaving?"

She tugged her arm, but his hold remained unbreakable. "Because I don't care to see my boyfriend snuggled up to another woman. Let me go, Vaughn. It's obvious you're enjoying yourself. Don't let me interrupt you. Go back to your date," she cried.

"Date?" Vaughn blinked, and then laughed.

"You think this is funny?"

"It's not what you think."

"Oh, like you being in Las Vegas?" she bristled. "I'm not blind nor am I a fool."

A man stepped forward. "Excuse me, is there a problem?" he asked, looking toward Sienna.

"There will be if you don't back off," Vaughn threatened in a calm voice.

"I wasn't talking to you, buddy. I'm speaking to the lady."

Vaughn didn't spare the man another second. His eyes were on Sienna. "Where are you staying? I'm taking you home, so we can clear the air."

"It looks crystal clear from where I'm standing. Get off me."

"That's it," the bystander announced. He placed his hand on Vaughn's arm and yanked him away from Sienna. Vaughn shoved the man to the floor.

"Vaughn," Sienna gasped.

"Darling, I'm getting bored."

Sienna turned around to see the redhead from the table at Vaughn's side with her fingers pinching his biceps.

"My apologies, Natalia. If you can give me a moment to —"

"I'm not about to share you. Whatever you're discussing with her is inconsequential," she said, dismissively. "You and I aren't done."

Sienna wrenched her arm out of Vaughn's hand. He moved to block her path and guided her out of earshot. "Doc, I'm asking you to let me explain all this later."

"No, Vaughn," her voice shook. "It's now—or never."

"I'm waiting," Natalia called loudly from behind them.

Vaughn looked from his new client to Sienna. He shut his eyes and sighed. When he opened them, his expression was resigned. "I—I can't do this now."

Sienna blinked rapidly to keep the tears at bay. "This? After all we've been through—I'm suddenly categorized as *this*?"

Vaughn stared at her for a brief moment. His expression held regret. He shook his head and walked away. She watched him go back to the

Piranha he called Natalia, and escort her back to their table.

Sienna watched them for a few moments. Eventually, she sidestepped the large crowd coming in and walked out the door. By the time Vivian and Sasha ran out, she was hailing a cab.

"Sienna, wait up."

She spun around sending an accusatory look to her sister. "You knew, didn't you? You saw them, and you didn't say anything."

"What was I supposed to say, Sienna? That I spotted your boyfriend in a tete-a-tete with some woman? That maybe we should all go over, pull up a chair and say hi? That would've caused you nothing but pain."

"You think I'm not in pain now?" she said, incredulously. "I got blindsided, Sasha—and you let it happen."

"I didn't tell you so there wouldn't be a scene."

"Wake up. It *was* a scene. A big scene," she cried. "I embarrassed myself in front of a restaurant full of people, found my boyfriend cozied up to a woman old enough to be his mother, and to make matters worse he doesn't respect me enough to tell me he was having an affair in the first place. Oh, let's not forget he told me he couldn't deal with me right now. Like I'm some big inconvenience? Yes, Sasha. I think this definitely qualifies as a scene."

She turned and walked away.

"Where are you going?" Vivian called after her.

"I need to be alone."

Vivian sighed. "What a mess."

"That would be an understatement," Sasha said, dryly.

"I knew we should've interrupted."

"Didn't you see what happened to the last guy that butted in?" Sasha shook her head. "No. They needed to speak in private. I'm sure they'll work it out."

"Don't be naïve, Sasha. I could tell by the looks passing back and forth that the conversation wouldn't end well. We've got to find out how that bimbo fits in to all this."

"No chance. I'm staying out of it."

"I'm not going to stand by and watch my best friend get humiliated. I'm getting to the bottom of this."

"I just tried to help out and got my head bitten off. You're crazy if you think Sienna needs someone interfering in her personal life right about now."

Sasha went to walk away, but Vivian grabbed her arm.

"I don't begin to understand every nuance of you and your sister's complicated relationship, but I know enough about it to know that the last time she needed you—truly needed you—you weren't there."

Sasha recoiled and staggered backwards. The tears that pooled in her eyes this time were genuine. "How dare you."

Vivian glowered at her. "Sienna is my best friend. You're damned right I'm gonna dare. If there's a remote chance in hell that I can do something to fix this mess you bet I'm going to try. Sasha, I promise you—if you stand by and do nothing—again—" Vivian struggled for composure. "It will kill her. Do you really want to make that same mistake twice?"

Hailing a cab, they arrived at the hotel in record time thanks to the generous tip Vivian offered the driver. They took the elevator to their floor. After opening the door, Vivian went in with Sasha in tow. Sasha checked the bathroom. When she came out, her gaze sought out Vivian. She shook her head. "She's gone."

# Chapter Twenty-eight

## The Voices of Reason

Vaughn entered his suite and threw the key card on the table by the door. Coming further into the room, he spotted his brother on the couch watching television.

"Hey," he said tiredly.

"How'd it go?"

Vaughn dropped into a nearby chair and shoved off his shoes. "I'm alone, Pierce. I'd say that sums up how things went."

"Sorry, man. You weren't able to explain?"

"Didn't get the chance. My new client was pretty clear on the fact that she wouldn't be kept waiting. I tried phoning Sienna several times after I took Natalia back to her apartment, but she didn't answer. It's obvious she's avoiding me."

"So what's your back-up plan?"

Vaughn stretched his legs out in front of him and then stared at the ceiling. "I don't have one.

She dismissed me, remember?" he frowned at the memory. "Well, actually, I dismissed her first. If only she had given me the benefit of the doubt. Exactly what does that say about our relationship?"

"Hey man, she was hurt at seeing you with another woman. Plus, you were here in New York when you were supposed to be in Las Vegas. Plus, from what you told me she thinks you're having an affair. Are there anymore pluses I should add? Besides, what if the tables were turned?"

"This client is possibly worth more money than Dexter for the company. What was I supposed to do, let her leave? Granted, I'm going to have to bust my butt to make this eccentric old woman happy, but I could be made partner after all is said and done, Pierce. Partner," Vaughn stressed. "I couldn't walk away from that."

"Dude, Natalia wanted you bad. Sienna knows that. I don't know how you're going to fix this."

"By doing one thing at a time. Sienna and I are in a committed relationship. We can get over this. Granted, Natalia was coming on a bit strong—"

Pierce laughed. "She was practically giving you a lap dance."

"It's business. You know that. How many women throw themselves at you trying to get you into bed?"

His brother did a double take. "You're kidding, right?"

"From a business point of view," Vaughn snapped.

"Oh. A few."

"Do you sleep with every woman that makes you a proposition?"

Silence enveloped the room.

"Well, I don't," Vaughn clarified. "To top it off, she didn't even make me a proposition. Regardless of what she saw, Sienna should damn well know my character by now."

"I hear what you're saying. My only question is why you didn't even try to set her straight? Doesn't she mean enough to you to try and work this out?"

Vaughn turned an impatient eye toward his brother. "She means everything to me—you know that."

"Yeah, but I'm not sleeping with you."

Vaughn was pensive.

"Look, I'm no expert on relationships," Pierce looked sheepish, "at least not lasting ones, but I do know that you love her, and it's obvious from the way she almost demolished Le Cirque tonight that you're more than eye candy to her."

"Which is precisely why she shouldn't have overreacted."

"You don't know your girlfriend very well, do you? Women are all about the proof. You gave her all the ammo she needed to think you were cheating. Regardless of how you try to rationalize it, you messed up by leaving before you had a chance to set the record straight. Trust me, I know the ladies."

"Pierce, the longest relationship you've been in with a woman is our mother."

"You don't think that qualifies me as an expert?" he countered.

"I think you need to quit worrying about my love life. It will work itself out."

Pierce looked at his brother skeptically. "I knew you should've gotten her some Be-Dazzled."


"This is it, right here," Sienna informed the taxi driver. He pulled into her driveway and stopped the meter. Retrieving cash out of her wallet, Sienna paid him and got out. The man had already exited the car and was retrieving her luggage from the trunk.

"You have a wonderful evening, Miss," he said, politely.

"Thank you," she replied wheeling her bag up to the door. She retrieved her key from her purse and let herself in. "Home Sweet Home," she said forlornly.

Oddly, the quiet was deafening to her. She rolled her bag into the foyer and left it at the bottom of her staircase. She went into the kitchen without bothering to turn on the light. Retrieving the container of bite-sized Snicker bars out of the freezer, she headed to the living room. She flopped down on the couch. Kicking her shoes off, Sienna pulled her feet up under her. She chucked a chocolate tidbit in her mouth and sighed aloud. Her anger had abated during the plane ride home. Sadness was left in its wake. Just then the telephone rang. Sienna contemplated not answering it. Eventually the ringing ceased. When it started up again, she got up and went into the kitchen. She picked up the handset. "Hello?"

"Girl, you had us worried to death," Vivian scolded. "What were you thinking running out like that? Sasha and I were worried sick."

"I needed to be alone."

"Yeah, you said that, but we thought you meant alone in New York, not back in North Carolina."

"I'm afraid I'm not good company right now."

"We can understand that, you just dumped your boyfriend."

"Vivian," Sienna began.

"You're right. Now is not the time. We'll see you when we get back home tomorrow morning. We're scheduled to fly out first thing."

"That's not necessary. You two stay and have a good time."

"Honey, I'd say that's a lost cause this weekend. See you tomorrow."

"You don't have to—"

"I know," Vivian countered before hanging up.

Sienna returned the handset to its cradle, and then placed her snacks back in the freezer. With heavy steps, she climbed the stairs dragging her suitcase behind her. She flipped the light switch on and walked into her bedroom. Wheeling her suitcase into her closet, Sienna stripped down and went into the bathroom to shower. Waiting for the water to warm up, she wrapped her hair into a bun and washed her face with cleanser. Sienna gazed at her reflection in the mirror. "Wow, you look as bad as you feel," she tried to joke.

Thirty minutes later, Sienna was cross-legged on her bed going over audio tapes of her last session. She tried to concentrate on what she was doing but it was too hard. Her thoughts kept straying back to the encounter with Vaughn in New York. One minute she was recounting the doomed conversation in her head. The next she was curled up in a ball crying uncontrollably.

\*\*\*

Vivian and Sasha rendezvoused at Sienna's house bright and early the next morning. After ringing the doorbell several times, Vivian turned to Sasha. "I don't think she's going to answer," she replied with dismay.

"Not to worry," Sasha replied opening her purse. She retrieved a key chain and shook it. "We got it covered."

Sasha unlocked the door with her key and let them in. The first level was quiet. "Let's try upstairs."

Vivian went up to check it out. "She's not up here," she called from the landing.

"Has the bed been slept in?"

"Looks like it."

Sasha walked over and opened the door leading to the garage. She flicked the light on and peered in. "Her car's still here."

"Then she hasn't gone far. We should wait." Vivian sat down on the couch. She extended a bag toward Sasha. "Want a muffin?"

"No, thank you."

Five minutes later, Sasha was holding her hand out for the bag.

They conversed lightly while eating.

"About last night," Sasha began.

Vivian glanced up at her. "Is this where you tell me I should've minded my own business?"

"No. It's where I say thank you—for butting in."
Sasha sighed. "You were right."

Vivian nodded, but refrained from comment.

A few minutes later, Sasha's cell phone rang.
She yanked it out of her shoulder bag and stared
at the number. "Sorry, I have to get this," she said,
excusing herself and going into the kitchen.

"What's up?" she asked in a subdued voice.

"How are things going?"

"Not so good at the moment."

"Have you been able to find out any exciting
tidbits for your story?" her agent inquired.

"The story is going fine, but my—Sienna is going through a bad patch at the moment."

"Really? Do tell. Is it something we can use for
the book?"

Sasha frowned. "No, we can't. She may have
broken up with her boyfriend. She's pretty distraught."

"That's good. Not for her mind you, but we
can use that. Did he cheat on her? Was it a love
triangle gone bad? Oh wait, don't tell me he's
married, and she just now found out," her agent
pressed. "Sasha, this could work. Does he have
any kids? Granted, it's not a new theme, but we
can put a spin—"

"No," Sasha ground out. "He's not married, nor
does he have any kids. Look, I've got to go. My
sister will be here any minute."

"Oh, okay. Just remember to take plenty of notes and e-mail me later."

Sasha hung up before she had even said good-bye. She slid the phone into her back pocket. She raked her front teeth over her lower lip in concentration. A few moments later, she took a deep breath and headed back to the living room.

"So, how do you want to handle this?" she asked Vivian upon entering the room. "Good cop, bad cop?"

"I'm not sure." Vivian folded her arms across her middle. "I suppose we should figure it out before she gets here."

By the time each had eaten a second muffin, the front door opened and Sienna strolled in.

She stopped short, her hand going to her heart. "Good grief," she shrieked. "What are you two doing here?"

"Eating," Vivian swallowed. "Want a muffin?"

Sienna closed the door behind her. She turned an accusatory glance toward her sister. "I thought I asked for my key back last time?"

"You did," Sasha replied, casually.

Vivian slid over and patted the seat next to her. "Where were you? We've been here a while."

"I went walking."

"Have you spoken with—"

"Sasha, why in the world would she call Vaughn?"

"Maybe he called her?"

"To say what? What he did was inexcusable and I wouldn't even entertain the idea of forgiving him," Vivian argued.

"It's not your decision to make," Sasha observed.

"Will the two of you quit speaking like I'm not even here?"

"We're sorry, girl. Well, look at it this way, most of your relationships don't last past two months. Your relationship with Vaughn lasted five. I'd say that's something to be proud of," Vivian reasoned.

"Yeah, rule number twenty-two: once it's over, it's over. Clean break. No going back."

"Good idea."

"Bad idea," Sasha retorted. "Sienna, you've just had a seriously big argument with your boyfriend. Breaking up with him seems a bit precipitous, don't you think? I mean you haven't even heard his side of the story."

"What's to hear? He dumped her for some surgery enhanced cougar. Why add insult to injury and allow him to tell her why?"

Sasha stared at Vivian. "It's no wonder you're alone with backwards logic like that. We don't have a clue what prompted Vaughn to leave with that woman—or why he was there in the first place."

"Will you two stop bickering? Sienna complained. "Enough is enough. I'm done. Vaughn and I are over, so let's drop it, okay?"

Vivian went over to Sienna. "Fine. Would you like to go out tonight? We can paint the town red. Finish up where we left off in New York?" When she saw the shadow that crossed her best friend's face, she frowned. "I'm sorry, sweety. I shouldn't have mentioned it."

"It's no big deal. I have to start dealing with it anyway. Might as well start now, right?"

"Sienna, I hate to be the voice of dissention—"

Vivian rolled her eyes. "Then don't."

Sasha ignored her. "I have to. I'm your sister. Granted, we've had a tenuous relationship for a long, long time, and I know you doubt my sincerity, but Vaughn made you happy. What you two have is real. You can't just discount that."

Sienna shrugged. "I don't want be appear rude, but I've got a business trip in two days and there's work I need to prepare. Would you two mind?"

Her sister stood up and motioned to Vivian. "Sure. You want me to tell Mom and Dad, so you don't have to?"

"No thanks. I'll deal with it when I get back." Sienna walked them to the door.

Sasha awkwardly hugged her sister. "I'll phone you later. Be prepared. Dad might call you. You know how he swears he can sense when there's trouble with either of us."

Sienna managed a smile. "I know."

Vivian stepped forward. She enveloped Sienna in a hug so tight, they both tilted off balance. "Call me. Anytime. I mean it, Crazy. Whenever you want to talk, I'm here."

"I will," Sienna assured her. "Thanks, Viv."

When they left, she shut the door behind them. She leaned against it for a minute listening to the loud sound of silence. Her phone rang. Somehow, Sienna instinctively knew who it was. She didn't answer it. *Rule number twenty-three: Pain, like disappointment, wears off.* With a determined stride, she went upstairs.

# Chapter Twenty-nine

## A Two Way Street

Vaughn took a moment to stare at the ceiling in his office. In three short weeks, his life had become completely unrecognizable. Natalia Simone had forewarned him that she was difficult to work with. That minute detail had been a complete underestimation of her talent to throw every nuance of his life off-kilter.

His days and the majority of his nights were spent fine-tuning the campaign for *Inner Beauty*. Which he noted wryly, changed daily.

He'd been correct in his assumption that a partnership was riding on the Simone account. His boss had intimated that if all went well, and Natalia continued to be enthralled by Chase & Burroughs, he'd make partner. Everything had gone according to plan. *Everything except Sienna.*

Vaughn ran a hand over his overworked eyes. That was the one piece of this intricate puzzle that he'd been unable to make fit. He'd tried countless times to contact her. She wasn't returning his calls and she didn't answer when he knocked on her door.

His pride had been hurt at the realization that she'd written him off. That she had moved on. Hurt turned to anger that she didn't care enough about him to allow him to explain the circumstances surrounding their encounter in New York. Her inability to trust him had caused him to cease trying to make amends.

*Life doesn't always go according to plan.* He told himself. Neither did his expectations. He'd expected to get it out of his system. He'd expected to allow himself some time and be done with missing her. He'd expected to not go by every single phone he came across and feel the urge to stop and call her. Most of all he'd expected not to still be as in love with her now as he was when she had her ATV accident. That incident alone caused him to admit the extent of his feelings.

*Dammit, Doc. Why didn't you hang in there?*

His telephone rang. He leaned forward and picked it up. "Deveraux."

"Hi, Uncle Vaughn."

He smiled. "How's my Angel?"

"Terrible."

He sat up. Worry lines creased his forehead. "Why? What's the matter?"

"I miss you. It's been ages since you've spent any time with me," his goddaughter complained.

He relaxed now that he knew it wasn't something physically wrong. "I'm sorry, I've been so tied up with work. I promise I'll make it up to you soon, okay?"

"When?"

"Soon."

"How soon?"

Vaughn smiled. "Is Friday night soon enough for you?"

"Ooh, that's perfect," she exclaimed excitedly. I have a recital after school and—"

"Whoa, wait a minute. Did you say a recital?"

"Yes, Uncle Vaughn, it's a dance recital."

"You're dancing now?" he was dumbfounded. "When in the world did that happen?"

"I've been going to the studio for ages now. This is our first recital. I'd really like if you could make it."

He quickly scanned over his date book. "Okay Angel, I'm there. What time?"

She filled him in on the details before letting her dad on the phone.

"Why didn't you tell me Angella's a ballerina now?"

"She's not really a ballerina. It's more like a musical. She wanted to tell you herself. Don't feel bad, it was a surprise to me as well. Still, she seems to be having fun and she's really good."

Vaughn flicked his pen between his fingers. His not being there for Angella weighed on him. "I'm sorry I haven't been available lately. Work has been incredibly hectic. Actually hectic would be manageable."

"No word from Sienna?"

Vaughn's pen hit the desk. "None. I guess I should resign myself to the fact that she's ended it."

"Since when do you resign yourself to anything?"

"I can't make her take my calls, or listen to what I have to say. She thinks I had an affair with Natalia. If she wants to assume the worse, so be it. It's obvious we weren't that solid to begin with."

"Sorry man, but you'll never convince me of that. She was crazy about you."

"Pivotal word being was."

Vaughn's second line rang. "I'll have to talk to you later."

"Sure thing, but remember what I said and we'll see you Friday."

"Will do," Vaughn agreed before disconnecting the line.

Friday arrived sooner than anticipated, but luckily Vaughn was able to clear his schedule for Angella's event. Now if he could just have a Natalia-free afternoon, all would be perfect. Carlton gave him the address with plans to meet up at the studio.

As he walked through to door with the other guests, he admitted to feeling enthusiasm at seeing Angella perform for the first time.

He saw his friend from across the room. He waved and headed in his direction.

"You made it."

"I said I would. When does she start?"

"In a few minutes. I got here early and saved two seats up front."

Vaughn followed Carlton down the hall and into a large room. There were rows of seating and a large curtained stage. The drapes were closed for the show, but he could see and hear slight movement behind them. Shortly thereafter, the spacious room was filled to capacity with parents, grandparents, friends, and kids. Digital camera flashes were going off in rapid succession around the room while people waited for the show to begin.

Seconds later, a woman walked elegantly across the stage. She was wearing black leggings, ballerina slippers and a long-sleeved top in a fusion of colors. Vaughn's chair screeched in protest when he reared back in surprise. A mother turned around and shushed him.

"Good afternoon everyone and welcome to our recital. For those of you that may not know me, my name is Cassandra Lambert."

"What the hell is going on?" Vaughn whispered loudly.

"How so?" Carlton replied.

"That is Sienna's stepmother."

"Yes, I know. Angella's taking dance lessons from her."

"Don't you think I should've known that tidbit of information before now?"

"Why? What difference would that have made? You wouldn't have come if you knew Angella's teacher was your girlfriend's mother?"

"Ex-girlfriend," Vaughn snapped. "And you know better than to ask me that."

"Okay, so what's the big deal?"

"It still would've been nice to get advance warning, Carl."

"Point taken. Now be quiet. That grandmother over there is giving us the evil eye."

While Cassandra was talking, Vaughn slowly perused the audience. When he didn't see Sienna anywhere, he visibly relaxed.

"You're pitiful," Carlton whispered.

"Shhh," Vaughn warned.

Several people turned to stare at Carlton. His expression when he looked at Vaughn was telling. He mouthed the words, "Payback."

"Bring it," Vaughn mouthed back.

All concern at running into Sienna was forgotten the moment Angella stepped out on the stage. She was dressed in a 1950s pink poodle skirt with an embroidered black poodle. Her short-sleeved polo shirt was black with a pink poodle. At her neck was a pink chiffon scarf. White cotton socks, saddle shoes, and pink cat eye glasses completed her outfit. Her hair was pulled back in the signature ponytail tied with a scarf. She danced with a young man also dressed in period attire. They danced to the song *At The Hop* and then they broke out into the Twist.

When they were done, the crowd cheered and clapped. Carlton beamed proudly. "That's my little girl."

"She was incredible," Vaughn enthused over the tremendous applause. He was cheering along with the majority of the audience.

There were another three performances by the students followed by a grand finale of Cassandra's teenage ballet class to *Deux Arabesque* by Claude Debussy. What made it difficult to sit through was that Sienna was the pianist. Throughout the entire routine Vaughn's eyes would stray to the piano off to the side of the large stage. Sienna's profile was relaxed as her fingers moved effortlessly over the keys. Her back was straight and at times her head would move in time to the music. It was clear she was caught up in the classical composition. It was all Vaughn could do to stay in his seat. Several times he shifted uncomfortably. He was in purgatory. A serene and well-choreographed hell set to beautiful music. It was almost more than he could bear.

At the conclusion of the piece, the troupe received a standing ovation. Much to Vaughn's dismay there was a reception afterwards. The whole procession filed out into another room where tables placed along the walls were laden with refreshments. He stood around trying to look at ease, but it was an act. He realized that at any moment he might see Sienna. Vaughn's calm outward demeanor was in stark contrast to the emotions warring within him.

"We're not at a tax audit," his friend chided. "Quit scowling."

"I'm not," Vaughn smiled in reaction. "Here's my Angel now," he said as Angella walked up. "These are for you, lovely lady." He handed her a bouquet of red roses. "You were sensational."

"Thanks, Uncle Vaughn. Oh my gosh, did you guys see me trip when we were doing the Lindy Hop?" she cried. "I was so nervous I'd mess up again."

"We didn't notice a thing, baby," her father assured her.

Vaughn gave her a hug. "No way did you look anything but incredible out there. I had no idea you were interested in the arts."

"I couldn't help it. Miss Sienna and Ms. Cassie made it sound so awesome, I had to try it. Don't worry Uncle Vaughn, I still love my sports."

Crouching down so that he was eye level, Vaughn tweaked her nose. "Angel, you can do whatever you want. You know your dad and I will always support you."

"That's right," Carlton piped up. He glanced over Angella's shoulder. "Sweetheart, I think we should go and thank Ms. Cassie for a job well done."

"Sure, Daddy."

As she turned around she spotted Sienna. "Hi, Miss Sienna. The show was great, wasn't it?"

"You know it. I'm so proud of all of you." Smiling, Sienna hugged Angella. "How does it feel to be a star?"

"The butterflies didn't leave until after our second performance."

"Well, by then you were an old pro," Vaughn joked.

"Come on, Angella, we don't want to miss speaking to your teacher."

The pair said their good-byes leaving Sienna and Vaughn alone. *Here it was.* Vaughn lamented. *That dreaded first meeting after the relationship post mortem.* He looked her over. "Hi, Doc."

A strained expression crossed her face.

"Sienna," he corrected, annoyed at her reaction. "Or would you prefer Dr. Lambert?"

She bristled. "How are you?"

*Was that a trick question?* He wondered. "Just fine and you?"

"Good."

Time slowed to an agonizing crawl. The two stood there staring awkwardly at each other.

"I'm surprised you didn't bring a date?"

Vaughn shrugged. "This was Angella's moment. I didn't want to detract from that."

Sienna nodded. "It was nice seeing you. Take care of yourself," she told him turning to leave.

"Sienna?"

Halting, she turned around. "Yes?"

He hadn't planned on stopping her, but he just wasn't ready for her to go.

"Vaughn?" Sienna repeated. "Is there something you wanted?"

*Yes . . . you.* He declared to himself. It was too late. The moment was gone. Resigned, he shook his head. "No. It was good seeing you, that's all."

"Likewise." With that she turned and walked away.

# Chapter Thirty

## Damage Control

"You have to be the most pig headed guy I know."

"No offense, but do I look like I need a lecture from you right now?"

Gordon gazed up from his mug. "What you need is to stop being stupid. Go apologize to my daughter and patch things up."

"With all due respect, I'm not the only one at fault here."

"Great, so you'll both resign yourself to being miserable for the rest of your lives just so each of you can be right?"

Vaughn took a sip of his beer and remained silent.

"You know what? The more details I hear about this big blow-up, the more I think you and Sienna are perfect for each other. You're both two peas in a ridiculously asinine pod."

"Name calling won't get you anywhere," Vaughn said in a clipped tone.

"Just tell her you had a client account on the line and be done with it."

"No. She didn't trust me enough to realize I would never cheat on her, or that there may have been more to the story. I don't suppose she cares for me enough, either," Vaughn groused.

Gordon was incredulous. "Are you two the only ones that can't see that you belong together?"

Vaughn stared down at the table. "Maybe."

At that Gordon signaled the bartender for another round. "So, what you're saying is you no longer have feelings for my daughter. That your life is better off without her?"

Vaughn's gaze turned polar. "That's not what I'm saying. Why does everyone ask me that?"

Gordon leaned across the table. "Well, if it's not, you're doing a real good imitation. Vaughn, I like you. You are a real stand up guy, but you aren't thinking this through very well. I suggest you take my advice and fix this thing before it's too late and you both lose out."

"It's not that simple."

Sienna's father scoffed. "You know I've had a chance to tour the world during my military career. It's brought me in contact with different cultures and ways of life. I was also fortunate enough to have good men serve under my command. One thing I do know is that there are many things in life that are downright difficult to bear. Admitting your feelings to the one you love shouldn't be one of them. How we overcome adversity to persevere is really what tests our mettle. It defines us. It makes us stronger and I'd hope wiser. I know you'll eventually see what's staring you square in the face."

"What, that I'm wrong?"

"No, that you can't ride two horses when you've only got one ass."

Vaughn's eyebrow rose. "Is Sienna supposed to be one of those horses? You already know I'm not cheating on her so who's the other one?"

Gordon looked Heavenward. "Sometimes I wonder about your intelligence. It's not who, it's what. Pride. The other thing I'm talking about is pride."

Sitting back, Vaughn swirled his beer around in its mug. "I knew that."

Sasha paced back and forth across her bedroom floor. Her conscience tugged at her. Glancing across the room, her gaze settled on her laptop. On it was an e-mail from her agent she'd only half read. Time was running out. Her outline was way overdue. She needed to start working on her book if she was going to be on schedule. A knock sounded on her door. She turned toward the sound. "Come in."

The door opened, and Cassandra stuck her head in. "Hello, dear. We missed you at dinner earlier."

Sasha faced her stepmother. "I wasn't hungry."

"May I come in?"

"Sure." Sasha walked over and sat heavily on her bed.

Closing the distance, Cassandra came over and sat on the bed next to her. "Do you want to talk about whatever it is that's eating at you?"

Looking up, Sasha was ready to deny it, but something stopped her. Bolting off the bed, she put some distance between them. "Oh, Mom. It's a mess. Everything is such a mess; I don't know where to start."

Cassandra regarded her daughter for a few seconds before a warm smile flitted across her face. "I find that the beginning is usually the best place."

Sasha nodded. "She was right."

"Who was, dear?"

"Sienna. She was right—about everything."

"Darling, I'm not quite following you," Cassandra said, in confusion.

"I lied, Mom. I was here to—to get material for my book. I intended it to be a book about being twins and all our sordid baggage, but . . . I—"

Cassandra gasped. A horrified expression on her face. "My God, Sasha. After everything Sienna's been through . . . you could do this to your sister?"

Sasha's eyes were burdened with unshed tears. "Oh, Mom," her tone was remorseful. Years of turmoil laced throughout those two words. "You don't know the half of it."

*Two days later . . .*

Sasha pressed the doorbell button and waited. After five seconds, she pressed it again.

"I'm coming, hold your horses," she heard through the door.

When it was finally opened, she said, "Took you long enough."

"Pardon me for being upstairs working," Sienna complained. "What brings you by?"

"What a minute," Sienna's eyes bugged out. "You rang the doorbell. You didn't use the key you won't give back."

Ignoring the barb, Sasha stepped past and came in. She watched Sienna close the door and head upstairs, so she followed behind her.

Sasha sat in the seat near Sienna's desk. "So, how was the recital?"

Sienna fixed her with a dubious stare.

"What?"

"Oh please, you're living with Ma and Pa Informant. I know you know exactly what happened at the recital."

"Okay, maybe I do," Sasha capitulated, "but the details are better coming from the source instead of a watered down version."

"There's not much to tell. Vaughn was there to see Angella perform. I figured there was a chance that he would be there—and he was. End of story."

"I hardly think that's the end. You two talked, right?"

"Trust me, there wasn't much to say."

Sasha sighed with frustration. I don't understand your reticence. You have feelings for Vaughn. I'd wager they are very deep. This isn't an insurmountable situation, Sienna."

"Why do you even care, Sasha? You and I have a strained relationship at best."

"I know that."

"Then I don't understand—"

"I messed up once, Sienna," Sasha cried out. "I—wasn't there for you. It cost us both a lot. I just—I'm sorry that I didn't support you."

Sienna sat utterly still. "Why now? Why tell me this now, Sasha?"

Sasha angrily wiped tears away from her cheeks. "Let's just say your best friend gave me a wake-up call."

"Vivian?"

Sasha nodded. "She put me in my place—and I deserved it. Do you know how it makes me feel sometimes, Sienna? That she's more of a sister to you than I've been? You don't think it gets to me?"

"I—you never—"

"Well, it does," Sasha said hoarsely. "I didn't do enough to salvage our relationship, but I can't let that happen again."

Hesitantly, the two sisters came together and put their arms around each other.

When they parted, both stood there, ill at ease.

"This will take some serious work," Sienna admitted.

"I'm willing to give it a try, if you are."

"I am."

"Sienna, you need to do the same with Vaughn. What you two have is real. It's worth fighting for."

Her sister backed up. Her face contorted with pain. "How do you know it can be fixed? You don't even have all the facts."

"And you do?" Sasha countered.

"Of course she doesn't," Vivian said from the doorway.

Sienna jumped. "Good heavens, don't either of you knock?"

"Hey, I did knock," Sasha protested.

"Girl, please. If God intended that people should knock on their best friend's doors, he wouldn't have granted someone the power to invent spare keys," Vivian leaned on the edge of the desk. She turned to Sasha. Her smile faltered when she saw their faces. "What did I miss?"

"Progress," Sasha told her.

Vivian nodded. "So, what's going on with Mr. Deveraux?"

"Nothing. There's no more discussion. It's over and it's time to move on, remember? Now if you two will excuse me, I'd like to mourn in peace."

"Mourn? What's to mourn? You think he cheated on you. I guess it's better you found out now before—"

"Before what? Before I made it worse by falling in love with him? You said it yourself, Viv, remember? I am in love with him." Sienna choked out. "I know I act like I'm not affected, but the truth is—I feel like I've been ripped apart inside." She wrapped her arms around her middle. "I've prided myself on my ability to withstand anything. I was the voice of reason in every situation. I even came up with these stupid rules to live my life by."

"They're not stupid," Vivian corrected.

"The heck they aren't. I tried to make sure life was all neat and packaged up so that I could control it," she turned to her sister. "I tried that with you, too. I was so far off, and I'm sorry. You know, Vaughn was right about me. I can't control everything—or everybody. He told me life isn't perfect. It just *is*."

"Sienna, if you feel so strongly about this then don't you think you owe it to yourself to hash this out with Vaughn?"

"He cheated on me. I can't forgive that. I won't forgive it."

"Were you there?" Sasha said, in a terse voice. How in the world can you surmise that Vaughn cheated on you during a three minute conversation in a restaurant?"

"That woman practically said it straight out. I don't need a road map, you know. It was obvious."

"You know, for a psychologist, you are extremely dense sometimes," Vivian argued. "Women have been lying since before the dawn of time to get what they want. Sure, maybe that barracuda wants your man, but how the hell do you know she's already had him?"

Sienna paled visibly. "Vivian, I know you mean well. You both do, but he put that woman before me. Regardless of what the redhead said, or didn't say, that speaks volumes. He said he didn't have time for me. That was no misunderstanding. He told me that looking dead at me. It's over," Sienna said, with conviction. "Now I'd appreciate it if both of you would give it a rest. I've got to go get packed."

"Where are you going?" her sister asked.

"I have a focus group to moderate. I'm leaving within the hour."

"Where to now?"

"New York. I've really got to get moving. I'll see you both in a few days." Sienna got up and walked quickly from the room. Sasha traded looks with Vivian after her sister had left.

"This just isn't right."

"Remember what you said earlier," Sasha countered.

"I know what I said. I was trying to get her to fight for her man by downplaying the attachment. I was wrong, okay? That reverse psychology stuff doesn't always work. I don't want her to kiss her relationship good-bye. She loves him, Sasha. I mean the forever type of stuff with the His and Her engraved towels and the no-sex tonight headaches. We've got to do something to fix this. With or without her help, I might add."

They were silent for some time. Sasha pinched the bridge of her nose. As she looked down at the table, she suddenly smiled. She picked up Sienna's cell phone. She hit a button and flicked her finger to scroll down. Sasha glanced at Vivian. For the first time that day, a bright smile lit up her face. "I've got an idea."

*Forty-Five minutes later . . .*

Pierce put his feet up on his coffee table. His arms were crossed with one hand supporting his chin. His face was a mask of concentration. "It won't work."

Sasha looked disappointed. "Why not?"

"It reeks of a set-up. You can't be obvious with it. It won't take long before one or both of them realize they've been played."

"Fine. Do you have a better idea?"

When he regarded her his expression was questioning. "I'm a bit surprised by this about face."

"What are you talking about?"

"From what I saw your first night here, and what I've heard, you two get along about as well as fire and baking soda."

"I know," she admitted. "I'm not saying we're inseparable at this point, but—we're working on it. Getting her and Vaughn simpatico again—just say it's my olive branch."

"Fair enough. Give me some time to mull it over."

"We don't have time," Sasha stressed. "If we wait much longer, they'll get past the point of no return. Sienna is already at the there-is-nothing-more-to-discuss phase. If we wait for one of them to grow up and get a clue they'll miss the boat, and what in the world is that horrific smell?" Sasha pinched her nose shut.

Pierce looked baffled. "What smell?"

Sasha got up from her chair and walked around his living room. Her face was a mask of concentration. As she walked by the couch she stopped. She sniffed the air and then leaned in toward Pierce. She recoiled immediately.

"Hey," he said, in surprise.

"It's you."

"What's me?"

"That smell."

"What? I don't think so," he scoffed. "I just showered. You caught me on the way out. I always smell nice before I go out with my ladies."

Her lip curled up. "Not tonight you don't."

Pierce bounded off the couch. "Are you serious? I showered, shaved and used a sample of the beta test for my new cologne."

Sasha leaned in and took a good whiff from his neck. She burst out laughing. "I'd say your chemist needs to go back to the drawing board. My guess is you were going for the woody crisp variety, but one of the base notes is overpowering. I don't know if it's the Olibanum or Patchouli. One of them needs to be toned down—way down."

"Oli what?"

"Olibanum. It's another name for Frankincense."

"I've heard of that one. How do you know so much about scents?"

"I'm a licensed massage therapist. I have a passion for mixing my own scents to use in my massage oils."

"Uh huh. So you think my cologne is too strong?"

"It's too something."

"Yeah, but does it make you want to—"

"No. Not even close."

Pierce looked deflated. Sasha tried not to laugh, but it was difficult. He was utterly crestfallen.

Without another word, he grabbed his cell phone.

"What are you doing?"

"Texting my assistant. I want her to let my R&D team know about this."

"Why don't you just tell them yourself?"

"Uh, date remember? Now I've got to shower again."

"We were in the middle of a brainstorming session. Can't the hot date wait? Vaughn and Sienna need our help getting back on track. You can't tell me that's not more important than a woman whose name you won't even remember come six o'clock tomorrow morning."

Pierce stopped and turned around. "Six? No woman has ever stayed at my place after four a.m. That's if she has her own ride. If I've got to take her home, that time gets pushed back to two."

Sasha's mouth dropped open. "Are you serious?"

"Like a triple bypass. Anyway, how would you know? Has my reputation preceded me, or are you talking from experience?" he countered with avid interest.

A smug expression appeared on her face. "The men I used to deal with didn't want me to leave at all, much less with a time frame in mind."

Pierce raised an eyebrow.

"Uh-uh. Those days are over. I'm a one-man woman now."

Pierce shuddered. "That seems to be going around."

Sasha pointed to his phone. "Call her up and cancel. We've got work to do."

"Fine, I'll cancel my date," Pierce agreed, reluctantly. "I'm still taking a shower, though. I can't smell suspect no matter what's going on."

Sasha almost bit her tongue trying to stifle a laugh. "I've been everywhere and I've never met such a high maintenance man. No wait, I take that back. There was this guy from Brussels—"

"I'm sure he wasn't as good looking as I am."

"No," Sasha agreed, "but he was just as full of himself as you are. Now hurry up. You've got fifteen minutes."

By the time they got in Gordon's borrowed Tahoe thirty minutes had elapsed. "So tell me again why we're headed to your parent's house?"

"I had time to call them up while I was waiting for you to get squeaky clean," she griped.

"How do I smell now?" he inquired, leaning in.

Reluctantly, Sasha took a whiff. She didn't back up this time. "Like Aquaman."

Pierce bobbed his head, but then frowned. "That's a good thing, right?"

"You are unbelievable. Does everything have to be about you?"

"Not everything," Pierce countered, "just most things."

"Like I was saying," she pressed on. "My dad thinks we should all rendezvous at their house to devise a covert maneuver. Vivian's on her way as well."

"For what?"

She let out an exasperated sigh. "To get them back together. Are you listening?"

Pierce's head turned toward her. "Sorry, I'm a bit preoccupied. I had to up and cancel my date—and it was with Ashley. She would've definitely made it worth my while."

"Oh, so sorry that's one less time you'll get your pipe cleaned this week."

"I'm glad you're so concerned about my lack-of-sex life."

"Will you please get your head in the game and start thinking of more scenarios."

He was deep in thought. Suddenly he glanced over at her. "Did you say a covert maneuver?

"Yeah. Why?"

"Just curious. I was wondering if we're trying to get two people back together, or infiltrate the enemy's stronghold in a neighboring village."

"Despite herself, Sasha's lips curved into a smirk. "Oh, shut up."

# Chapter Thirty-one

## Darkest before the Dawn

The five conspirators were sitting around the Lambert's kitchen table. Cassandra sat a plate of oatmeal raisin cookies in the middle of the table. Pierce immediately grabbed one as did Vivian. "Cassie, your desserts are always delicious."

Cassandra beamed at the praise. "Thank you, Vivian. I've made coffee, or would you care for some tea or milk?"

"Coffee would be fine," she murmured stuffing another cookie into her mouth. She got up out of her seat and headed for the refrigerator. "Don't bother, I'll get it."

"I'll take milk, please."

Sasha gawked at Pierce. "Milk?"

He tilted his head to the side. "What's the matter with that? I always drink it with cookies or cake."

"Nothing. Just unexpected that's all," her body shook with mirth.

His eyes narrowed. "I suppose in your travels you've never come across a man who drank milk?"

"Only in tea." she informed him sweetly.

"Now that figures," Pierce laughed between mouthfuls.

"Will you two stand down? We've got more important things to discuss than each of your conquests."

"Gordon," Cassandra admonished.

Vivian cracked up laughing. Sasha and Pierce were dutifully silent.

"Now, our common dilemma is how to get Sienna and Vaughn back together. Sasha came up with waylaying them at a family function, but that would be too obvious."

"What about something work related?" Cassandra piped up. "Considering that's how they met in the first place, we'd come full circle. That would be so romantic."

"I don't think that will work, Mom. She's done with Best Kept Secrets," Sasha added.

"Yeah, and Vaughn's on another assignment," Pierce told them.

Vivian tensed. "We know, with his Barracuda."

"She's only a client. Nothing is going on between them. There's no way my brother would cheat on his girlfriend."

"That was obvious to me too," Gordon agreed. He turned to his wife. "Darling, when's the next recital?"

"Not for another three months. We can't wait that long, dear."

"I think we can all agree on that. Hey, what about Angella? Both of them are crazy about her. Maybe we could enlist Carlton and Angella to help us devise an opportunity for the two of them to run into each other?"

Everyone glanced around the table. One by one they nodded in agreement. Cassandra turned to Pierce. "Can you call Carlton and set it up?"

"Consider it done. I'll let him and Angie come up with the venue."

"Wait, when's Sienna due back? You two said she was in New York, right?"

Vivian nodded. "Yep. She'll be there a few days at least."

"Great. We're all set." Gordon looked relieved. "We'll execute our plan when she returns. I've got a good feeling about this. My instincts tell me they'll be back together in no time. And you know my instincts are never wrong."

"We know," everyone but Pierce chimed in.

***

Since Sienna knew in advance she would be in New York she treated herself to a Broadway show. Considering the current turmoil in her life, she picked an upbeat musical. She purchased a ticket for a seven o'clock performance of "Hair." Having wrapped up her focus group for the afternoon, Sienna went for to Sushi at Haru on Broadway. Seated at her table, she scanned the large room before she had even picked up her menu. Not recognizing a single soul, she relaxed and perused her dinner options.

Deciding to go with the Philadelphia roll and the Crunch Spicy Salmon roll, Sienna ordered and then handed her menu to the waiter. While she sipped ice water, she took an opportunity to observe the patrons. Time and again her eye wandered to the bamboo wall dividing the dining room from the Sushi bar. She found its beauty a true work of art.

When dinner was over, Sienna glanced at her watch. She still had time to kill before the show. The restaurant was only a block from Forty-second street. She decided to walk to Times Square to check out the mega billboards. Immersing herself in the bustle around her was oddly just what she needed to unwind. By the time she got to the theater, she was at ease and looking forward to an evening filled with laughter and gaiety.

There was a fifteen minute intermission in the middle of the show. So Sienna took the opportunity to go to the bathroom. She'd just gotten situated in her stall when she heard two women talking.

"I'm telling you it was her. I heard it from my manicurist who got it on good authority from her personal trainer. Natalia Simone has a new sex toy. She's almost half her age."

Sienna's ears perked up at hearing the name of Vaughn's redhead. She had no doubt they were talking about the same woman. How many Natalia Simones could there be in New York City?

"So who is this mystery girl?" the other woman prodded. "Model?"

"Of course."

"American?"

"European," the first woman snorted. "Where have you been, in rehab? It's just hit the newsstands. They've been out everywhere together. Parties, charity functions, fashion shows. I'm sure I can't wait to see her. I hear she's stunning."

Their conversation was cut short by another lady coming through the door. Sienna waited until it was completely silent before she flushed the toilet and came out.

She walked over to the sink to wash her hands. While she dried them, she willed her stomach to cease twisting itself into knots. *What should I do?*

Leaving the bathroom, Sienna noted that there were still people milling around. "Great, I've got a few minutes," With a plan of action in mind, Sienna walked quickly toward the exit. As soon as she was on the sidewalk, she retrieved her cell phone and dialed Vivian. When she didn't get an answer she tried Sasha. *Darn.* She said to herself. *Vaughn's girlfriend is cheating on him—with a woman—and there's nobody to tell about this?* Immediately, she set about trying to locate a magazine stand.

Luckily, she found one close by. She flipped rapidly through every fashion magazine they had.

"Hey, this isn't the library. You'd better be paying for one of those," a surly man complained as he peered down at her.

"Of course," Sienna told him while checking the latest rag in her hand. She waved it in front of him triumphantly. "Here it is."

The man rolled his eyes. "How thrilling for you . . . cash or charge?"

There in all her boyfriend-stealing glory was Natalia Simone. She had the same impatient expression she had the day they met. She scanned over the article with avid interest. The article mentioned that Ms. Simone had definitely been seen around town with her latest girlfriend. Sienna retrieved cash out of her wallet and paid for the magazine.

She hightailed it back to the theatre. While en route, Sienna retrieved her cell phone. She decided it was best to call Vaughn and tell him about it. A few seconds later she hung up. *Rule number twenty-four: When your ex-boyfriend has an affair with a gay woman, wait until you're in person to burst his bubble.* With that Sienna placed the magazine in her bag, turned her phone off and dropped it in.

Vaughn was on the telephone leaned all the way back in his chair. "Yes, Natalia, I'm one-hundred percent certain I sent those changes to you."

"Darling, I'm sure you didn't. I have looked and they aren't here. Maybe you haven't sent them yet?"

"I don't see how that could've happened. I sent them via e-mail, and we faxed them to you."

There was a large commotion on the phone. Vaughn pressed his receiver closer to his ear. "Natalia, can you speak up? I can't hear you too well. Are you at a party?"

"No, I'm at a charity auction. Darling, I trust that my staff knows what they are talking about. If they say we don't have it, that's the way it is. Are you calling my staff incompetent?"

"No, I am in no way suggesting that your office is incompetent. I'm merely asking you to have them look again."

"Fine," she said, impatiently. "I'll call them now."

"Thank you, I'll hold." Vaughn unbuttoned the first two buttons on his shirt.

Moments later, she returned to the line. "Vaughn, I'm so sorry, darling. The young assistant that screwed up is so sorry for his mistake. It turns out they did have those changes."

"They did? Great, I'm glad they found them."

"So am I. I should fire him for making me look bad."

Vaughn could not tell if she were kidding or serious. "I'm sure that isn't necessary, Natalia. Accidents happen all the time. Besides, I don't think anyone could make you look bad even if they tried."

She paused for a second and then laughed into the phone. Her voice held a hint of amusement. "Flattery will get you everywhere with me, darling."

A member of Vaughn's team came into his office. Vaughn sat up in his chair. "Natalia, I'm so sorry, but I'm going to have to call you back. My boss, Linda just came in and—"

"Well, did you tell her that I am on the phone?"

"Actually, she is holding up the approved storyboard for your next commercial so yes, it is still all about you."

"Oh, well that's different. You can go then. I will expect to be apprised of the outcome tomorrow morning."

He motioned the man further into his office. "Of course I will." Finally, he hung up the phone. He leaned back in his chair and expelled a loud breath. "That woman is going to be the death of me."

"Won't be the first poor unfortunate soul that's had to deal with her royal highness."

"Nor the last," Vaughn countered.

"By the way, why'd you have to make me a woman?"

"Because nobody lower on the totem pole than Linda would've been good enough for Natalia to let me get off the phone."

"Point taken. Man, I don't know how you deal with it on a daily basis."

"I've got millions of reasons, and they're all in Natalia's bank," he joked.

"Yeah, but who knows if you have enough stamina to go the distance with the Dragon Queen to get them. Besides, what's the point of being partner when you're in a psyche ward?"

Vaughn laughed heartily. "Touché."

"Anyway, I just came in to tell you goodnight. We'll have the copy for Inner Beauty to you in the morning by ten."

"Great. She loved the end concept for Inner Beauty. I'm just hoping she'll go with my suggestions for the other line."

"One could only hope. We've been going non-stop since she awarded Chase & Burroughs those two lines. Personally, I should've taken you up on your advice to take a day or two off before we got going. There's no telling when that'll be now," the man grumbled.

"Hate to say I warned you, buddy."

"Yeah, yeah. I'm gone. Good night."

"See you tomorrow," Vaughn called out. Once he was alone, Vaughn turned his attention back to the neatly arranged piles on his desk.

There was a tap on his door. Vaughn shook his head. "What did you leave this time? I tell you that memory of yours is the pits."

"Actually, it's quite good."

Vaughn's head snapped up. His gaze zeroed in on his office door. "Sienna. What are you doing here?"

She walked further into the room. "Am I disturbing you?"

Vaughn stood. "Not from anything I wouldn't mind being pulled away from. Can I get you anything? Coffee? Tea? Soda? Wine?"

Sienna looked surprised. "You have wine in your office?"

He walked around to the front of his desk. "Actually, we do. One of our latest clients owns a vineyard. Thankfully, it's pretty good. Makes my job a lot easier," he said with relief.

"That's convenient. There are a lot of perks to your job, aren't there?"

Vaughn didn't answer right away. He was curious if there was some double entendre intended in that phrase. "Uh, I guess there are. He leaned against his desk for support. "It's been a while, hasn't it? I'll be honest, Sienna you are just about the last person I expected to see."

"That last person being your sixth grade teacher, Mrs. Whittier?"

He couldn't help the smile that lit up his face. "Yeah, with her being dead and all." His shook his head in surprise. "I can't believe you remembered that."

She shrugged.

It was suddenly silent. Eventually, Vaughn recovered himself. "Forgive me, my manners are horrible. Please sit down, Do—Sienna." He corrected before calling her his pet name for her.

"Thank you," she said, lowering herself onto his couch. "I don't mean to intrude."

"When have you ever? Well, except that first time when you came in to read me the riot act during the Best Kept Secrets campaign. "Wait." He turned wary. "Is this one of those times?"

"Not—exactly. Look, there is something you need to know so I'm just going to come right out and say it. Lord knows the rehearsing I did on the plane ride home didn't help, and who knows where Sasha and Vivian are or why they aren't answering their phones but—"

"Sienna?"

She looked up. "Yes?"

"You're rambling."

"Well, it's not my fault," she snapped. "This isn't exactly something I feel comfortable discussing with you—considering the way things are."

The color drained from his face. "Oh, my God. Sienna . . . is it . . ."

She frowned. "What?"

"What you came to tell me." He strode over and sat next to her on the couch. He picked up her hand in his. "Is it that—are we? I'm sorry I mean are you—pregnant?"

Sienna snatched her hand away like the skin had been burned. She bolted off the couch. "No," she practically shrieked. "I'm not pregnant. I—I came to tell you that your girlfriend is cheating on you."

Vaughn sat perfectly still. "What?"

"With another woman," she blurted out. "I'm sure you must be shocked."

He stared at her. "Another woman?"

Sienna nodded. "I didn't believe it at first either, but I have proof."

He perused her from head to toe. "You—have proof?"

"Yes."

Vaughn ran a hand over his face. "Why are you just now telling me? I assume you've known about this for some time?"

"No, I haven't. I just found out two days ago . . . in New York. I was at a musical, "Hair" to be exact and—"

"So it was a spur of the moment thing?" Vaughn stood up and began pacing. "You're telling me you met a woman at a musical in New York days ago, you two hit it off immediately, and now you're . . . gay?"

"What?" Sienna shook her head in confusion. "No, Vaughn. I'm not gay."

His patience was thinning. "If you're not pregnant, and you're not attracted to women. Then, what the hell are you saying?"

Sienna looked at him in bewilderment. "I'm not talking about me. I said you're girlfriend, not your ex-girlfriend."

"Dammit Sienna, they are one and the same. Now quit playing games with me and tell me what the heck you're talking about."

Her anger rose to the surface in reaction to his. "I'm talking about your redhead, Vaughn. I overheard these two women at the theater in New York. They said that she's dating some European model. Can't you see? She's playing you for a fool. Actually, I find it ironic. You cheated on me, and now she's cheating on you except she's not into men it seems—at least maybe not one hundred percent."

His expression was incredulous. "Sienna, for the last time, I am not cheating on you. Not with Natalia—or anyone else."

"You expect me to believe you—"

"Yes," he roared from across the room. "That's exactly what I expect you to do. You know for some bizarre reason I thought you'd give the man you were in a relationship with, the actual benefit of the doubt. Instead you latch on to the first stranger you find and believe her like she's the patron Saint of Miracles."

"It's Saint Anthony," she said automatically.

"What?"

"The patron Saint of miracles is Saint Anthony."

Vaughn threw up his hands. "I can't believe you. Here I am telling you that I'm not cheating on you. I am open and honest, not that you deserve it in the least, and all you can do is correct me about some saint. You aren't even Catholic."

"Well what do you want me to do?"

"To believe in what we had together. What we still have."

"It's over, Vaughn," she said, tearfully. "Once it's gone, you can't get it back."

She turned to leave. Before her hand had touched the knob Vaughn had crossed the room. He hauled her up against him. Leaning down Vaughn kissed Sienna passionately. He stopped a few seconds later. "Tell me it's gone."

"Vaughn, I—"

He kissed her again. He trailed kisses down her neck while running his hand up and down her back. This time when their lips met Sienna's mouth opened. His tongue played with hers before he moved to nibble her ear. "Tell me, Sienna," he whispered. "Tell me there's nothing here."

When she remained silent his hands unbuttoned her blouse. His fingers slid inside the silk top and flicked over her bra to tease her mercilessly. His name escaped her lips as a half-moan, half-plea.

Vaughn reached down on either side of her skirt. He raised it to her waist. He picked her up, slammed his office door shut with his foot and leaned her against it in one fluid motion. Her legs immediately anchored themselves around his waist. Her eyes drifted shut. Their breath mingled together. "Sienna, look at me."

Reluctantly, she did as he asked. When she did, the intensity of his gaze held her far more securely than his arms. "Doc, if you don't want this, tell me it's over and I'll stop. I swear to you, I will."

She stared at him so long her eyes teared up.

Vaughn waited. "Say it."

Her voice came out in a shuddered whoosh. "I—I can't," she confessed.

Vaughn kissed her. It was slow, solemn and held a touch of sadness. Gently, he released her. His hands swiftly returned her clothes to their original position. His thumb tilted her face up to meet his. "I'm sorry, Sienna, but it still bothers me that you don't know that I would never, ever, hurt you. As much as I want you, and believe me,

Doc, I want you in the worst way—it can't be like this. Not with any doubts or hesitations."

Sienna smoothed her hands over her skirt. She looked up at him. "I'm sorry, Vaughn."

His expression was grim. "Me too." He leaned around and opened the door. She turned and slowly walked out.

# Chapter Thirty-two

## Covert Maneuvers

Sienna was driving home trying her best to focus on the road in front of her and not the grief she felt at her and Vaughn's final farewell. *It doesn't have to be.* She told herself. "Yes, it does. It's too late." Just then her cell phone rang. The Bluetooth in her car picked up the call. "Hello?"

"Okay, what's so important that I had to interrupt a pivotal scene with Genevieve on holiday in Monte Carlo?"

"Who's Genevieve?"

The heroine in my book. I'm working on a scene. Genevieve just got finished sleeping with this hotelier's son, Miguel. The father's security detail is in the middle of doing a sweep of the house. He's got to get her out before the father's henchmen see her."

"Why?" Sienna inquired. "What's the big deal if she's caught?"

"It's the day before Miguel's wedding. The bride's family would call off the ceremony, and Miguel's father would lose the inside track on her father's exclusive line of spa products for his hotels." Sasha explained.

"Of course."

"Do you like her name?"

Though nobody could see her, Sienna hunched her shoulders. "I guess."

"Pierce said it sounds like a nanny's name, but I think it's sexy."

"Pierce? What you two are friends now?" Sienna inquired.

"Sort of. You could say we have similar points of interest. So what's up?"

"Vaughn and I broke up."

"Again?"

"This is final, Sasha." Sienna said, tearfully.

"Sis, I'm not getting this whole break up thing. It seems like a big misunderstanding that could be cleared up with a heart-to-heart talk. Why aren't you willing to try?"

"I don't know," Sienna sniffed. "Look this is painful enough without analyzing it to death."

"You're right, I'm sorry. Why don't you come over? Mom and Dad are out tonight. I think they're on a date," Sasha chuckled. "Hey, maybe I should come over there?"

"Would you mind? I hate pulling you from your book, but I'm trying not to wallow."

"No problem. I can bring my laptop in case inspiration strikes. Besides, I don't want them coming home trying to get all amorous while I'm here," she joked. "That's creepy."

Sienna's thoughts drifted back to her encounter with Vaughn at his office. Her skin tingled everywhere he'd touched her. "Stop it," she admonished herself.

"Stop what?"

"Sorry, not you. I was talking about—never mind. I'll see you soon?"

"Yep. Want me to bring anything? Ice cream? Pizza? Gummi Bears?"

"No thanks. I couldn't eat anything right now."

"Suit yourself, but if you change your mind call me."

"Sasha?"

"Yes?" her sister answered.

"Um, thanks. I—appreciate it."

"You're welcome."

Sienna said good-bye and ended the call. As she was driving, Vaughn's words replayed in her head. *"Sienna, for the last time I am not cheating on you. Not with Natalia or anyone else."* She then recalled the woman at the restaurant staking her claim to Vaughn and him letting her. The pain she felt at his abandonment had been real. Her world was turned upside down that night. Vaughn made his choice, and he hadn't picked her.

Later that evening, Sasha and Sienna were on the couch in her living room painting their nails and listening to jazz on Satellite radio. "I'm glad you came over." Sienna admitted.

"Me too. Do you know how long it's been since we painted each other's nails?"

"It was twelfth grade. You were about to go on a date with—what's his name?"

"Quimby Carson, the third," Sasha retorted. "His name may have been dull but he sure as heck wasn't."

"Really?"

"He was such a great kisser."

"I just couldn't see it. He was such a nerd."

"Yes, but he had a car and his parents were loaded."

"Then, why did you break up with him?"

"He wanted more and I wasn't ready to give it. I don't know, I guess I panicked, kind of like you're doing now."

Sienna looked up. "It's not the same and you know it. You didn't run into Quimby several states away with a woman in his lap."

Sasha was thoughtful. "True, but I may have listened to the explanation had he offered one."

"Let's change the subject. I'm thinking of taking a rock climbing class."

"Uh, why?"

"Because it's something to do, plus it looks like it would be challenging and fun."

"How about scary and dangerous?"

"It's in a controlled environment. It's perfectly safe."

"Make up with Vaughn and get him to take you. That craziness is right up his alley."

"Well, that's not happening, so that only leaves you and Vivian to be daring with me."

"I'm thinking no, not just a normal no, but an emphatic no-way-on-the-planet kind of no."

"Come on, Sasha."

"Uh-uh. If I want an adrenaline rush I'll go skiing in the French Alps with my boyfriend's soon-to-be ex-wife."

Before Sienna could reply, her telephone rang. She eased herself off the couch and duck waddled to the kitchen to answer it.

"You really should invest in a cordless phone for in here," Sasha said, loudly.

"Hello?"

"Hi, Miss Sienna."

"Angella? Hi sweetie, how are you?"

"Just fine. Well, maybe not completely fine."

Sienna's forehead creased with concern. "What's the matter?"

"I'm in an awful bind, Miss Sienna. You see I've got a dance coming up and Daddy took me to go pick out my dress, but he's completely helpless when it comes to—you know—the getting ready part. I could really use a woman's help. Can you come over?"

"Um . . . yeah, sure. When is it?"

"It's Friday night. I'm really nervous," Angella lamented. "I have some friends meeting me here and I don't want Daddy hovering," she whispered into the phone.

"Say no more. I'll be out of town most of the week on business, but I will be back by then. I promise."

"Oh, thank you, Miss Sienna. I feel better already."

"Glad I could help. I'll see you then."

She hung up and made her way back to the living room.

"Who was that?"

"Angella. She has a dance this weekend and wants me to help her get ready. She doesn't want her dad getting freaked out."

Sasha got a far off look on her face. "Remember how Dad acted whenever we had a dance or a date?"

"Do I? He would sit there doing everything but cleaning his guns."

Sasha regarded her sister. "It wasn't all bad, was it? I mean you and me."

"No, it wasn't. Funny how we remember the bad things with such clarity and the good times we just gloss right over."

Sasha nodded. "I'm glad we're getting reacquainted, Sienna. I know it will be a bumpy road, and that nothing will get fixed overnight, but regardless of what we've said to each other, we both know how we were before—"

"Before the beauty pageant," Sienna supplied.

"And what happened after it," Sasha's voice filled with remorse. "I'm so sorry."

"You're right, Sasha. I think it's about time we tried to heal the wounds."

They were quiet for some time before awkwardly hugging each other.

"Agreed, but I still want my crown back," Sasha said, in a serious tone.

Sienna sat back on the couch. "You'll get it back when I get my house key."

Sienna was the first to shake with mirth. Eventually, Sasha joined in and before too long they were laughing so hard they were crying.

A loud melody interrupted the sister's revelry.

"I just got a message." Sasha leaned over the side of the couch to grab her bag. Gently, she eased her cell phone out of her bag while trying not to smudge her recently painted fingernails. She hit a button on her phone to pull up her text message.

"Hi, Honey, it's Dad. This Friday is a go. Angella spoke with Vaughn and he'll be at Carlton's house at five fifteen. He thinks he's driving Angella and her friends to the dance. I just tried to call the house. Where are you?"

"At Sienna's house." Sasha texted back.

"Are you two okay?"

"Relax. We aren't at each other's throats, Dad."

"Did she take the bait?"

Sasha typed out, "We've got her hooked. We're a go."

"Roger that. Dad, over and out."

She couldn't help but chuckle reading her father's message. *You can take the man out of the military . . .* she mused.

"Who was that?"

"Just my agent. She wanted to check on my progress."

"So, we've painted our nails, now what?"

"Now," Sasha replied heading for the kitchen, "comes the popcorn and old movie on the Classic channel."

While her sister was microwaving the popcorn, Sienna walked over to her purse. She retrieved her cell phone from inside. There were no messages. *Rule number twenty-three: Pain, like disappointment, wears off,* she reminded herself. With a wistful look, Sienna returned the phone back to her bag.

The rest of the week was a fast-paced blur. Monday, Sienna flew to Detroit for a meeting with a potential client. She was home on Tuesday, but left on Wednesday to conduct a focus group in Chicago for a company specializing in outdoor adventures. Her focus group consisted of six men and women. Their ages ranged from twenty to fifty-five. The youngest was an entry level computer programmer. The oldest was a retired grandmother of three that traveled doing bodybuilding competitions and promoting senior fitness. A high school science teacher, a park ranger, a convenience store clerk, and a stay-at-home mother rounded out the group.

Ordering a Mediterranean pizza from room service, Sienna scanned over her questions for her respondents. Her stomach twitched with nervous energy. "Hello, old friend," she said, looking down at her abdomen. "Don't worry about a thing," she started singing her favorite Bob Marley tune. "Tomorrow will be fine," she said, taking a deep breath. "Relax, relate, release."

The next morning, Sienna made it to the facility with time to spare. This allowed her to slowly unwind and get prepared for her group. By the time the hostess ushered in the six respondents, she was more than ready. Once she'd welcomed them and introduced herself she allowed everyone to do the same.

"Now that we've had a chance to meet the people we're going to be up close and personal with for the next few hours, I'd like to get started. My first question is—where are my adrenaline junkies?"

Several people raised their hand. "Fabulous. Now, tell me how many of you have ever rode on or driven a motorcycle? Don't worry folks; even if it was on that cute little sidecar, I still want to know about it."

Laugher sounded around the room. "You all are doing wonderfully. Let's keep that energy going, okay? Now, tell me about the most exciting outdoor adventure you've had. Keep in mind; I'm referring strictly to recreational pastimes. I don't need to know about any extracurricular activities that don't include clothing."

"I went jet skiing in Wisconsin," the programmer replied.

"Great, who else?"

"I went white water rafting," the stay at home mom added. "It was the longest I was ever without the kids."

"Who watched them?"

"My husband's parents. They treated us to an all expenses paid trip for our anniversary. It was incredible."

"It sounds like it. Now, from a recreation standpoint, let me see by a show of hands; how many of you would consider doing something out of the norm if someone else covered the cost?"

Everyone raised their hands. Sienna made a few notes. "Looks like you all really let your hair down when you don't have to worry about who's going to foot the bill, right? I know I'd be the first one out there hitting the slopes if the price was right."

"Now I'd like to know the longest recreational trip you've ever taken. Was it five days, four nights? A week? Two weeks?"

"I went on a five-day ATV adventure in Baja. We rode in the desert. It was so much fun."

"I'll bet. I went ATVing in Arizona recently. It was a blast," Sienna confessed. As others chimed in with their comments, she found herself thinking about her weekend in Sedona with Vaughn. Quickly, she pushed the painful memories aside.

Time flew by quickly for Sienna. She had really enjoyed her latest group. They were lively and had some great responses for her. Her client only had an additional question or two that they had asked her to incorporate into the discussion. By the time the session had concluded, she was looking forward to returning to her hotel to go over all the audio tapes of their session. She went back into the observation room to say good-bye to her client. By the time she returned to the session room, it was empty. *Great. No guys loitering around trying to ask me out.* It was a perfect end to a very productive day.

She sat back down at the table to organize her notes and pack up. She was scribbling some additional comments in her notebook when she heard a man clear his throat. Slowly, Sienna lowered her pen to the table. *Fantastic. Another living Adonis here to sweep me off my feet,* she grumbled to herself. Taking a deep breath, Sienna plastered a relaxed smile on her face and looked up. The smile immediately disintegrated into a look of utter disbelief. Her eyes were riveted to the man standing before her. When she spoke, her voice was barely recognizable. "Vaughn?"

# Chapter Thirty-three

## Interview with Love

Rising to her feet, Sienna stared at Vaughn as though he were an apparition.

"How are you?"

"Just fine" she snapped out of her reverie. "Thanks for asking. You?"

He shrugged. "I'm hanging in there."

It took a few moments for Sienna to speak again. "So um, what brings you to Chicago? Are you here on business?"

"You could say that. How was your interview?"

"It went well. I had a very animated group. That always makes for great sessions." Realizing she was still holding her notebook, she set it down on the table. "I have to admit that I'm really shocked to see you. How did you know where I would be, or that I was even in town for that matter?"

"Your client told me."

Sienna looked baffled. "Excuse me?"

"I know them. Some of the managers are friends of mine. Occasionally, we go on excursions."

"Of course you do," she said, dryly.

"Anyway, one of my buddies told me they hired you to conduct a focus group. I told him you and I were—well acquainted and the rest is history."

A frown line creased her forehead. "You told him we were how well acquainted?"

Vaughn expelled a harsh breath. "I told him the truth, Sienna. I told him that you mean the world to me. I might have mentioned how important you are in my life, that you and I had a major fight, and I may have touched on desperately needing to find a way to make things right."

Sienna sagged against the table. "You told him all that?"

Vaughn nodded. "I kind of paraphrased."

Quiet overtook the room again. Vaughn observed her studying her shoes with avid interest. "Sienna, what would you say to thirty seconds of total honesty?"

She glanced up at him. "I'd say at this point we have nothing to lose."

"Great. Ready?"

She took a deep breath and stood up to her full height. "Let's do it."

Vaughn went first. "I have missed you more than I ever thought possible."

"I look at my cell phone every day to see if you've called, Sienna admitted."

"Every room in my house reminds me of you."

"Sasha and Vivian think I was crazy for not hearing your side of the story—so do I."

"Natalia Simone is a fashion mogul worth millions of dollars to the agency. My making partner was dependent upon landing her as a client. Sienna, I am so sorry I walked away from you that night. I thought I would be able to explain myself later—it didn't work out that way."

Her eyes grew moist. "No, it didn't. You hurt me, Vaughn,"

"I know," he said in a low voice. "I'm sorry, Doc."

"I'm sorry I didn't trust you."

"I can't lie, Sienna. You immediately assuming the worst bothered the hell out of me."

Before she could retort he stopped her.

"Hang on a minute." Vaughn turned and strode out of the room. Sienna stood there baffled. When he returned, it was with his redhead in tow.

Sienna looked at him questioningly.

"Sienna, this is Natalia Simone. Natalia, this is Dr. Sienna Lambert."

Natalia briefly pressed her fingers against Sienna's hand.

"Charmed, darling. Vaughn has been telling me about your problems. I'm sorry if you misconstrued my involvement with your boyfriend as something sexual in nature," Natalia eyed Sienna very nonchalantly. "That happens a lot. What can I say? I'm very desirable and it is in my nature to flirt, but we aren't lovers," Natalia slid an approving gaze over Vaughn. Her eyes smoldered. "Not that I wouldn't mind—if things were different. He and Pierce are amazing to look at, aren't they? Like Adonis himself."

Sienna tried not to smile at the reference.

"You have nothing to worry about, dear girl. My affections are otherwise occupied. Though I must tell you, she tends to be somewhat jealous. I can't help but admire that. Women want me, men find me irresistible, but trust me, darling; I never sleep where I work. I have extremely high expectations from everyone around me. Their vision, their creativity, their ability to give me what I want has to remain the priority. Once they have indulged in the fantasy, I can assure you, it would alter the reality. They would want to remain at my side like forlorn puppies," she laughed. "Horrendous for my bottom line."

"I can see your point," Sienna agreed.

"What can I say? It's a hazard in my life that can't be avoided. Anyway, I've got to go, darling. I have reservations at Charlie Trotters. Vaughn, I will call you later. Sienna, you really should work on your hair. That bun is just hideous. Try something a little fuller around your face. You are too statuesque to be so severe. You need to embrace your inner beauty." She turned to Vaughn. "Darling, see to it that she gets a complimentary gift set. Ciao."

Vaughn kissed her on the cheek. "Thank you, Natalia."

"No need. I do charity work all the time, darling." She winked, and then sailed past them in a blur of stilettos and fur.

Somehow, Vaughn beat her to the door and opened it. He followed her into the hallway. When he returned, he glanced at his watch. He grinned. I think we have another ten seconds."

Sienna was awed. "I can't believe you brought her here."

"I wasn't taking any chances. There was no way I was leaving until you and I were copacetic."

Her face reddened. "I apologize for not believing in you—in us."

"I'm as much to blame for this, Doc. I was stubborn and refused to tell you about the details surrounding Natalia. I guess my pride ran amuck."

"I didn't want to hear the truth, Vaughn. I was scared and wanted a reason to run from you."

"Is that your professional opinion?"

"I'm embarrassed to say it, but yes."

Vaughn went to her. He tilted her face upward with his finger. "Sweetheart, our first weekend at my house—do you remember it?"

She looked aghast. "Of course I do."

He leaned closer. "You bared your soul to me. I promised you then that I would never let anyone hurt you again. I meant it."

"I know you did."

"Then you have to know that you and I coming together afterwards—what we shared was—" he grasped her head in his hands and rested his forehead on hers. When he released her, his eyes brimmed with emotion. "I was right there with you, Doc. Do you understand what I'm saying?"

Tears cascaded down her face in earnest.

He lowered his head and kissed her solemnly. "So, am I forgiven?"

"That would depend. Am I?"

He kissed the bridge of her nose. "Yes. I forgive you for being stupid enough to think that I would ever disrespect you or what we have by lying and being unfaithful."

Sienna wrapped her arms around his neck. "That's good to know, because I forgive you for not telling me sooner that Natalia was your client."

"Fair enough."

"Did you make partner?"

He moved his hands around behind her and undid the bun. He fluffed her hair out around her shoulders. "Yes, I did, but I really miss my old partner. The problem is I love her, and I want her back."

Sienna didn't know she had been holding her breath until she gasped. "You love her?"

"Yes, I do. I've never stopped."

"So what you were trying to tell me about that weekend was that I . . . I didn't fall alone."

"No sweetheart, you didn't."

They hugged each other tightly, each allowing themselves to finally relax.

"One final question for you, Doc."

Her hand glided up his shoulder. "I'm ready."

"When are you going to say you love me?"

She beamed with happiness. "I love you, Vaughn Deveraux. I have for quite some time. How could I not be in love with you, darling?" she mimicked Natalia. "You're a living Adonis."

They returned to her hotel room where Vaughn helped her pack up. They caught an afternoon flight back to Raleigh. After they landed, Vaughn decided to take Sienna out to dinner. By the time they arrived at Vaughn's house, it was late evening.

When they arrived, Vaughn sat their luggage in the mud room. Sienna was about to grab her overnight bag to take it upstairs but he staid her hand. "Uh-uh. Later," he told her. He took her hand in his and kissed it. "Follow me."

They went upstairs and Vaughn pulled her toward the bathroom. He turned the water in the shower on. As it warmed, he helped relieve Sienna of all her clothes. When he was done he removed his.

"Are we taking a shower in the Mini Cooper again?" she teased.

"Yes," he said, lasciviously nudging her under the warm rain shower. The water cascaded down the both of them. He hugged her to him. "You don't know how much I've missed this."

Sienna exhaled a pent up breath from deep within her chest. She returned his hug with equal reverence. "Yes, I do."

Vaughn outlined her lips with his thumb. "I love you, Doc."

"I love you, Vaughn."

\*\*\*

It was a while later before either wanted to exit the shower. Vaughn retrieved a fluffy beach towel and dried them both off.

She glanced at her fingers and laughed. "My skin is all pruney."

"I still love you—wrinkles and all."

"You say that now. Just wait till I'm all old and have the ones that last twenty-four hours a day."

He wrapped the towel around her using it to guide her towards him. He kissed her neck. "I'd still think you are hot."

Vaughn picked her up and took her out of the bathroom. When he passed the bed Sienna raised an eyebrow. "Where are we going?"

"You'll see."

He took them out onto his covered deck.

Sienna looked up at the star studded sky. "I truly think the observatory is my favorite place in your house."

"After what transpired the last time we were out here, I'm going to agree with you."

He sat her down. "Meet you in the middle?"

"You're on."

They worked on either side of the outdoor room lighting the candles. They ran into each other at the foot of the canopied lounger.

Vaughn relieved her of her portable lighter and sat it on a nearby table. When he returned, he wrapped his arms around her waist. "Hello beautiful."

Sienna leaned up to kiss him. "Howdy, stranger."

"It's been a while hasn't it?"

"Yes, a long, exhausting, arduous, lonely while, Vaughn. Let's not do that again." Her eyes glistened with candlelight-hued tears. "Ever."

He took her hand in his again. Easing the canopied curtain back, he motioned for her to lie down. While she got comfortable, he tied the curtains on either side before joining her on the bed. He gathered Sienna in his arms. Silently, they observed the night sky. They were content just to be with each other and stare at the constellations.

Sienna's hand entwined with his. "Is this where you say this is pretty amazing?"

Vaughn leaned down and kissed her lips. He gave her a big bear hug, and then whispered into her ear, "Not yet." When he leaned back, there was a large diamond engagement ring between his thumb and index finger.

Sienna stared at the ring and then at him. She bolted up into a sitting position. He followed her. "Vaughn?"

"Sienna, I love you. You make me happier than anyone I've ever met. You're smart, sexy as hell, you're compassionate, funny and you are addictive. The more I'm around you, the more I realize how essential you are to my life. His voice shook with emotion. "I know how hard it's been for you to trust enough to open your heart to me—to anyone, after what happened years ago. I swear I wish I could have saved you from having to suffer through it. You have to know that I'm here now, and that I promise to protect you. Nobody will ever harm you like that again. You believe that, don't you?"

She raised a shaking hand up to his face. She rested it on his cheek. "Of course I do."

"Then Sienna Lambert, will you marry me?"


"Vaughn, you mean everything to me. You are my Adonis—shiny red cape and all."

Vaughn looked baffled. "Red cape?"

She couldn't contain her glee. "I'll tell you that one later."

He kissed her lips. "Who would have ever thought one silly company outing could have turned my life upside down?"

"I never thought we would end up here," she cried. "I convinced myself it would never happen, that I'd never experience what my parents felt. My father was blessed enough to find love twice in a lifetime. I believed I wouldn't find it once, that somehow I didn't deserve it, that nobody would ever touch my soul, but—you did, Vaughn. You saw behind the camouflage to the real me."

"Sweetheart, I hate to tell you this, but that so-called camouflage wasn't even that good."

They both dissolved into laughter. Tears of joy rolled down her face. She hugged him tightly. "I love you, Vaughn Deveraux."

"Is it enough to marry me? Because I'm still waiting for an answer on that one."

"Yes, yes, yes," she cried. "It is way more than enough to marry you."

He visibly relaxed. "Good. I was getting worried." He took her left hand in his and slipped her ring onto her third finger. He brought her hand to his lips and kissed it. "A perfect fit."

She touched his face lovingly. "Just like us."

He nodded. His eyes were as moist as hers. "Now, this is pretty amazing."

# Chapter Thirty-four

## The Best Laid Plans

Gordon was pacing the floor. He glanced impatiently at his watch for the fourth time. "Are we ready?"

"Everything is a go. Vaughn called and he's on his way, and Sienna said she would be here shortly," Carlton assured him.

"Dad, are you sure you parked far enough away? Sasha inquired. One look at that tank you drive and we're busted."

"I planned for every contingency, sweetheart. We brought your mother's car. It's a perfectly non-descript car that will blend in."

Cassandra cleared her throat.

"Sorry, sweetheart, your car is very beautiful—just like its owner."

She blew a kiss to her husband. Sasha shot a glance at her father. He winked.

The doorbell rang. Everyone jumped.

"Okay, showtime," Gordon whispered. "Cue Angella. All nonessential personnel report to the guest room PDQ."

Everyone but Carlton and Angella filed out of the room.

Angella glanced at her father. "What's PDQ, Daddy?"

"Pretty—darn quick," he replied.

When he opened the door, Sienna walked in carrying a small bag. "Hi, Angella. How are you?"

"Great, now that you're here."

"Don't worry, Ange. I've got you covered. I have curling irons, hair accessories, lip gloss, and even a sewing kit should we have any last-minute emergencies."

"You've thought of everything," Angella giggled.

Just then Gordon, Sasha, Cassandra, Vivian and Pierce came into the room. Sienna jumped in surprise.

"What are you guys doing here? What in the world is going on?"

Carlton called us last minute. He wanted everyone to be here to see Angella off to her first dance," Cassandra lied, smoothly.

Sienna went to hug her family. "Well, that was sweet. I'll be right back I need to run to the bathroom."

The doorbell rang again. This time Angella went to answer the door. "Uncle Vaughn," she said, excitedly.

"How's my little dancer?" Vaughn hugged Angella to him. "All ready, Angel?"

"Um, not yet."

Vaughn looked up to see his brother and Sienna's family standing off to the side.

He was surprised. "Is there a party I didn't know about?"

Gordon stepped forward. "This is an intervention."

"An intervention?" Vaughn remarked. "Why exactly?"

"We're sorry, son, but we've given you and Sienna ample time to get things patched up. Nothing's happened thus far, and time is running out. You two have to get past your differences. There is nothing to be had by holding grudges and letting your pride get in the way of your happiness, and everyone else's for that matter."

"Gordon, I appreciate this whole—maneuver, but really it isn't necessary. Sienna and I—"

"Need help," her father continued. "Both of you are all screwed up. You need guidance. That's where we come in. We're here to set you on the path. You two belong together. It's time you faced it."

Vaughn tried not to laugh, but it was hard, especially when Sienna came back into the room. Baffled, she looked around. When she saw Vaughn, she ran right to him. He gathered her in his arms and kissed her soundly on the lips. The room got so quiet they were able to hear the distinctive ticking of Carlton's old grandfather clock.

"Damn, that was fast," Pierce said, dryly.

Gordon gaped at the scene before him. "What's going on?"

Sienna turned to face the dumbfounded crowd. "Isn't it obvious, Daddy? Vaughn and I are—we're back together."

"Back together? When? How?"

"He came to me when I was in Chicago," Sienna looked up at Vaughn. "He surprised me with declarations of love and Natalia."

Her father looked deflated. "So all is back to normal?"

"Yes sir," Vaughn spoke up encircling her waist with his arm, "for good this time too. No more lack of communication between us."

"Now, there's just an engagement between us," Sienna informed them holding her ring up for everyone to see.

Cassandra practically screamed and ran over to her daughter. She threw her arms around her. Vivian was next in line and then Sasha.

"This is such joyous news," her mother said, tearfully. "Gordon, isn't it wonderful?"

He shook his head. "You mean we executed this big elaborate plan for nothing?"

"Congratulations, man," Carlton said, patting his friend on the back.

Angella moved in to hug Sienna. "You're going to be my Aunt now. I'm so excited."

Sienna's eyes were bright with tears of joy. "Thanks, sweetie," she kneeled down in front of her. "Did you really have a dance tonight?"

"Of course not, that was part of our elaborate scheme to get you and Uncle Vaughn back together."

"One that backfired," Gordon frowned.

Sienna kissed Angella on her cheek. "I guess since you're all dressed up we'll have to have a party here."

Pierce came over to his brother. He punched his arm. "You did good."

"Thanks, little brother."

"By the looks of that ring and her smile I'd say you dazzled her big time."

Vaughn and Sienna made eye contact from across the room. He winked at her. "Yep, I dazzled her." He let out a hearty laugh. "Seriously, Sienna and I appreciate everyone showing an interest in our happiness." He hugged his brother. "Thanks."

"This calls for a toast," Vivian announced com-ing out of the kitchen with a tray full of juice boxes. "And since Carlton didn't have any champagne, we're going to Plan B. She handed everyone a juice box.

Sasha sidled up to Pierce. "I suppose if you asked nicely Vivian could find you some milk."

He flashed a signature grin.

Sasha covered her eyes, and then faked a swoon. "Oh, somebody help me, I've been daz-zled."

Despite himself, Pierce burst out laughing. "I like you. You're just twisted enough to be allowed to hang with me."

When everyone had received a juice box, Gor-don stepped forward. "A toast to Sienna and Vaughn. True love is a special gift from God. It isn't to be taking lightly, or without respect. We are all glad you two finally realized what we all could see, that you two are each a half of the one thing. Brought together by chance, but bound to-gether by love. Congratulations on your engage-ment, kiddo," his voice was gruff with emotion. "We wish you and Vaughn all the best."

Loud thuds from carton hitting carton echoed around the room. After that, they all sat down on Carlton's couch and chairs. Gordon glanced over at the happy couple. His chest puffed out with parental pride. "You know I never had a doubt that things would work out. I was telling Cassie that just last week. It took a solid plan and I must say everyone came together to get the job done. Even if you two hadn't kissed and made up, I think we still would've been victorious. You know my instincts told me that you two would be back together in no time. And you know my instincts are never wrong."

"We know." the entire crowd said in unison.

# About the Author

Being a native of Washington D.C. fed Lisa Watson's romantic imagination. Creating interesting, realistic characters that challenge personal and spiritual growth are her forte. Lisa has parlayed her love of the romance genre into her first solo novel, *Watch Your Back* (Urban Soul, Sept. 2009).

Lisa resides in North Carolina with her husband, son, daughter, and dog, Boomer. She is an Asset Management Specialist for Logistics Applications, Inc. and is a sub-contractor with HP for ATF. When she isn't working, she is doing her favorite things: Writing, hanging out with other authors and readers as co-publicist for the yearly RT BookReview Magazine's annual BOOK-LOVERS Conventions, spending time with family, and catching up on all the Tivo'd shows she never has time to see.

Lisa is working on the second book in her Interview Series, *Interview with Danger*.

## ORDER FORM
## URBAN BOOKS, LLC
97 N. 18th Street
Wyandanch, NY 11798

Name (please print):_____

Address:_____

City/State:_____

Zip:_____

| QTY | TITLES | PRICE |
|-----|--------|-------|
| | 16 On The Block | $14.95 |
| | A Girl From Flint | $14.95 |
| | A Pimp's Life | $14.95 |
| | Baltimore Chronicles | $14.95 |
| | Baltimore Chronicles 2 | $14.95 |
| | Betrayal | $14.95 |
| | Black Diamond | $14.95 |

Shipping and handling-add $3.50 for 1$^{st}$ book, then $1.75 for each additional book. Please send a check payable to:
### Urban Books, LLC
Please allow 4-6 weeks for delivery

## ORDER FORM
### URBAN BOOKS, LLC
97 N. 18th Street
Wyandanch, NY 11798

Name (please print):_____

Address:_____

City/State:_____

Zip:_____

| QTY | TITLES | PRICE |
|-----|--------|-------|
|     |        |       |
|     |        |       |
|     |        |       |
|     |        |       |
|     |        |       |
|     |        |       |
|     |        |       |

Shipping and handling-add $3.50 for 1st book, then $1.75 for each additional book.

Please send a check payable to:
### Urban Books, LLC
Please allow 4-6 weeks for delivery